K'S

LANDING

■ A N O V E L

MIKE YOUNG

Deux Voiliers Publishing
Aylmer, Quebec

First Edition

Copyright © 2013 by Mike Young

Published in Canada by Deux Voiliers Publishing, Aylmer,
Quebec.

www.deuxvoiliers.com

Library and Archives Canada Cataloguing in Publication

Young, Mike, 1946-, author
        Kirk's Landing : a novel / Mike Young.

ISBN 978-1-928049-39-5 (paperback - Ingram)

        I. Title.

PS8647.O74K57 2013   C813'.6   C2013-907228-4

Cover Art, Photograph and Design by Ian Thomas Shaw

Cover Photograph of Haida artist Corey Bulpitt painting wall
mural of running salmon—used here with the explicit permission
of the mural's artists, Corey Bulpitt and Larissa Healey.

FOR MY MOTHER
MARIE (1915-2010)
WHO ALWAYS
ENCOURAGED MY
CREATIVITY

CHAPTER 1

Dave slouched in his chair, surrounded by tattoos and testosterone. Only full patch members were left in the room—all the rest had been sent out.

All except Dave, as once again he'd deliberately faded from their notice. He didn't know exactly how he disappeared—whether peoples' eyes just slid away from him or if light actually bent around him. His grandmother had never told him. All he knew was that it took a lot of concentration and he couldn't fool cameras.

"Last call for beer," said Weasel.

Dave quietly sipped his water. He was tired and needed to stay alert to focus his magical power, as today's meeting was a key one. The gang would be discussing how they could expand their drug network, targeting new markets beyond the big cities. Dave tipped his chair back, scratched his full beard, and then, despite his good intentions, his thoughts wandered. He reviewed in his mind the number and location of firearms in the room. He then considered the number of members there with known or alleged murders on their scorecard. He'd joined up only a few weeks ago, with a referral from another chapter, but already it looked like his work would pay off well.

Sasquatch—their very large and very hairy leader—finally called them to order. "Okay, let's get going. Weasel, Spider, good job last week, torching up that club. Now they'll show us a little more respect, and cash. Oh, and welcome to our newest member, Badger."

Sasquatch had taken back control last year when he'd been released from prison—with an MBA earned on taxpayers' dollars. Badger was even newer than Dave, recently arrived from some First Nations group out in

California. He'd already been made part of the inner circle, based on an impressive criminal record. They'd met earlier, and he'd given Dave a peculiar look at the time.

"Spider, phones off, and no photos," said Sasquatch.

"Sorry boss." Spider put down his cell phone. "Just thought you'd want to see us all together." He stared at the picture, then pointed across the table at Dave. "Hey, what's he still doing here?"

Dave woke up with a jolt, crashing back onto the floor, and definitely losing his concentration. With his sudden unfade everyone stared—frozen for a moment.

He knew that every person present would kill him without hesitation. He was on his own in this. He stood and spread his hands, smiling around the room. "Hey guys, lighten up! I just dozed off in my chair. What's the big deal?" This was not going to work, judging from the angry looks he was getting—especially from the new guy. Badger gestured angrily at him, and Dave swayed with a wave of dizziness. His pause gave Sasquatch long enough to block the only door.

Dave glanced behind him at the large window, almost floor to ceiling, with rows of painted over panes. He grabbed a chair, swung as if to go after Badger but then turned and hit the window as hard as he could, shattering the old wood trim and glass. Good thing he had practised this in simulation exercises. Now was the time to see if his leather jacket was worth the price.

He covered his face with an arm and pushed through the frame, landing on a pile of garbage bags behind the sushi restaurant. He scrambled to his feet, reeking of fish, and raced down the alley, slipping in the January slush. Angry shouts filled the air, as the rest of the gang piled through after him. No gunshots—yet. He burst out onto Queen Street, risking a quick glance over his shoulder to confirm they were still close behind him. He turned back, just in time to see the side of a big red TTC streetcar. Dave slammed into the side of the 'Red Rocket,' and fell back to the pavement. There was a screech of tires and a car bumper appeared, inches from his nose. A Toronto Police bumper. Within seconds an anxious officer was looking down at him.

"Whoa, slow down buddy. You all right there?"

As Dave's vision cleared he looked up at the concerned cop, then back at the alley. Most of his pursuers had stopped at the entrance, but Badger and Sasquatch walked toward him, calm as could be.

"That's okay officer," said Sasquatch, "our buddy wasn't paying attention. Our apologies. We'll take him across the street to the local clinic and take good care of him."

Dave looked at them, then up at the cop, still bending down with a concerned look. Choices, always choices.

"Up yours, pig," he snarled, and swung a fist at the innocently smiling face.

CHAPTER 2

Dave's nose had finally stopped bleeding. His ribs still ached though —less from the collision with the streetcar than from the knee of the cop who had held him face down on the pavement. Once they'd taken the cuffs off, Dave had cleaned up a bit, but the smell of well-aged sushi still clung to him.

There was a rattle in the lock, then a guard smiled down at him. "Come on, pretty boy, some suit wants to talk to you. Try not to bleed all over him."

Dave slouched in his chair, silent, staring at the RCMP inspector across from him. Dave noticed him glance up at the camera—a reminder of how this would have to go down. The inspector leaned forward, seemingly calm, but Dave knew him well enough to know he was upset.

Chuck Williams was in fact very upset. What a mess—not just Dave, the whole situation. With Dave's scuffed jacket, torn jeans, long hair and a beard, he looked like street trash. And he smelled of fish. Broad-shouldered, tall and muscular in a wiry way, he also had that haunted unhealthy bad boy look around his eyes that made people believe his story of an adolescence spent indulging in drugs. And those tattoos were just icing on the cake. Dave was more than just Chuck's best undercover worker though, he really liked the kid. He'd been worried sick about him and this hair-brained infiltration plan, so far off the risk grid it would never have been approved without Chuck's signature. He shook his head. Punching the uniform officer was typical Dave, brilliant yet way out of the box. Maybe there was still a chance to salvage the case. But, first things first. Get Dave out of here.

Chuck leaned forward. "So, Bear, I guess you figured moving to Toronto we wouldn't find you. You underestimate the RCMP. I have a federal warrant being forwarded to the Toronto Police as we speak and I am here to escort you to Chicoutimi personally. Don't plan on doing anything creative for the next five years." He was glad to pull Dave out of the reach of the Nomads but he was even more relieved to find a way to get Dave out of undercover before he got too careless. It was about time Dave grew up and thought about rounding out some skills for the rest of his career.

Dave smiled back. He liked his new alias 'Bear.' It fit well. He'd picked up on the hint too, that neither of them knew how secure the Toronto police cell-block was. Bikers had associates everywhere.

"You've got nothing on me," he said. "Those guys just started chasing me; I never saw them before. Chased me right into a streetcar. I was so groggy then, I thought that cop was coming after me, so I hit back —just in self-defence." He folded his arms and put a foot up on the table. "It's all a misunderstanding."

The Inspector shoved Dave's foot back off the table. "Nice try, but I've heard all your stories before. You're done for. Whatever you were trying to set up here is finished."

Dave argued back for a few minutes more, but eventually went along with the move to get him out of Toronto.

Later, after Dave had been paraded publicly in handcuffs to the waiting RCMP vehicle, they had a chance to talk more freely.

"Well Corporal Browne," said the Inspector, "here's another fine mess you've gotten us into. Did you at least get any details on their new plans?"

"Sorry, Inspector," said Dave, "Didn't get much, other than the names of key players close to Sasquatch. The meeting was just starting when I got busted."

"They're really pissed off, Dave. Too bad they made you. I hope you're not losing your touch. I'm afraid, that's it for you around here, as it's only been a few hours and word is already out on the street about you. They still seem to buy your cover story, so are now trying to find out which rival gang you're working for. At any rate, while you do great work —even if somewhat unorthodox—you're no longer any good to me on the streets here. So now what do we do with you? Any ideas? How about the SWAT team up in Ottawa?"

Dave shook his head, he'd heard about them from a friend. Lots of simulations, and nice toys, but no real action. Plus, compared to Toronto, Ottawa was boring—he'd been there once, and once was enough.

"No, SWAT's not my thing, Chuck."

"You're right, you'd probably blow something up. All right, then here's another choice, a better one for your career. I can set something up for you working uniform in another province. There's an opening in Manitoba in a little town, next to a reserve and provincial park. You'll be the Commander there, in a small detachment far off the beaten track. It's an easy posting. Just think of it as some time off—you could do with a break. Plus you'll have a chance to finally develop some supervisory skills. The main industry there is a big new eco-friendly mill, a showpiece for the government. The town is quiet until the summer tourists roll in, so it should be easy for you to get used to running a detachment."

"Can I think about it?" said Dave.

"Not really," said Chuck. "You need to get off the streets right away. You've time to just pack a bag and leave—we'll send your things up after you. Do a good job, keep things running smoothly, and I'll make sure you get a good chance at a promotion—wherever you decide to go. Just no more undercover."

"Hey, wait a minute, Chuck. Undercover's my thing—you know I'm good at it. I'm top of my game here. I'm the best you have. I'm a quarter First Nations, so I can do Native, Mexican, South American, whatever is needed."

Chuck was just shaking his head.

"Come on buddy," said Dave. "You owe me. At least give me drug squad somewhere. Patrol work is for the B team. It's house league. Especially in some rinky-dink place in Manitoba."

Dave liked being a loner, and liked the advantage his secret power gave him. He couldn't just give that all up. He could see that Chuck still had on his stubborn face, though. "Chuck, who had your back in that argument with the Chief? Who got you the information about who was padding their overtime claims? So yes, I admit I'd better disappear from

Toronto, but keep me in the file. I'll do six months, that should be plenty."

Chuck held up a hand. "Dave, once you get going, you could talk the stripes off a zebra. We both know that getting you out of Toronto is not only the best thing for your health, but it's SOP. Fine, I'll keep you on file—I'll give you that. But you'll do a year. Pick up some people skills, maybe even learn something about aboriginal issues while you're there. Just manage your team, learn how to wear a uniform again, and impress the District Commander. Don't make any waves."

"No problem," said Dave. "I guarantee it will be a quiet year."

CHAPTER 3

Dave woke up with a jerk, confused, falling. The call of a loon echoed in his head.

"Ladies and gentlemen, we have now started our descent into Kirk's Landing, please ensure your seat belts are securely fastened—"

He tuned out the rest of the announcement, stretched, and ran his fingers through his short dark hair. He had a crick in his neck, a sore butt, the start of a headache, and was dying for a smoke. These 20-passenger planes might be great for smaller airports, but they were built like a little tube, cramped for someone his size. He glanced at his neighbour. "Guess I fell asleep."

"You sure did. You were tucked up against the window for most of the flight. Hi, I'm John—you getting off here too?"

Dave nodded. "Not for long though." He crouched down and peered out the tiny window of the Bearskin Airlines turboprop. The view hadn't changed much for the last hour. Snow, scruffy pines, ice-covered lakes, and more snow, still a blinding white in the late afternoon sun. He supposed this was a great area for tourists, but for him it would just be very cold and very isolated.

His boss Chuck had been his usual efficient self. Within a day he'd orchestrated a cover story for Dave's disappearance from Toronto and the Chicoutimi prison, persuaded Toronto Police that charges could be dropped because Dave was too groggy from being hit by the street car to form intent, arranged transfer documents, convinced the local RCMP to post him to the Kirk's Landing detachment as the 'Corporal in charge', ordered up some winter-weight clothing to be delivered to the

12

detachment, and emailed briefing notes to read on the plane.

The notes hadn't been encouraging. Just another sleepy small town, with money from the mill and tourists, and probably nothing more exciting than a speeding ticket. He reminded himself that sleepy and boring would be good while he was up here. Definitely a change from the hustle of Toronto life, but bearable, he supposed. It was too late to change his decision anyway so the best he could hope for would be to get Chuck to reconsider in six months. He would miss his independence though, and the excitement of undercover work.

The plane rolled to a stop just short of the small terminal building and a ramp was wheeled up. Judging from the cold draft that swept in the open door it would be a brisk walk to the terminal. Dave stood, swayed with a bit of dizziness, but managed to help his seatmate wrestle down a bulky package, covered in a layer of packing tape. Dave was tall to start off with, but as he wrapped his new down coat around him he started to take up most of the aisle.

"Thanks for the help," said John. "I was down south on business— I'm in engineering here at the mill—and I decided I might as well bring a new supply of coffee back." He patted Dave's shoulder. "That's a serious parka there. You look like a big bear in it. Better be careful in hunting season. You look a little over-prepared with it though—must be from down south."

"I've been around," said Dave.

"Those southern winters are all slush and rain," said John. "Up here we expect it to be like this every year, so we dress for it. But it's not that bad out today, really, for mid-January, maybe 20 below with the nice hot sun. It should really drop tonight though, with this clear sky. Maybe minus 40 if we're lucky".

Dave shivered a bit. "I'm not sure if I'd call that lucky." There were only a few others getting off with him, but all wore lighter coats, with a tuque here and there.

He ducked his head as he stepped out onto the stairs. The cold and brightness made him pause for a second at the top step. Winters at Depot in Regina had been brisk at times, but never quite like this. His nose tingled, his eyes watered, and there was a definite draft up his pant leg. One of his first priorities would be to dig out his long johns.

***

The snow crunched under Dave's feet as he walked toward the small metal terminal building. Aside from a control tower, some small planes under tarps, a couple of storage sheds, and a small hanger, that was it for the Kirk's Landing airport. All was quiet as he approached the terminal entrance—a big change from the noise and hustle of Pearson in Toronto. The air was almost painfully crisp, clear and clean, the colours bright in the sun. Next to the wall a flock of small birds busily fluttered and chattered around a scattering of donuts. Above them, on the edge of the roof, sat a larger black and white bird, looking like a chickadee on steroids. It cocked its head at him, whistled, and flew off.

"Hello to you too," Dave muttered. As he opened the door he noticed a small sign in the window, saying 'Welcome to Our Hell-hole'.

John was still behind him, struggling with his big parcel. "We got that label last year from a rather outspoken Cabinet Minister," he said. "Her plane had stopped off, just to wait out a storm. She got bored and went into our little town, and I guess just assumed we would all reschedule to suit her. When she saw the plane almost ready to leave her behind she threw a bit of a temper tantrum and started yelling at everyone. Didn't bother us much, we've been called worse things by better people."

Dave held the door for him. "And?"

"Thanks. Ironically, she's now looking after Northern Economic Development. She gets to inflict herself on all sorts of charming little hamlets. In fact, I think she's due back here in a few months."

The terminal was small but fairly new looking, with windows along the front, rows of plain plastic seats, and some sad-looking potted plants. At one end sat the obligatory coffee shop, and a small store with chips and drinks, magazine racks, rows of postcards, and a few shelves of bedraggled souvenirs. Dave doubted if there was an executive lounge for government officials to wait for their flight.

"John, back from the big south?" Dave turned, as a very young looking constable approached them. "Hi, Corporal Browne? I'm Constable Reese, Jim Reese. I was hoping I'd be the first to welcome you to your new detachment but John here beat me to it."

Dave smiled and shook Reese's hand. John suddenly looked

nervous, very nervous. He'd gone a little pale, and Dave could already see a few beads of sweat on his forehead. "Yes, I met him on the plane," said Dave, "He's brought a fresh supply of coffee with him too."

"Really? I thought you were a tea drinker, John," said Reese.

Dave carefully turned toward his seat-mate, stumbled a bit, and managed to not only knock the big parcel to the floor but fall on it with one knee. "Oh, sorry, John."

Dave smiled to himself as the bag split open, revealing several smaller bags of coffee and two clear baggies of brown-green leaves. Maybe a few ounces worth. "Is that some of your tea, John?" He looked over at Reese, then pointedly back at the evidence.

"Wait a minute, Mr. Hammel," said Reese. "What do we have here?" Reese took John by the elbow and led him aside. "Why don't you have a seat over here for a sec." He turned back to Dave. "Want me to call Norris to come and get you while I deal with this?"

"Don't worry about it," said Dave. "We don't even know for sure what we have here—although I doubt that it's Orange Pekoe. You probably don't want to be going through his suitcase in this tiny airport lounge, anyway. How about we take John and his things back to the detachment, where you can find out his story and see exactly what this is. I'll have a cup of coffee there and a smoke, lock my gun away, and we'll talk about what you're going to do next. You do have several options, you know."

"Good plan," said Reese. He smiled and turned back to John. "Mr. Hammel. How were you getting home from the airport?"

John was close to blubbering. "I, I was taking a taxi I guess."

"Well, I'll save you the cost," said Reese, "and give you a ride to the detachment office. We can have a chat when we get there."

Dave beckoned Reese back over. "If he coughs up good intelligence you can always cut a deal with the charge, since falling on a package is not a customary search technique."

"Sounds good," said Reese. "although I suspect John doesn't have any drug links. I'll confirm what's in these baggies, then I can talk with him. Thanks for the tips."

"No problem," said Dave. He lowered his voice again. "And I'd appreciate it if we kept quiet about my undercover work in Toronto. I just got burned there by the Nomads, and don't want them tracking me to here."

"It's hard to keep anything quiet in little towns," said Reese, "but I'll do my best." He straightened up in his role as 'briefing constable'. "We've no biker gangs up here, though. Not any gangs at all, really. Apparently there are drugs in town, mostly weed, bit of cocaine in the summer, but nothing really organized. Just a quiet little place."

Dave nodded.

Reese continued. "A nice place, though. I just graduated eight months ago, so this is my first posting. I know I look young for my age, but I'm 20."

Dave smiled. "We all have to start somewhere." He'd hoped just to hide up here and do as little work as possible, but looked like he'd have to watch out for Constable Doogie Howser. At least Reese's six months coaching stint was over, so Jim could now assume full duties on his own.

"Want a coffee?" said Reese.

"No thanks," he replied, "Not really a fan of weak airport coffee."

Reese grinned, "You'll need to check out Rosie's then. He brews a mean cup. None of that big city grande triple triple double shot fluffy soy foam type stuff."

Dave listened with half an ear as Reese carried on with his chirpy introduction to the area. His briefing notes had already covered the basics for him. There were about 800 people in the town, a small pulp and paper mill, some hunting and fishing, and about 300 natives on the nearby reserve. He hoped there would be no issues with them. He couldn't remember which First Nations it was—maybe Ojibwa? The town, and reserve, were both just inside the edge of Whiteshell Provincial Park. His detachment had two constables and a part-time clerk—not a lot for the area, but maybe that meant it was quiet.

"The other constable, Norris, was your field coach?" asked Dave.

"Yes," said Reese. "She's been to a few detachments already. She's a big help, but it's been pretty easy so far. It's great! I've wanted to do this since I was a kid."

"And the clerk?" said Dave.

"She's the mayor's wife," said Jim. "She seems mainly to be there so that she can keep him in the loop with what we're doing and pass on what council thinks is important."

Great, thought Dave, a micromanaging council to deal with. Might be more work to this than he thought, even to just keep a low profile for his sentence.

Dave managed to pop outside for a quick cigarette while they waited for his bags to make the short but slow journey from plane to terminal. It calmed his nerves a bit, but didn't ease his headache. When he went back in, John was sitting quietly, staring at the floor, the only passenger left in the terminal. Dave's bags finally showed up, including his pistol. "Let's go Mr. Hammel," he said. Dave picked up his bags. Reese picked up John's, and they headed for the parking lot.

"I'm over here," said Reese, pointing at a brand new looking SUV.

"Mr. Hammel, in here please." John seemed in a daze as Dave helped him into the backseat.

Dave climbed in front with Reese and looked back through the plastic partition. "Sure looks like a first timer to me, Reese. Hey, nice truck."

"Just got it," said Reese. "These roads just killed the last one. We've two vehicles for the three of us," said Reese. "but Norris says with the summer rush we could even do with a third one. We look after the town, help the band police, patrol a section of the main highway, and also work with Conservation agents in the park. Oh, and we've a boat to tow around in the summer and a ski-doo trailer in the winter. At least we don't have to patrol any ice roads."

"That's good," said Dave. "Wouldn't want to risk this nice shiny truck. Or me."

"Just hope I can keep it shiny," said Reese, as he pulled onto the road in a spray of gravel.

CHAPTER 4

Reese reached for the radio mike, "Just a sec, Dave. 23-alpha-2, to Dispatch, checking in."

"10-4. Hi Reese, Sharon here. Scratched up that new truck yet?"

Reese looked embarrassed. "Ah, I have the new NCO in the car with me, Corporal Dave Browne. Just got off the plane and he's already on patrol."

"Hi Corporal Browne." She had a warm motherly voice. "Welcome to Manitoba, and to Kirk's Landing. Come in and visit us sometime in Winnipeg and we'll give you a tour of division HQ."

Reese explained to him that the radio and dispatch service was mostly done out of Winnipeg, although staff at the local detachment could patch in as well. In the evenings the dispatchers always wanted to know who was in what car and what shift they were working. "They even time me when I'm out of the car on break!"

Dave smiled. He suspected this was a safety thing more than coffee break monitoring. He would definitely try and visit them, though, as it was always good to put a face to a voice. Dispatchers were essential to operations, so it was always wise to be in their good books.

He stared out the window as they drove along the twisting gravel road, between high snowbanks and thick dark stands of trees. The snow was turning blue in the fading light, and the shadows seemed to shift and move between the trees as he watched. Not nearly as comforting as the familiar darkness of the back alleys of Toronto. He'd enjoyed his work there, working independently, using his fade to carefully infiltrate groups. As a shy little kid he'd learned to just not be noticed, as a useful way to avoid a teacher's question or a bully's fist. Then one summer his grandmother had inadvertently turned that skill into a real power, the ability to literally disappear. His dad had been posted off somewhere—again—but instead of the usual summer camps Dave had been sent to stay with his mother's side of the family. Nana had taken him fishing, and taught him how to be quiet, to blend in until the fish didn't see him. To her surprise, neither did any people. He just faded from notice. She was impressed with how strong the power was in him, but warned him to be careful, and to keep it a secret. So far, all anybody else knew was that he had an unusual ability to blend in, an ability that had gained him an early shot in his career at undercover work in Burnaby. Now he was part of the elite Combined Forces Special Enforcement Unit—a dream job.

Unfortunately, that job was on hold now, as here he was, a marked man, hiding out in Kirk's Landing for a year.

"Not far," said Reese. "We're lucky there's a long gravel esker here. It makes a natural runway so we ended up on most of the airlines routes as a stop on the way to Winnipeg. Great for tourist traffic."

Dave grunted as he watched the already boring scenery. "Sure are a lot of trees up here."

"Mostly spruce," said Reese, "and in between are some poplar and aspen, with a few leaves still hanging on. In a couple of months spring breakup will start. Come April everything seems to explode into green at once."

Reese paused as they came to a paved road, glanced for traffic, and turned left. "This is Route 44. The town is a few miles further on. Eventually this will get you to Winnipeg—not the most direct route mind you, but it's through some beautiful country. Bikers love to tour through it. My home in Kenora is like this too. Me and my buddies pretty well lived in the bush—whenever we wanted to skip school, we never went to the mall, we just walked out of town. I was surprised that I got this area as my first posting, but I love it."

He glanced over at Dave, "Where did you want to go first, right to the detachment office?"

Dave glanced in the back seat—John was actually dozing off! He must have had an exhausting visit in Toronto. Most people don't fall asleep when they get arrested.

"A quick tour of the town would help," said Dave. "I can't see that taking very long. Then we can drop off John, and after he's been processed, head on to the hotel. I've booked a room there for a few days until my stuff arrives from Toronto."

"That would be the Grande," said Reese. "Our one and only hotel, right on the shores of Raven Lake. It's a beautiful old place. You can also get a room up at the motel by the turnoff, but I wouldn't recommend it, not that nice, really. It's mostly used when summer campers get tired of sleeping on the ground. The Grande has a great pub too, the Raven's Roost. JB runs that, along with the hotel. Jacqueline Bourbeau, but we all call her JB. A local girl, maybe in her late 20's, nice person. It used to be her dad's place, but she took over when he disappeared last year."

"Disappeared?"

"Yeah," said Reese, "he was up here doing research on pollution from the mill. He headed out one day last winter for more samples and never came back. There was a big search done of the area, but nothing found. Local guy, so he supposedly knew the bush. The case is still open, but no new ideas have popped up. JB will be talking to you about it I'm sure, once you settle in, as she's convinced the mill is somehow involved. Here we are, the main turnoff."

The harsh glare of the street lights revealed a Metro grocery, a Petro-Canada station, a small motel and restaurant, and five or six small houses. The highway continued on into the dark, and a smaller side road led off to the right, presumably to the town. Reese pulled over across from the turnoff.

"The town, the lake, everything is down there. The gas station here has movie rentals, and our mayor owns the restaurant. Running the town isn't a full-time job, and it's a handy place for him to do his wheeling and dealing with his buddies. You can get takeout pizza from there with free delivery too, just ask someone at the restaurant to your party. The Metro store is fairly new—they get some business from the town as well as a lot of tourist traffic from the park and local cottages."

The motel was a long row of units—a few with lights on but most dark and snowed in. At the end of the row was a combination restaurant and bar. The parking lot in front was filled with ATV's and snowmobiles, and closer to the road was a row of flashy SUV's and muscle cars.

Reese nodded at the off-road vehicles. "The biggest problems up here are not on the roads. People get hammered in the bar, jump on one of their toys, and then drive off into the bush. Some end up flipping over, or getting lost and running out of gas. Or worse, they charge across the highway right in front of one of the logging trucks."

Reese started up the truck again, and headed down into the town. As the road dipped downhill, Dave's home for the year came into view, framed between the walls of the rock-cut. There was a scattering of house lights, and plumes of smoke rising straight up from chimneys into the cold air. The empty main street continued on straight down to the lake, where a full moon reflected off the water. Dave had an urge to whistle, suddenly feeling like Ichabod Crane heading into the unknown.

"So this JB runs the hotel?" said Dave.

"Yup," said Reese. "She's a real ball of energy. A little outspoken at times but gets along well with most people. She's looking forward to meeting the new guy—like most of the town".

Dave didn't relish the thought of having to pretend to socialize with people whose perception of police work came from television. Maybe he could use his fade and avoid some of the chit-chat. The town looked quiet, tidy, woodsy. Unlike those of Toronto, most of the trees here were tall and thin, poking above the deep snow. There were a few side streets, lined with high snowbanks, but most of the town was clustered along the main street. He listened, half asleep, as his tour continued in the fading light. There was another gas station, a building supply that sprawled over a whole block, a scattering of small shops and houses, two churches—a typical small town. He'd been posted to a couple since graduating, counting the days in each one until he could leave for the next assignment.

"It's pretty quiet now," said Reese, "but wait until summer. Norris tells me this place can keep the whole detachment hopping."

"It looks fairly prosperous," said Dave. "Expensive cars, well kept main street."

"There are rumours money was skimmed from the mill project into some local pockets," said Reese, "but nobody's really looked into it."

Dave just nodded at that, resolving to add mill corruption to his list of things he was not going to worry about. It could wait until his replacement came.

Reese pointed out the detachment office as they drove by. "Norris is still on duty, she'll be there another half hour at least, fighting with her paperwork. Not her favourite part of the job."

"Mine neither," said Dave.

The streets were empty except for a black SUV parked in the next block. It was lost in the shadows until the top of it lit up like a Christmas tree and a siren whooped from it.

"Dammit," said Reese, as he stepped on the gas.

Dave was suddenly wide awake, as was John. "I though you only had one SUV here?" said Dave.

"We do," said Reese. "That one is the mill security, Tony Barretto. He's a bit of a problem for us. Big talker, buddies with the mayor, and often gets carried away with trying to 'help' in town. We keep warning him to stick to the mill property, but he doesn't seem to listen."

They screeched to a stop by the two people in front of the mill vehicle. One was obviously the security guard, big and burly, decked out in a ball cap, black uniform, Kevlar vest, and police issue boots, with a selection of gadgets and cases dangling from his belt. The other was a tall but thin youth in a denim jacket, torn jeans, and scuffed sneakers. The guard was holding the youth by the collar with one hand, a bike with the other.

"Looks like he's after JB's brother again," said Reese. He poked his head out of the window and shouted, "Let go of the kid!"

***

Barretto watched as Reese and some new guy got out of the SUV. Too bad they'd showed up before he could put a real scare into this punk. "Hey Reese. About time. Good thing for you I was here, I managed to catch another one for you."

Reese walked closer. "Barretto, let him go. Now."

Tony gave Junior another shake then let go of his collar. "He was sneaking around—probably heading off to score some drugs or something. I think we should frisk him."

The stranger stepped forward and stared at Tony. "We—as in you and I—won't do anything of the kind."

Tony puffed out his chest. "Who the hell are you, another wet

22

behind the ears recruit?" He tried to hold the stranger's glare, but finally had to look away.

"I'm Corporal David Browne, RCMP, new Detachment Commander of the Kirk's Landing office. First, who are you, and second, why did you assault this youth?"

New commander? This guy could be a problem. He might not be as easy to push around as Reese and Norris. "Well, this kid is part of a gang of troublemakers, his people are always—"

"Pay attention," said Dave. "First, who are you?"

Tony adjusted his belt. "I'm Tony, Tony Barretto, chief of security at the mill."

Dave nodded. "Mr. Barretto. Now, getting back to my jurisdiction, what exactly are you doing here?"

His jurisdiction? This guy had some learning to do, this was a mill town. Best not to push too hard, though. "Okay, sorry Dave. I know your people have been short staffed lately, so I've just been trying to help out however I can, sort of a partnership. I saw this kid trying to steal a bike."

"Hey, it's my bike," said Junior.

"And you would be?" asked Dave.

"Junior Bourbeau, I live on the reserve and was just heading home on my bike—the one with my SIN number on it right here—when this goon jumped me. For the third time this week."

Goon? Tony was about to erupt again when the new cop held up a hand. "Junior, wait with the constable for a minute, would you? Mr. Barretto, step over here with me please?"

"Tony," said Dave, "I'm sure you mean well, but I think now that I'm on board we can manage just fine. As for your gang concerns—my gang experience included knives and guns, cocaine and heroin— somehow I think those are not issues in your quiet little town."

This was sounding like a brush-off. "There's a lot of concerned people here that think otherwise," said Barretto. "Gangs, I mean, not the drugs. We're clean there." And he'd make sure it kept looking like that. "It's these kids, they just think they can run wild, whooping it up, leaving their gang tags all over the town."

"I'm sure I'll hear everyone's concerns in the next few days," said Dave. "We can talk later about this."

Tony was confident that once the mayor had a talk with this new guy, he'd take his proper place in their town. "Sure, no problem."

"We don't want any confusion in the eyes of the townspeople," said Dave, "as that could waste valuable minutes in an emergency. I'll let you get back to your own duties in the mill now, so that I can have a talk with Junior. I'll let you know if I need any more information, or if he wants to pursue any assault charges."

That startled Tony—but he decided the cop was just bluffing. With one more glare at Junior, he turned back to his own SUV. He'd better call the mayor and the mill manager to warn them about the new guy.

CHAPTER 5

Junior watched the security guard drive off. Typical of Tony—tough until the cops showed up, then suck up to them as Mr. Helpful, as just a concerned citizen.

"Okay Junior," said Dave, "now suppose you fill me in on what happened here."

"Nothing." They'd only believe Tony's side of it, as usual.

"Really?" said Dave. "Humour me."

"Just charge me or let me go," said Junior. He just wanted to go home.

Reese put a hand on Junior's shoulder. "Come on, work with us." He turned to Dave. "The kids here are not that bad, a few have some real issues but this guy's okay. They've all been getting a bad rap from Barretto and some of his friends, who are more vigilantes than concerned citizens. When some people here see a few tags, they get all worried about gangs and a big crime wave."

Junior liked Reese, but he was ready to dismiss this new guy as just another loser cop, here for a year, ready to yap off about synergy and public engagement and all that crap. Someone who'd rush around shutting down all the parties and only listen to dip-wads like Tony Baloney. But he hesitated, as he could sense something different in this guy's manner. And then there was the colourful tattoo peaking out around his collar bone. Junior straightened up. Maybe this would be interesting. "We're not all taggers and potheads, you know."

"I know," said Dave. "I've seen some pretty creative artwork in back alleys. But still, using a spray can where it's not wanted is vandalism, whether it's a tag on a mailbox or a mural on a shed."

Junior sighed. More pompous cop talk. "Look, we just want to do art, add some colour and excitement to the town."

"Not tags, though," said Reese. "We had those spreading all through Kenora when I left. The town had to spend a lot on painting it over and patrolling. That's what the mayor here keeps pushing us to do."

"So what's up for us, you're going to start busting us all?" said Junior.

"Let's focus on tonight," said Dave. "What's your story?"

"I was just out late at a friend's and heading home, that's all," said Junior. "I took a shortcut through some yards and Barretto spotted me."

"Well, for starters, try to stay to the main streets at night," said Dave. "Don't give Barretto and his group an excuse. And get a light on that bike, will you? As for Barretto, we saw him come after you. Do you want to press charges?"

Junior was startled, he hadn't thought of that. "No, he's just being a bully." He hopped back on his bike. "I'll wait and see what you do." He started to pedal away and added, "You might find our town is not all that it seems."

***

Dave watched him ride off. He seemed like a nice kid. "Interesting," he said.

"He's OK," said Reese. "He's just finishing high school. He had some problems a few years ago. He's son of the band chief, had an older cousin that ran a gang here—some mixed role models. Junior ran off to the streets of Winnipeg for a year, then smartened up and came back. Might be on his way to being a good example for the younger kids, both from the reserve and the town. Most of them are okay but there are two or three that have a real hate-on for cops. I'll get you some names. But tell me, what's with this back alley art you were talking about?"

"It's part of a redirection program," said Dave, "for kids that are starting to get into petty crime. They select those with artistic talent and pair them up with a community to do murals instead of tags."

"Does it work?" said Reese.

"Supposedly," said Dave. "Less tagging, stronger communities and some interesting art."

"Sounds great, why don't we try it here?" said Reese.

"Whoa now," said Dave. "Not sure if it would work up here. And remember, I'm only here for a year, if that, so don't have time to launch a new program. Let's stop off at the detachment office and process poor John. I don't think he needs any more of a tour. You can drop me off at the hotel after. Hopefully the rest of the night will be quiet."

"It's usually pretty quiet until summer," said Reese. "Then we get maybe another two or three hundred people here, between the cottagers and campers from the park dropping into town. Norris told me we usually hire extras each summer to help out—she has a list of names for you to look at I think. Somewhere in her pile of paperwork."

Dave hoped the budget had room for at least two extra. Two more for him to manage, but might make it easier for him to stay back and not get involved. He assumed the summer crowd would be like the Toronto clubbers, with lots of parties, too much drinking, a few soft drugs. Some of those Toronto people might even be here this summer, come to think of it. He was glad he'd shaved off his full beard, as it wouldn't do for someone to recognize him and tell their friends back home.

"We get some party people but also just regular families," said Reese. "Sometimes the teenagers they drag along get bored and get into trouble. We try to organize some programs for them."

"What, like dances and stuff?"

"Yeah," said Reese. "Last summer JB put on a whole hip-hop festival over the long weekend in August. She got the local builder's supply to donate some materials. The Lion's Club built a plywood wall for painting. Somebody had a sound system, and one of the local kids hooked up some old turntables. JB bought special spray paint and organized the artists so everyone had a chance to paint and to learn. I dropped by to check it out. They even had some kids spinning around on their heads on the dance floor."

"Did you join in?" said Dave.

"No, not really my thing, but some liked it. Even a few of the old folks dropped by and were positive about it—both local and from the reserve. We ended up with some nice art on the wall, which never did get tagged. The mayor eventually made them cover it up though—some obscure bylaw about signage. I don't know if JB will do the festival again.

She should."

It sounded interesting to Dave, but he really wanted to keep a low profile. He could probably just connect JB online with some contacts in Toronto that had done these sort of projects.

Reese pulled up to the detachment office. It was a square brick building, with a two-car garage on one side. Attached to the other side was a small bungalow, with a satellite dish bolted to the roof. His new home for a while.

The front yard—like the whole town—was buried in snow, but Dave could see the tips of some shrubs trying to poke their way out of it.

"Here you are," said Reese. "Your office and home sweet home."

Dave smiled. He'd not had much time to pack more than a couple of bags. He'd just left all the rest, unpacked, for the movers. He'd likely find they had packed the kitchen garbage can, with its garbage inside, into one of the boxes.

He wouldn't have far to walk to work at least, and the two constables would be close—he'd noticed the two 'official' bungalows just a block away. He'd still need to get his own transportation, though. He'd had a vintage GTO as part of his cover in Toronto, but that had been on loan. And likely not that suited to winter here in the boonies.

"Jim, if you know of anybody selling their vehicle, I'd be interested."

"I'll ask around," said Reese. "Corporal Miller left his old one here, but I think it needs a lot of work." He pulled up to the office. "Here we are, go ahead in and meet Norris. I'll bring in our drug lord."

CHAPTER 6

Dave stomped the snow off his boots as he entered the detachment. There was a counter across the front of the room, a few desks in the middle, and an office and holding cells at the back. A short blond officer sat at one of the desks, digging through a pile of papers. She looked up and smiled.

"Hi, I'm Constable Norris."

"Corporal Dave Browne," he said, extending his hand. "Dave please. Nice to meet you, it's Violet I believe?"

"Yes," she said, "Just V is good. Shy Vi is not."

"V it is." He looked around. "Coffee smells good."

"Our little luxury," she said. "Want some?"

"Sure," he said. "No, don't get up, I'll grab it."

He walked around the counter to the machine, a shiny chrome device covered in dials and buttons, with a half-full pot on a warmer.

"Nice machine," he said.

"We all chipped in," she said, "and Rosie sends the beans over from his cafe."

He wasn't surprised to see someone still on duty. Corporal Miller, the previous commander, had left last fall on extended sick leave, so they'd been short-handed for a while. Good for overtime but tiring. No wonder they were glad to see him.

"I'm here another 20 minutes until 7," she said, "then we close down and forward the phone line back to headquarters for the night. Reese is on call. Speaking of which—"

"He's just bringing someone in. We managed to squeeze in a drug bust at the airport, a John Hammel."

"John? From the mill?" she said. "No way."

As Reese brought him in, the engineer just stared at the floor, avoiding Norris' eye. She nodded to Reese. "Why don't you take John in back and process him while I get Dave up to speed. Oh sorry, if that's all right with you, Corporal? It's your detachment now."

"That's fine," said Dave. "You can get back to your paperwork."

"It can wait a bit while I brief you," she said. "I'm just trying to catch up on this mountain of forms. Not something I enjoy, I admit. I can stay longer if you want, too."

"No," said Dave, "I'll just be here a bit, I'm sure you've other things to get to—you're a single mother aren't you?" As soon as he mentioned that, she bristled a bit.

"Yes, I've an eight-year old son waiting for me at home," she said. "But we do okay, never been a problem. My parents looked after him while I was in training, and I've managed to always get good babysitters on my postings."

"Just asking," said Dave. "We also have a part-time clerk here. Sheila Palin, right?"

"That's correct," said Norris. "She does some paperwork, covers the phones, and is our liaison."

"Liaison with the reserve?" he asked.

"Unfortunately not," she said. "If anything, she does tend to be less than sympathetic to their culture. As does the mayor and his cronies. No, her main focus seems to be acting as liaison with the mayor, her husband, to make sure we're staying focused on the right things. Standard small town politics."

Dave shook his head. He'd have to really work at keeping a low profile in this place—good thing he had his fade. At least he'd be able to get out of the office for some fresh air without being pestered too much.

"They're mostly good people here," said Norris. "The full-time residents, I mean. They just take a while to warm up to someone new. Give them time. Here, I did an info pack for you, and here's a set of keys, for the office as well as your place next door. There's a connecting door for it through there. It's a nice home, with a big living room, full fireplace, bit of a deck out back, and a BBQ. Corporal Miller used to use it for some staff meetings as well as parties. He didn't go to the local bar often. He got along well with everyone, but just didn't feel he could mix like that."

Dave had liked the crowded bar scene in Toronto, but that had been part of his undercover persona. Up here, in this small town, he'd likely be spending more time at home. He'd need to get the satellite dish hooked up and some high speed Internet. On the other hand, it might be nice to occasionally get down to this JB's place for a cold draft.

"I may drop by the bar once in a while," he said. "Reese tells me there's a bit of a drug problem in the summer?"

Norris nodded. "We get a lot more people here then. Nothing too serious, and no big suppliers locally. I think people just bring their drugs up with them."

"I saw some pretty flashy cars and SUV's on our way in, too," said Dave, "up by the restaurant. Looks like a rich town."

"Depends who you are," she said. "The new mill certainly saved this town, with lots of government money, big salaries, and generous bonuses. The mayor and council made sure most of the work went to local contractors too. But just wait until you see the places some of the locals have now. They're cottages in name only, look more like mansions by the water. By the way, I hear you were undercover in Toronto. How was that?"

"I'm trying to keep it quiet," said Dave. "Not sure how well that's working."

"Sheila had started talking about it," said Norris, "but I stopped that pretty quick. It is a small town, though."

"Thanks, V," said Dave. "Is that your monthly report there?"

"Yes," she said. "A little late as usual. I'll leave it for your late night reading."

He sipped his coffee and reviewed her report and the info pack. Both were well done. December had been quiet, with a few parties, domestic disputes, and a few DUI's. The rest of the winter was just as quiet. They had some speeders in a trap on the highway, logging trucks with incomplete papers, noise complaints, some cottage break-ins. Nothing too exciting.

He dug a little further and found the file on that missing person,

JB's father. It had happened almost a year ago, while he was out on a snowmobile in April—cripes, did they still have snow here in April? He checked the file quickly. Jacques Bourbeau, out doing some sort of environmental survey related to pollutions issues at the mill, never came back. Looked like the search was quite extensive, directed by the chief of mill security in fact, but they found nothing. He closed the file. It would wait another day or two, if not longer.

He was about to go look for Reese when the young constable showed up in his doorway.

"All settled?" said Dave.

"I think so," said Reese. "How did you know to check that package?"

Dave explained that he just used his eyes. It was a huge bag of coffee, why not pack it in the luggage? He also knew that coffee was often used to transport drugs in the mistaken assumption the aroma hides smell of drugs from the dogs. And John was all friendly and chatty with him, then was suddenly nervous when he realized who Dave was.

"Okay," said Reese. "So then you fell on the bag on purpose?"

"No," said Dave. "That would have been an illegal search. I really did stumble. But we were fortunate to take advantage of that accident."

Dave was not being completely honest. When he got off the plane he'd suddenly felt a rush in his head. Something mental—like his talent for fading, but different. Similar to what he'd felt in Sasquatch's meeting when Badger had challenged him. He'd felt twinges of dizziness too. This was very weird. He'd never felt like this before, but would wait and see if it went away on its own. He didn't really want to testify in court that their drug seizure had happened because some sort of mental condition made him fall on the bag of coffee.

"What's your plan with John?" he said.

Reese seemed hesitant. "Well, I searched his things and there was just three baggies of marijuana. Ten grams each. I bagged and tagged them and put them in the temporary locker." He paused and continued. "John isn't a bad guy. He's a single dad, raising a 12-year-old son by himself. He said he met this lady on-line, and wanted to impress her that he smoked dope."

"Really?" said Dave.

Reese rolled his eyes. "Well I guess he's lonesome so he's trying everything. He never actually had done any drugs, and he didn't want to buy it here where everybody knows him so he got this in Toronto. The coffee and duct tape thing was something he saw on some TV show about drug smuggling." Reese paused again. "The thing is, I feel sorry for this guy. He's not bad. This might cause him to lose his job. He said he's never going to touch dope again and I believe him. I was wondering if we could work out some deal with this."

Dave was relieved. He didn't want to micromanage Reese and tell him what to do, but the seizure had flaws. At the same time he could see Reese wanted to learn more about drug work, which just happened to be Dave's speciality.

"How about this," said Dave. "We let John go home. You tell him you have to consult with me about what charges if any we will be looking at. In the meantime, what kind of information might John have that we would be interested in? The name of the person he bought the dope off? Does he know about any local criminal activity? Then make an appointment to talk in a couple of days and see if he has anything interesting to tell us. It's a small place. He's not leaving town and we can always find him." He paused. "Good work on this, Reese."

Reese beamed with delight. "Thanks. It's a first for me. I'll give John the good news and let him go. Then I have to get back out on patrol, I'm on until one. If you're ready now I can run you down to the hotel, or drop by later."

"Now is good," said Dave. "I'll be out in a sec. I'm starting to fade, it's been a long day." He smiled to himself—wouldn't that be a shocker if he actually faded. He'd have to be careful to keep his ability a secret.

He filed away his briefing notes and closed the door on his already messy office. He was about to see if Norris wanted a ride when the door banged open and in walked Barretto, the security chief. Dave caught a quick look of annoyance on Norris's face, then she smiled and said, "Dave, this is Tony Barretto, chief of security over at the mill."

"Thanks, we've met already," said Dave, "Tony was doing some policing on his own, so we had a discussion. " Norris just smiled.

"Hi Dave," said Tony. "Didn't expect you to be starting your new job tonight. Did you put a scare into that kid for me?"

"We talked," said Dave.

"Let me guess," said Norris. "You were hassling Junior again."

"He's a bad apple," said Tony. "Don't let him fool you Dave, he's got history. Remember, anytime you need help I'd be happy to work with you on your cases around town. Glad to be part of the team."

Dave raised an eyebrow. "I'll let you know about any mill issues. I'll want to meet the manager there in a few days, so that might be a good time for you to give me an overview of things." He deftly steered Tony to the door. "In the meantime, Constable Norris has to go, and I've got to check some files."

Tony frowned for a second, then smiled at Norris, "Want an escort home, dear?"

"As usual, no, Carmine," she said, "and once again, that would be Constable Norris." She grabbed her things, and smiled at Dave as she walked out the door. "I've already called dispatch to say we're closing up, alarms are just here on the way out. Good to meet you Corporal. You go ahead to the hotel with Reese, I don't mind the short walk home. It will clear my head a bit."

"I'd better get going too," said Tony.

"Hold on a sec," said Dave. He wanted to give Norris a head start, as it looked like this Tony could be a bit of a pest. "I just wanted to say that with one more person here—me—we can extend our coverage, so any evening patrols you were doing won't be necessary."

"Don't mind at all," said Tony. "Glad to help."

"Let me be a little clearer," said Dave. "My staff and I will look after the town. You will look after the internal mill security. We can certainly cooperate on an as needed basis—I'll let you know." He clapped Tony on the shoulder. "Got it?"

"Okay," said Tony. "We can talk more when you visit my mill. Or over a beer at the bar when you're off."

"We'll see," said Dave. "I just got here and have a lot to cover." Tony started again about all the local problems he wanted fixed, but Dave soon cut him off. "All good input. We'll discuss this once I settle in. Now, if you'll excuse me, I have to close up."

He watched Tony drive off. Not as simple a town as he'd hoped. Even that missing person file looked a little peculiar. Funny that Mr.

Security hadn't included it in his list of open issues, but maybe he'd been rushed out the door too fast. Right now Dave needed a cold beer and then a warm bed. He checked the doors one last time and turned out the lights. Someone had left a checklist on the wall that included in bold letters TURN OFF COFFEE. He checked—it was off. He set the alarms, zipped up and headed out into the cold again.

CHAPTER 7

Reese was eager to continue his tour. "This is Pine," he said. "It's a busy intersection, with a church, town hall, post office, and bank. There's talk of even putting in our first traffic light here."

Dave nodded but couldn't really focus. He'd felt a little off since yesterday, but had put that down to his collision with the side of the streetcar. Now he could feel the beginnings of a bad migraine headache, a pressure building up in his skull. It was strange. He never used to get these.

"And here we are, the Grande," said Reese.

The hotel was an old two story log building, with large windows, a wide porch on three sides, and a newer looking kitchen tacked on the back side. The main floor windows were all lit but the upper floor looked unoccupied. Dave hoped he would not be sharing a room with mice.

Dave nodded. "Thanks for the tour. I'm ready to just check in, then crash. Pop the back, would you?"

Dave stepped back out into winter to get his bags. Wide steps led up to a pair of entrances, one labelled Reception and one further down, Raven's Roost. He picked the former and pushed in.

While the outside had been freshly painted, the renovations had skipped the lobby. There was an old cracked leather sofa, a tattered carpet, and two straight back chairs at a side table. The wallpaper was faded, and a sad-looking fern sat in the corner. The reception desk was empty, but he could hear noises through the heavily curtained doorway behind it. He put his things down and leaned on the counter for a moment to rest. It had been a rush to get out of Toronto, with only time to grab a couple of hastily packed bags. He rubbed the back of his neck and yawned.

He was about to ring the bell when a head popped through the curtain. "Hi, you must be Dave, be with you in a sec."

He saw a fleeting figure of a young woman, dark haired and native. She'd flitted in, cocked her head, and disappeared before he could say a word.

In a moment she was back, "Sorry, was a busy day, your room's not quite ready."

"Am I the only guest here?" he asked.

"For now," she said. "We do more rooms in the summer, once tourist season starts. I've a place upstairs, but the public section has been closed since the fall. I just need to get some fresh towels and let your room warm up. Why don't you pop in the bar for a beer while you're waiting?"

Then she was gone again.

Dave stared after her. She was kind of cute. It was too bad he had this rule against dating co-workers, waitresses at his favourite bar, landladies, elected officials, people with criminal records, television announcers, and pretty much anybody else who might compromise his work or get clingy if things didn't work out. It was a pretty long list. He let out a huge sigh. It was sure a long way from Toronto—the Centre of the Universe. He supposed it wouldn't hurt to have one drink with her.

He hunched his shoulders, ducked outside, and went back in through the Raven's Roost door. The pub was all one large room, dimly lit, with a bar along the far wall. Next to it, in the corner, was a table top curling game and a pool table. A set of wide patio doors led outside, onto the porch he supposed, but they were covered up with clear plastic. There was a mismatched collection of wooden chairs and a scattering of plain pub tables, all of them empty except one at the back, with a group of four quiet drinkers. There were several flat screen TV's on the walls, tuned to various sports channels but all muted. He could hear some piped-in music, 80's rock style. The air was heavy with a blend of beer, wet winter clothes, and something deep-fried.

Most of the walls were covered in art—big colourful canvases, almost abstract looking. One had a big spoked wheel on it, while several others featured different animals. The style was a blend of back alley mural and First Nations art, but it worked. The bar itself had the standard collection of bottles behind it, some draft taps at one end, and a row of low-backed stools in front. The only other patrons tonight were a couple of older guys sitting at the end of the bar, staring at a TV, baseball hats on their heads. JB was behind the bar, on the move, flitting back and forth, whistling a little tune to herself.

She waved to him. "Want a seat or are you still thawing out before you can speak?"

"Sorry," he said, "it's been a long day. Just sort of zoned out."

"You'd think this cold would have perked you up," she said. "Join us."

He walked over to the bar and pulled out a stool, then looked around the room again. "Nice place. Not too fancy, just a tavern. I like the art too."

"Thanks," she said. "Some of it is mine, a lot is by my little brother, Junior. He's good. As for the furniture, we do get the occasional bar fights here so need some relatively cheap."

He decided to not mention he'd met her brother already. "I hope you call us to help calm the crowd."

"Sure, we do, but it's often over and done by the time someone gets here. The only thing for you guys is to decide who gets to have a ride in the Buffalo cab back to lockup for the night. Now, the summer crowd? That's another challenge."

Dave smiled at the cab reference. He'd once had a drunk wave his police car down and climb into the back before realizing where he was, and that the back doors wouldn't open for him. Dave had recognized him, ran his name in the system, and discovered two outstanding warrants. It was the easiest bust he'd ever made.

"So, I guess tonight's crowd will show up later, eh?"

"Nope," she replied. "This is pretty well it for tonight, no big hockey game on the wide screen, and we're in between paydays and government checks. I provide free Wi-fi, but that's mostly for the summer tourists. Most evenings people, when they do come in, split a pitcher and nurse it all night." She nodded over to the table in the corner.

While he listened, Dave had been taking off his parka and hat and scarf and mitts, building a mound on the stool next to him. "I was freezing before," he said, "but now I'm dying in all this. How do you manage to not spend all your time dressing and undressing?"

She smiled at him mischievously. "We've just met and you're already undressing me?"

Dave blushed and stammered, "No, I mean, I just — "

The two drinkers next to him laughed and high-fived each other.

JB smiled. "Calm down you two. Just teasing you, Dave, that's my style. Paul, Scottie, meet Dave, new guy in town. He's taking over for Chris, to run the detachment, so be nice to him."

"Great, hope we see you in here more than the last guy," said Scottie.

"Perhaps," said Dave.

"It's a friendly crowd," she said. "Paul here, he works part time for the town office, helping with the books. Used to be a big broker down south, but now is just easing himself into retirement. Scottie—far from retirement."

"Damn right," said Scottie. "I spend all summer doing cottage renos, in between fishing trips. Winter is more upgrade work—indoors—and the ski-doo club. Plus listening to my pal Paul try to convince me to set up a retirement plan."

"Just want to make sure you can always afford to buy a round or two for us," said Paul.

"Nice to meet you guys," said Dave. "Right now, I need a pint myself to help end the day. JB?"

"Not much selection on tap in the winter I'm afraid. There's Ex, Blue Light, and Two Rivers, from a micro-brewery in Winnipeg. My grandfather loves it." She hesitated, then pointed over to the lone table of drinkers. "If I could make a suggestion, as much as you'd be welcome here at the bar, it would be a good gesture to join him and his friends for a bit, as long as you're here anyway."

"I suppose I could say hi," said Dave.

"Here, could you bring them a new pitcher too?" she said. "On the house. They're drinking Two Rivers."

Dave carried the draft over to the four men. One looked to be his age, one middle-aged, and then two older ones, natives. First Nations, he corrected himself. Those two looked like a Mutt and Jeff pair, one tall and lean, the other short and squat. Everyone looked up expectantly as he approached, jug of beer in one hand, a glass in the other.

***

JB watched Dave as he walked over and sat down at the table.

"He'll have to work at blending in," said Paul, "but the beer will help. We'll have to make sure to invite him to buy some for us next time."

"Not sure how much he'll be drinking here," said JB. "Chris was pretty much a teetotaller, and tried to keep official and social sides very separate. Personally, I think it doesn't hurt to wander in once in a while—to show he's a person."

"I saw you watching him wander across the room," said Scottie. "Enjoying the view?"

"Shut up," said JB, as she gave him a poke. She did have to admit she'd followed Dave's progress, though. "I'm in no hurry for another guy. After that jerk in Ottawa dumped me I decided to swear off men."

"For good?" said Paul.

"For now," she said. "Let's just drop it, okay?"

She could see that Dave was trying to get a conversation going. Poor guy—she knew her grandfather was cautious with new people, as he'd seen a lot of do-gooders from the south. They'd show up, fresh from some course, eager to make their mark, trying to please too many bosses, full of prejudices and plans. She'd been like them in a way, heading off to University ready to change the world. However, once she got there, she'd soon become bored with her courses. They didn't seem that relevant to her. She'd spent most of her time enjoying the clubs, the cafes, the art scene.

"What about Ottawa," said Scottie. "Are you heading back there again to study?"

"I don't know," she said. "It was a big change. Ottawa is not Kirk's Landing."

"Lots of parties, I bet," said Scottie.

"I did hit a few," she said. "But I was older than most of the kids, so it felt a little weird. I hung out in a few cafes, or at some hip-hop events. I met some very talented people at those: dancers, poets, musicians, graffiti artists."

40

"What—taggers?" asked Paul.

"No, not kids with markers doing mailboxes, artists doing big outdoor murals on walls—for money."

"Sounds the same to me," said Paul.

"Trust me, I'll bring in some photos. Some of them even get work into galleries. Now, I need to go and finish up Dave's room. Scottie, you leave the draft taps alone."

She glanced over at Dave's table as she left. They all seemed to be getting along, chatting back and forth, her grandfather quietly watching —as usual. She hoped this guy was different and not up here just to put in time. He did seem kind of distant, but maybe he was just shy. He certainly was cute enough, even kind of hot, once he got all those extra clothes off. She took in those wide shoulders, and imagined the muscles underneath—

Stop it, she told herself, it's been a long winter and a long time since Pete had dumped her. Not a very good year, either, with failing her courses, being away from her family, and then her father's disappearance. She had thought coming home was where her path led, but she still felt restless, unfocused. She definitely didn't need another complicated relationship.

***

Dave walked over to the group, set the beer down on the table, and smiled. "JB sent over a pitcher. Mind if I join you for a drink?"

They all smiled and slid their glasses forward. "That's a good introduction," one of them said. "Have a seat."

"I'm Dave Browne, RCMP."

The youngest stretched his hand out, "Hi Dave, just heard today we were getting a new chief of police. Glad to meet you. I'm Mike, this is Rosie and George, and the band chief, Charlie Bourbeau."

Rosie and George put out their hands, but the band chief just nodded.

Dave nodded back. "Sir." He felt a wave of dizziness as George and Charlie looked at him—he really should have grabbed a sandwich with this beer.

Dave poured a round then sat back and sipped his drink. He'd rather be asleep in bed by now, but would try to make the best of it. Develop some of those social skills for his file.

"I don't officially start here until tomorrow," he said, "but already had a tour. Nice little town."

Smiles, but no comment.

"I look forward to working with you all," he said.

The chief just nodded. He certainly wasn't a chatty one. As they sipped their beer, the others began to thaw a bit and share a few details. Mike worked at the mill, on some sort of database, Rosie had a restaurant in town, and the shorter native, George, did a mix of things. He was a former chief, and despite his apparent age and diminutive size, still ran logging trucks in the winter, did some snow plowing in town, and guided tourists in the summer. He was also something called an elder. Dave talked a bit more about life on other postings, but left out any specifics, especially the undercover part. He also tried to throw in some ideas about policing in a small town but he was winging it there—his postings had been mostly to cities. It turned out Rosie had come from Toronto a few years ago, so they exchanged some stories of familiar places. The two natives were relatively quiet, especially Chief Bourbeau. He just sat and watched, occasionally nodding or grunting in agreement with something George said.

"So, are you eager to dive into the little issues of our little town?" asked Mike. "Or will we be too quiet for you?"

"I wouldn't mind quiet for my time up here," said Dave. "You're town is fine, but I'm really more of a city guy."

"We do have a few city-style problems," said Mike. "Especially once the summer folk roll in. Drugs, fights, lots to keep the detachment busy. In addition, there are some issues with the mill's government funding. Not as squeaky clean as some claim."

"And there's the disappearance of the Chief's son," said George.

"Yes, I heard already about that," said Dave. He nodded at the chief. "Sorry to hear about that, sir." The elder nodded back.

"I'll be reviewing all the open issues in the next few days," said Dave. "If you've any new information, please feel free to drop by and talk to us."

"Don't need more talk," said George. "Time for action."

"Sure," said Dave. "Just let me check the files first, I'll get back to

42

you."

They all acted friendly, but guarded. He'd seen that before in small towns. Not really his problem anyway, as he wasn't up here to make friends, just to keep his nose clean.

Soon the pitcher was empty, and Dave could feel his eyes drooping. George had started a long complicated story and Dave had already nodded off once—hopefully without being noticed. He was tired from the long day, as well as trying to keep the conversation going. Dave excused himself, with handshakes all around and a nod from the chief, and walked over to the bar, where JB was busily checking her stock and cleaning up.

***

Dave looked done in to her. "Calling it a night?" she asked.

"Yup, getting tired and not a lot left to talk about."

"Give them time," she chuckled. Maybe he was really trying.

"One of them, George, was telling some story about a bear," said Dave. "It was sitting in a circle with some animals—some kind of meeting I think. They were all advising him, like a town council or something, but the story just went on and on. I honestly had no idea where he was going with it. I may have even dozed off. Not a great first impression."

"He does like to tell stories," she said, "but can be long-winded at times. On the other hand, he may have seen you were tired and droned on just for the fun of it—he's tricky sometimes."

She'd have to remind the elders that this was a city boy, still used to fast paced entertainment, rather than a leisurely story.

"Teasing you would be a good sign," she said. "Be patient. They need to see where you fit in and if your actions and words match up. They're simple people, but not simple—if you know what I mean."

"I do," said Dave. "I've some First Nations blood in me too, from my grandmother. She was Ojibwa."

"Really?" said JB, "She was Anishinaabe?"

"I think so," said Dave. "Was on my mother's side. Didn't see her that much. My mother died when I was a teenager, and my dad was in the armed forces, so we kept moving every few years. Good practice for being independent. He and I don't talk much now."

"That's too bad," she said. "You should tell George about your grandmother though. He knows lots about our history—seems like a slow plodding sort of guy but he's observant. And smart. So is Grandfather, just more reserved at first."

"Is that what I should be calling him, Grandfather?"

She laughed, "No, not yet, sir is just fine, as a show of respect." Now why did I say 'not yet', she wondered. Calm down girl. "Here's your key. Top of the stairs, turn left, you've the executive suite so even get your own bathroom. Did you get any dinner?"

"No," he admitted, "somehow I missed that today."

"Well, we don't do much here," she said. "Especially in winter. Weekends we do have an awesome meatball sub—it's messy and greasy but very popular. For tonight I can do up a sandwich. How about roast beef with provolone cheese, on sourdough bread?"

"Yes, sounds good," said Dave. "Rare if you've got it, please. I'll just wait here and bring it up with me."

"You're the only guest right now," she said, "but I'll make sure there's fresh coffee and some muffins or something at the end of the bar for you in the morning. Help yourself. And feel free to drop by while on your rounds to grab a coffee. Give me a sec now and I'll make that sandwich."

When she came out Dave was sitting by himself at one of the tables. Scottie and Paul were completely ignoring him, which was a little strange, as they usually tried to talk the ear off anyone nearby. There was some sort of shadow around Dave too, but when he saw her watching him he stood up and whatever it was—bad lighting she supposed—was gone.

"Thanks," he said, rubbing his head. "Pretty worn out, time to crash I guess."

"No problem," she said, and watched him walk over to the stairs.

She noticed her grandfather and the others getting ready to leave, so she went over to their table.

"What do you think of Dave?" she said.

"Dave?" said George.

She blushed. "Corporal Browne. So—first impressions?"

"Seems like a nice guy," said Rosie.

"Not too eager and keen either," said Mike.

"We could do with a bit of keen, though," she said. "We don't need somebody that's just filling in time for a year. How about you, Grandfather—what do you think."

He shrugged. "He doesn't talk much. I like that in a man." He paused as everybody laughed. "He sounds reasonable to me, but not that willing yet to get involved. His spirit could be a problem. George and I saw something dark there, something we didn't like. The last time we saw that it was in your cousin."

"Who's that?" said Rosie.

"He left the year before you arrived," said JB. "I thought I saw something too just now but blamed it on the lighting. I hope you're wrong about this."

CHAPTER 8

Dave was surprised, as his room wasn't that bad for a small country hotel. It was plain but clean, with a queen-sized bed against one wall, a desk in the corner, a big TV with a leather chair next to it, and a loveseat by the window. He prodded the mattress—it would do. He was about to check his cell for messages, then realized he didn't have one anymore. He'd had a burner phone the gang had supplied, and an active, but fictitious, Facebook identity. He'd had a long list of contacts from his club persona—suburban kids, dancers, bouncers, investment brokers, high-rollers and posers—all looking to score a little action, to get their buzz on. All that was gone now, left in Toronto, part of his old life back there, a life of fun times but also of stress. No point in worrying about his choice, he just needed to tough it out for a few months. He'd had worse postings. As for that Badger character, hopefully he would forget about Dave. The biker had looked really pissed and, unlike the others in the room, had stared right at him.

Unpacking only took a few minutes, then he sank into the big chair and munched on his very good sandwich. This place might work out. Maybe not so much of a sleepy town after all, but still far enough off the grid that the Toronto bikers would never find him. He picked up a pen and started making some notes, a useful police habit for closing the day. Barretto, the chief, his staff, JB—a lot of new people to deal with—a whole town full. His fade would help him deal with it all, although when he'd used it tonight he'd felt a sharp pain, right between his eyes. He sat back, and felt some of the tension drain away as he relaxed, free from the worry of being caught out, of someone pouncing on him in a dark alley.

Out of the corner of his eye, he saw a pale shape at the window. Before he could even worry about who might have betrayed his location he reacted instinctively. He rolled to the floor and within a second was against the wall next to the window with his pen at the ready. He stared ruefully at it. This was a ridiculous weapon. Why did he leave his gun at the office? That was the last time that would happen. There was a scratch on the glass. Peering sideways he saw a small cat—white as a ball of snow—pawing at the window.

He lifted the sash and beckoned, "Okay—it's pretty cold out there. Come in. Just for the night though. I'm a lone wolf, so don't need a pet to have to look after."

The cat paused, then leaped onto the floor and rubbed against his leg.

"Just as long as you're cool with that," he said. "Here, finish my sandwich, then just find a corner and settle down. I'm tired and need my rest."

And he needed to stop talking to a cat.

***

Dave tried to run faster, but the deep snow pulled at his feet. The moon did little to dispel the shadows from the tall pines that surrounded him on all sides. In the distance, wolves howled to each other, but that was not what he was fleeing. Whatever chased him was closer, almost at his back. He'd turned a few times to face his enemy, but there was nothing there. He could hear something breathing heavily, yet it ran silently, always closer. There was a growl, hot on his neck, and he yelled in fear.

Dave woke up with a jerk, confused, afraid, then realized where he was, safe in bed. He'd left the window open just an inch, a habit from Toronto, so had been glad for the warmth of the thick duvet. Too much warmth, as now he was covered in sweat—probably from that nightmare. He shivered, then looked over to the frost covered window. Last night the cat had fallen asleep even before Dave had, but was now meowing loudly, eager to get out. There was the occasional faint noise from the bar downstairs, and the sound of some birds outside, but no sirens, no streetcars, no traffic.

He smiled as the cat meowed again. A lot of noise for such a little

47

ball of fur. Snowball, he thought, would be a good name for it.

"Yes, Snowball, I'm up and it's time for a pee for me too."

He let the cat out, then closed both windows all the way, cranked up the heat, grabbed his toiletries, and headed into the bathroom.

When he came out—refreshed by the hot shower—there was no sign of the cat. Just as well, he thought, I don't want her in here when I'm gone. He stared pensively at the clothes he'd brought. A suit would be a little much for Kirk's Landing, his biker garb—not enough. He settled on a shirt, tie, sweater and slacks. With any luck his new uniform would arrive today.

True to her word, JB had left a muffin, shrink-wrapped on a plate, a banana, and a note, saying "Coffee's behind the bar, have a good first day at work. Let me know if you want us to pack lunches for you. JB." The note finished with a little happy face. He poured himself a coffee, and met Sid, the day guy.

"You're not the first city visitor to say that it's almost too quiet up here," he said. "I'm from Halifax—I noticed the difference too when I arrived. You'll get used to it."

***

Dave had hoped for a quiet walk to work, but the few people on the street all waved and called out greetings to him. After a while it just got to be too much, so he used a lull to turn on his fade and finished his walk in peace. His power still felt different to him than in Toronto, even after a good night's sleep. Now it included both a headache and a bit of a buzz—different, but still useable. Worth it, just to be left alone. These people certainly were an in-your-face crowd, compared to those in Toronto. Down there the best you could hope for on a crowded street was to not get pushed aside or have your toe stepped on. He preferred the big city crowds though, as he could walk along by himself, headphones in, and ignore everyone right back. Except for the occasional smile at a pretty girl, of course.

48

CHAPTER 9

ave walked into the detachment at seven—still carrying his muffin
and a cup of delicious coffee from the Grande. He certainly couldn't
fault the locals for their coffee. There might be hope yet for the north.
Norris was at her paper-covered desk, and just behind the counter stood a
matronly looking woman. Dave nodded to the constable, smiled at the
woman. "Hi, I'm Corporal Dave Browne, you must be Sheila Palin."

"Yes, that's me," she said. "Nice to meet you young man. Glad they
finally decided to send someone here. It's disgraceful how we are always
neglected, treated like a small town in the middle of nowhere when we're
an important hub for the area. My husband, the mayor, works literally day
and night for us all. You would think that we would get more
appreciation. I hope you'll do better than the last one they sent us. He was
always fussing about speeders on the highway or those Indians out on the
reservation, never paying attention to the important things here in town."

Dave waited patiently for her to run down. "Well ma'am, I realize
folks may have felt we were a little short-handed for a while here, but I've
done a quick review last night of the files. Looks to me like the two
constables have done a good job working extra hours to look after the
town."

When Sheila looked ready to start up again, Norris quickly
interjected. "Dave, could you look at this report for a second?"

He walked over to look at the paper, an old report, and realized she
had only been running interference for him. "Yes, looks good," he said.
He lowered his voice. "Oh, by the way, I thought the mill security guy
was called Tony?"

"His middle name is Carmine," she said. "He hates it, so I'm using it when he's being particularly annoying. Trying out some behaviour modification techniques that I learned from a training course."

"Hmm," said Dave. "Let me know if they work on Carmine."

He ducked into his office, closing the door. He heard Sheila starting up again, and realized his coffee was still out on the counter. Dammit! Maybe it could wait a bit.

***

By 10 am, Dave had made a good start at organizing his office. He'd also reviewed the current duty rosters and hot issues, retrieved and enjoyed his coffee, and was starting to wish he'd had more for breakfast. Norris had brought him up to speed on a number of issues, but thankfully nothing was too urgent. She and Reese seemed to have been filling in fine on their own—although with extra hours. Hours approved without question by sub-division headquarters.

Dave was painfully aware that for most of his career he had been on his own, mainly working the drug squad. He was counting on this team to keep him out of trouble for the year he was stuck up here. He smiled to himself as he remembered one of the first pieces of advice given to him by Chuck. "Just keep your reservations to yourself, son. Fake it 'til you make it and nobody will be the wiser." Dave sincerely hoped this would be the case.

Sheila bustled into his office and smiled at his attempts to sort papers on the desk. He'd suggested she help out, but apparently sorting his paperwork was not part of her job description. She handed him his office cellphone, along with yet more forms, and added, "Oh yes, that reminds me. The District Officer and NCO are coming out for a visit day after tomorrow."

Dave looked at her enquiringly.

"The superintendent will want to welcome you officially to the division, " she said. "He's your line officer and does your annual performance assessment. But the District NCO, he writes it for him. He's the one you call first if there is a major file or questions we can't answer."

She hurried back out and Dave smiled. Chain of Command 101.

He looked at the pile of papers still to be sorted through, and decided he needed to get out for a bit. He missed his former office—the comfortable streets and back alleys of Toronto. He was about to get up when Sheila poked her head in the door.

"The mayor and the mill manager have asked to meet with you," she said.

He really had been hoping to delay any official visits for a few days at least.

"Can you set something up for next week?" he asked.

"They're here now—are you in?"

He sighed. He'd have to get her to do some scheduling for him. As for right now—they were here so might as well get it over and see what their big issues were. Hopefully would be no more than small town things like petty theft or jaywalking.

"Be right out," he said.

Dave straightened his tie and strode out to meet his visitors. Mayor Rob Palin, and the mill manager, Frederick Klein, were all smiles and booming voices. After handshakes all around Dave pointed them toward his office.

They all managed to fit in, in spite of the mayor's size. Palin had a flat topped brushcut, bulging eyes, and a round face, flushed and sweating. His collar and suit jacket looked like they were losing the battle to contain his bulk as he settled carefully into a chair. Klein, on the other hand, was thin, with a carefully groomed goatee, slicked down hair, and an expensive looking pin-striped suit.

"Sorry, it's a bit cramped here," said Dave.

"Why don't we have the mayor's wife set up our weekly meetings down the street in the town hall?" said Klein.

"Good idea," said the mayor. He moved as if to call back into the main room.

"Hold on," said Dave. "Thanks for the offer, but I'll see first what my workload looks like. I'll be sure to find a way to keep you in the loop on things. Apparently we used to have monthly status meetings with you and your council, so I'll at least keep it at that."

"Okay, but it's just that I like to keep my finger on things in the town," said the mayor. "Helps to have the wife working in here too, that way if I can't reach you directly I can get her to pass the issues on for me."

The mill manager beamed. "Anyway, we wanted to pass on some great news. We're in line for a big award this spring, plus $2.2 Million in funding under Canada's Economic Action Plan for a PPGTP project."

Dave stared at him blankly.

"That's our Pulp and Paper Green Transformation Program."

Dave wondered what he meant by 'our' —whether it was as a fellow Canadian or a wannabe confidant of the present government.

"Great for the townspeople, great for the economy," said Klein.

"A real feather in our lapel," said the mayor.

"A chance to grow into the biggest and most important mill town in the province," added Klein.

"Special visit by the Minister—big city stuff," said the mayor.

"A vote of confidence for this new technology," said Klein.

As Dave watched them volley back and forth like a tennis match, he had a good idea who was really in charge.

He nodded at Klein. "It does sound impressive. I've already heard some talk of pollution problems here, so it's good to hear there's money to clean that up."

Whoops, not a popular topic. Both Palin and Klein sat back and those happy smiles disappeared.

"You might want to be careful who you listen to around here," said Klein. "There are some that like to complain and gossip. With this promised funding, we certainly don't need rumours spreading and distracting the press. Fact is this mill went in 10 years ago with state of the art equipment, designed to the latest specifications for pollution control. We were the first site in the company to go TCF. That's Totally Chlorine Free."

"That's right," said the mayor, "we're state of the art here, totally TCF free."

Klein looked at the mayor then continued. "We recycle everything back into the process. Our discharge into the water and the air is targeted to be well below the limit. The local band demanded we do that, as the outflow goes through the land we let them have for a reserve. They did some heavy lobbying somewhere for sure to block us initially, caught us off guard, so we had to do some fast negotiating."

"They just can't see the big picture," said the mayor. "We had a hard time convincing them that this would be a win-win, for them and the town and a chance for them to finally get jobs. Once they saw the numbers on how clean the mill could be, and how well this process ran elsewhere, they were convinced."

"So it has been good for jobs for them?" said Dave.

"In some areas, yes," said the mill manager. "You have to understand this is a complicated operation, you just can't put anyone in charge of this equipment. Head Office sent in their own team for the management positions. They still do need people out on the floor to run the equipment, so there are lots of jobs left, ones the natives can handle just fine. But they still aren't happy, so are always trying to shut us down, threatening protests, making up stories of pollution and filing grievances every time one of them decides they'd rather sit at home than put in an honest day's work."

"What you need is a tour," said the mayor. "See the operation for yourself."

"I'll have Sheila set something up," said Dave. "I understand there's still an open case on a disappearance last year—a Mr. Bourbeau?"

Again, a sore point. Both men looked uncomfortable.

"Nothing in that," said the mayor. "Some guy went out on his own and just got lost. Tragic but it happens often up here in the north. Every summer we have to go look for some tree-hugger off on a nature hike."

Dave refrained from pointing out that the missing man was not only a local, but First Nations and likely familiar with the surrounding area.

"Like I said, we consider it an unfortunate accident," said Klein. "It's over and done. Just need to leave it be. Oh, look at the time, we better run."

And with that they were gone, leaving him to his quiet office again. He might need to dig a bit more on this unsolved case. As for the alleged pollution, that was not really his concern. It had been interesting though, to see how jumpy they had been about both issues.

***

Dave wondered if he could just stuff his whole in-basket into a box and start over again. Yesterday's visit by the mayor and mill manager had managed to add to both his stress and his suspicions. While he still was more that willing to stay uninvolved, his detective instincts were nudging

53

him to start poking around a bit.

The phone rang out in the main office, then Norris called in to him, "Dave, politics on line two."

"Hello, Corporal Browne?"

"Yes."

"This is Emily Grant. I'm aide to the Minister for Northern Economic Development. I need to touch bases with you about her planned visit to your town."

"Yes, I just heard about it," he said. "Is she hoping for another quick in-and-out tour? Because I hear timing at the airport can be tricky this time of year. "

There was a pause. "No," she said, "it will be for the full day. This is an important event. The award portion is to recognize the mill for all their advances in pollution-control technology, but there's also a new funding initiative from this Government, part of PPGTP—"

"Pulp and Paper Green Transformation Program?" he said.

"Ah, yes, that's it, glad news has spread about it. The Minister will be announcing the funding on April 25th—that's a Friday—in a press conference at the mill. She'll be arriving on the morning flight from Winnipeg, and taking the evening one back. We're counting on your support on this. There have been some rumours and gossip about pollution from the mill, encouraged by the opposition parties of course, and not based on any facts."

Yet more people talking about a problem they insisted didn't exist. Dave sat up. "Go on."

"I would hope that you and your men can ensure everything runs smoothly and there are no incidents."

"And women," he said.

"Pardon?"

"And women—one of my constables is a woman."

"Excellent," said the aide, "the Minister will definitely want her there at the opening. Can she wear her dress uniform?"

"I assume you mean the Red Serge," he said. "Sorry, but she'll be on regular duty, so can't wear that. But I will make sure she's assigned to your group. As for the pollution issues, or any others, we will focus on ensuring the visit goes smoothly, but we will of course also continue with any open investigations."

They weren't really that far into any investigations, but he thought he'd see what he could stir up. "We do have excellent cooperation from all groups involved," he said, "especially from the band members. However, we have not yet determined if in fact charges should be laid."

"Charges?" she said. "No, no, this is all just rumour as far as we know. We certainly wouldn't want to influence the excellent work you and your team are doing, but we'd prefer the focus to be on the Minister and her visit."

After he assured her of a smooth visit, the talk grew more casual. She was a Toronto girl originally, and had heard he'd been posted there at one time. She was convinced they must have bumped into each other. He tried to be vague about his time there, but she managed to imply that she had some inside information. He hoped he hadn't met her in a drug bust somewhere. That could be awkward!

"Maybe when I'm up in your little town we'll have time to catch up on old times over a drink," she said. "I hear it's pretty cold up there, but I'm sure we'll be able to find a warm fireplace. Thanks for your cooperation on this, we're looking forward to the opportunity for your community and our government's proactive pollution control program. Oops, gotta run, Dave, another vote is about to start in the House, thanks for all your help."

And with that she was gone, leaving Dave looking at the phone in his hand. How did she know about his fireplace? Hopefully just a lucky guess. As for her 'advice,' he was tired already about the mill visit. He hoped people were getting the message that he had no intention of making waves.

He got up and headed for the detachment door. "That's enough office work for now folks, I'm off for a walk down Main Street."

CHAPTER 10

Dave scratched a big X on his desk calendar. Day Number Three, and it was looking to be just as busy as the first two. The visit from the mayor, plus that call from the minster's office had added to the already complicated job of running a detachment. He'd had a chat with Sheila too, in an effort to find out what she thought her job description was. He was pretty sure that had been a waste of breath, as she'd spent the whole meeting rearranging the binders on his shelf in order of height and colour, and talking about her husband the mayor. If only Dave could convince her to organize his desk. All of the desks, for that matter—hers was the only tidy one in the office.

First thing this morning three large boxes had arrived from RCMP Stores and Sheila was now giddy with delight. She opened the boxes, piled the clothes on the counter, and set all the clips, pins and hats in little lines on his desk. Then she called Reese in from patrol and assigned him to polishing Dave's ankle boots.

"He doesn't really have to do that," said Dave. "The new ones are non-polishing, and Reese has better things to do solving crime."

Sheila gave him a withering look of disdain. "He was on a vandalism call at the gas station. Everybody knows that the Reynolds kids did it, and their parents will just cover for them again. There's nothing Reese can do there so he's better off here getting you ready for the Superintendent's visit this morning."

Dave stared at her in amazement as she hauled out an ironing board and began to attack the shirt and pants she obviously had in mind for him to wear today. He was pretty sure this was not in her job description, but there seemed to be no stopping her.

Sheila voiced his thoughts. "And don't you think this is in my job description! This is a one-time only favour because I don't want the Superintendent seeing you wearing those old pants and a sweater for his first visit. You only have once chance to make a first impression!"

She continued grumbling to herself while Dave took the extra clothing through the door to his private residence. When he returned Reese had finished polishing the boots and belt and was busy adding rank pins to his jacket and hat. Sheila was meaningfully holding out the freshly ironed shirt, so Dave peeled off his sweater and took it. The room went silent and Dave looked up to see both Sheila and Reese staring at him—her with shock, him with fascination.

"What?" And then he remembered his tattoos. When you wear them every day you forget the impact of them on a first viewing. Since he only had a singlet on, the raven on one shoulder was easily visible wrapped around his bicep. The brown bear on his back extended up into his neck, there was a Celtic band encircled one arm, and a couple of birds on one collar bone. Not to mention the scars on both arms. What they didn't see were several lash scars on his back where his father had beaten him with a belt when he was young. Hiding those marks was the main reason for the first tattoo.

"Drug squad," he explained to Reese, who nodded dubiously and went to help Sheila tidy up the main office.

***

Dave hurried down the detachment steps. He'd managed to convince Sheila that he had time to pop over to Rosie's before the big visit, and assured her he would keep everything clean. He could already feel the cold nipping at his ears, as he headed for the cafe.

Rosie's was a small place, looking more like the converted front of a house. It sat at the end of a row of houses, typical of the mixed zoning— or lack of it—that he'd seen in small towns. The clapboard was painted blue, with a clean white trim, and the roof looked new. The sign on the big front window said Rosie's Cafe, written in a bold red script with a rose painted at the end. As he got closer he could see that there were some booths under the window and a long counter with a row of red stools.

He was just reaching for the door when he heard a voice behind him.

"Hey, nice uniform Dave. On a break?"

"Oh, hi JB," he said. "This just came in today. Might as well look like I'm in charge. Big meeting later so I'm out for some fresh air. It's pretty cold air though, so I thought I'd drop in here to warm up."

"I did hear the brass are coming to visit," she said. She held the door for Dave behind her. "Hi Rosie, here's a new customer."

Rosie bustled around the counter's end, wiped his hand on his apron, and held it out, "Corporal Browne, good to see you again. Glad to see you out and about. Welcome to my humble cafe, a culinary experience and home of the best coffee in the area."

JB smiled, "The cafe may be humble, but Rosie is neither humble nor quiet."

"What can I say?" Rosie spread his hands out. "If I didn't like people, I wouldn't be in the business of serving them."

"And the name?" Dave asked.

"Bit of a story, but glad to fill you in," said Rosie.

"Here we go," said JB. "Pour us a couple of coffees while you're revving up would you?"

"Honest, I'll just give you the Cole's Notes version," said Rosie. "I still have to prep for supper. Grab a perch."

Dave sat on a stool next to JB. There was a shiny espresso machine behind the counter and list of today's specials on the wall, along with some black and white photos. Looked like they were of downtown Toronto. The booths, all along the window, were done in red to match the stools. At the end of the room was a low table, covered with magazines and papers and flanked by several comfy looking chairs. Two were occupied, one by a knitter, the other by John Hammel, from the airport. The latter looked furtively down, grabbed his coffee, and headed out the door. Dave made a mental note to check that Reese was following up on him.

"Nice place," said Dave.

"Thanks," said Rosie. "My wife Rosie and I had a fancy little cafe in downtown Toronto. We did breakfast, catering, gourmet lunches—mostly the office crowds. She was the real cook, I just made sure things ran smoothly. Some guy started calling me Rosie too as a joke, and it stuck. We covered for each other on everything anyway."

"So, what brought you guys up here?" Dave asked.

"It's just me," said Rosie."Our goal had been to sell the business and the property and retire somewhere with a small quiet, cafe. We'd wanted to move to a small town like this, eventually, but the busier we got, the harder it was to take time off. Then a few years ago my sweetie got sick, a hidden heart defect."

"Oh, sorry'" said Dave.

Rosie nodded. "It was fast, she only lasted a few days. I promised to still follow our dream, so I found a rich buyer, packed up our secret recipes, and here I am."

"It is a nice place," said Dave, "and I'll be eating here until my stuff arrives, I guess."

"You're in luck," said Rosie. "Tonight's special is steak."

"Excellent," said Dave. "I've a craving for one. That and good coffee." He held his cup out for a refill.

"Let me guess," said Rosie. "You're a Starbucks fan?"

Dave nodded. "Yonge and Adelaide."

"I know it," said Rosie. "Nice view from the row of little bistro tables lined up inside. A great place for people watching. People on serious business meetings, or first dates, lots of cute young office workers all dolled up in the latest fashions."

"Not like here," said JB. She looked down at her plain clothes.

"You look just fine to me," said Dave. JB blushed. Actually, she looked a lot better than 'just fine.'

"She's quite a catch," said Rosie. "Anyway, my business is pretty good, even in winter. Just plain good food. I try not to be too trendy in the kinds of coffee drinks I serve either, no matter what fancy blends and names the tourists want. Geez, some of them sound like Nigel on the old Frasier show."

JB pointed to a shelf behind the Rosie. "And for those that miss it, he keeps a tin of the Tim Horton's blend."

"Some prefer it," said Rosie, "A bit of citrus, sort of nutty, but not to my taste really. I brew it on request—but I charge a premium for it."

Rosie smiled. "So, like I say business is okay here. The mill is a big help to the town—too bad it doesn't do as well for rest of the area. "

"What do you mean?" asked Dave.

"Well, the stacks occasionally belch out some pretty foul stuff, but the wind usually carries that away from us. However, we're pretty sure they're polluting the water downstream. Fishing has been down, a lot less frogs in the spring, water in the lakes there often has a strange taste now."

Dave looked suspiciously at his coffee. "This water?"

"No, you're okay," said Rosie. "Town water is good, but the reserve gets theirs from wells, and they're downstream from the mill. Seem to be more people sick in the last few years, more just tired and rundown, but some cases of cancer too. Doctors of course refuse to discuss any of the cases, citing patient confidentiality. And the manager is pretty close-mouthed about operations at the mill."

"How about the newspapers," said Dave. "If there's any story, won't they dig it out?"

"Not really," said Rosie. "Too local an issue. Townspeople had pushed for years to get the old mill reopened, but problem was the location. The effluent would flow right through the reserve lands, and then into the Park, so local First Nations groups—and the province—made sure it never got approved. Until this new design was done, that is."

"I'm told it's all the latest state of the art design," said Dave. "What would be the problem now?"

"The design is good," said JB, "Plus this was promoted to us as a big boost to the local economy. Unfortunately, most of my people get put in relatively unskilled jobs on the main floor—low paying jobs."

Dave was hearing a story similar to the one mill manager had told, but with a different spin.

"And no training programs either," said Rosie.

"Exactly," said JB. "And the mill messed up the whole retrofit program. Nothing specific, but there were problems during start-up, and after that too. There always seems to be whole areas of this fancy new equipment shut down and waiting for some crucial part on back order, or they're doing preventative maintenance, or realigning and recalibrating something. The reports all looked good at the annual shareholder meetings, though, the data shows that all is well within the limits."

"But nothing criminal found?" asked Dave.

"Nothing proven," said JB. "The company sent their own investigator, but they never disclosed what he found—not so far. Initially he asked some questions, held a few information sessions, but now he seems to spend most of his time being wined and dined by the managers in their big fancy homes. The company is proud of this mill as an example to other mills, as is the government, so I suspect no one wants to know the truth. In the end we ended up with a mill not much better than the previous designs from the 50's had been, but a lot more expensive."

It sounded to Dave like even if there had been some shady dealings, it would take a lot to dig it up and prove anything.

"What about your dad?" he said.

"My dad was looking into the pollution, especially in the water, when he disappeared."

"He was working for the mill?"

"Ha, no way!" she said. "No, he fought them. He'd earned a science degree a while ago from Guelph in Environmental Biology, and decided to go back and do a Masters. He was looking into the actual impact of these newer, supposedly cleaner mills." She paused. "Maybe he should have stayed in Guelph."

Rosie reached over and squeezed her hand.

"Her dad was collecting more samples," he said, "up from university, last spring. He'd been here the summer before, said he only had a few minor gaps to fill. He'd decided to go out for one last field trip before flying off to a conference on pollution. He'd already done a lot of trips. Last one had been in February."

"In the winter?" said Dave. "Isn't everything frozen and dead?"

JB shook her head. "Not to a biologist, and not to the 'Nish, my people. For us, the winter is still alive, just different. My father was looking at the fish, to see how many had survived over the coldest part of the winter, and taking samples. It was at the beginning of April, but still was cold enough for him to travel easily. Spring break-up wasn't due for another couple of weeks. He could still go onto the ice—carefully—and drill holes for his gill nets and sampling poles. He had already found some disturbing results the summer before, pretty high values in heavy metals and other toxins he said. He'd talked to people in town about it, too. Maybe he shouldn't have been so vocal, because he went out one day and never came back."

Dave said, "I looked into some of it already in the file, it looked to me like a pretty thorough search."

"Oh, it was," she said. "The mill shut down most of the shift and sent everyone out to the area around the lake he'd been going to check out. Hundreds of searchers. They found nothing."

"And his samples and results so far?" Dave asked.

"Gone," she said. "I checked his stuff here, but couldn't find anything. I called his supervisor back in Guelph, he said there was nothing there, that he must have had it all with him." She paused. "Deep down, I know he's not just missing. Somehow, he died out there in the bush. I just need to find out what happened to him. Will you help me?"

"I'll try," said Dave. "There's not much in our detachment files to build on, but I'll be working with Barretto on mill issues, and I'll get him to check his files on this."

"You might want to be careful how close you get to him," she said. "He may not be all that sincere."

"Thanks," said Dave, "but he seemed pretty willing to help. I'll see. Right now, I need to get back to the office. Thanks for the chat."

Rosie watched Dave walk across the street. "What do you think," he said. "Will he help us?"

"Not sure," said JB. "I'll let you know after I talk to him some more. I'm getting a mixed vibe so far."

CHAPTER 11

Superintendent Dickenson and Staff Sergeant William Scully arrived at 11:00 a.m. Sharp. Sheila claimed that it was so they could do exactly one hour of criticism, go to Rosie's for lunch, and then return to the district office before end of day. Reese was long gone, supposedly to check out a complaint at the other end of their territory. As both men peered intently around the office, Dave saw why Sheila had been busy dusting and straightening. He was waiting for somebody to pull on a white glove and start wiping window ledges for dust.

The superintendent leaned against the side of a desk and cleared his throat. "Corporal Browne, I would like to thank you for volunteering to help us out at this detachment."

Dave smiled to himself. Volunteering was a bit of an exaggeration. As the superintendent continued the welcome, the staff sergeant paced around the office, peering at the shift schedule taped to Sheila's desk and sniffing with distaste at the stack of files on Norris's desk. Finally he came and stood beside the superintendent, who finished up quickly and headed back to inspect the cell-block. Dave had no doubt this was a well-rehearsed routine and the staff sergeant's welcome would be less cheery. He indicated that they were to now proceed into Dave's office.

"Corporal Browne."

"Sir."

The staff sergeant narrowed his eyes and resumed his pacing. "Don't 'sir' me, I work for a living. You will call me Staff Sergeant Scully or Staff. You will not call me Bill unless I have already addressed you by your first name and never in front of the public or junior ranks. That is unlikely to happen. I expect regular reports from this office about major events. I expect you to handle minor events without pestering me. There will be no media announcements unless cleared through my office. There will be no going over budget—you've enough staff now to cover the shifts. Let's get something else clear—I don't like self-centred drug squad prima donnas showing up unexpectedly from Toronto. You may be a corporal but you have no credibility and no supervisory experience. There will be no thinking outside the box here until you know what is inside the box. You are not in charge of this detachment—the RCMP is in charge. We are the glove of justice and you are only a finger, the tip of a very small finger that happens to be in this neighbourhood. You do not do weird sensationalist drug squad things here. I want no complaints against the Force, and if there are any I will be investigating them myself. Do I make myself clear?"

Without waiting for an answer, Staff continued. "You have two weak constables here. Constable Reese has potential but he's painfully young and just off field training. He has a tendency to be abrupt with the public, and drives vehicles carelessly. Constable Norris is a poor performer. She seems to have done a credible job training Reese, but she has a reputation for slow paperwork, and does not show enough drive. Her level of self-initiated files is low. Keep an eye on her."

As Staff continued the rant Dave stood at attention. He knew this speech. The drill instructors in basic training made sure every recruit was able to take orders. Keep quiet, respectful, avoid eye contact, do not interrupt. There were a lot of rules here.

"Finally, Corporal, why are you ignoring all my requests on the intranet?"

Dave paused to make sure this really was a question and it was time for him to talk. In fact, he'd forgotten there was an internal network at the office, and nobody had brought it up. As he thought of a good answer the superintendent came back, followed closely by Sheila who held a tray of coffee and cookies. Did she just bake cookies in his oven?

Sheila smiled. "Staff Sergeant, I couldn't help but overhear—you have such a commanding voice. We have a request in for Corporal Browne to get connected to the intranet but he arrived so quickly it hasn't been processed yet."

Staff made a harrumph noise as he munched his cookie. "Well, okay then." He looked at Dave's uniform closely. "Good turnout." He looked around again. "Where are the constables?"

Dave cleared his throat, "Norris is on evening shift. Reese is on patrol."

Staff harrumphed again then stomped off to inspect the exhibit locker.

The superintendent finished his cookie and asked Sheila if there was more coffee. As she busily rushed off to refill the superintendent's cup, he looked curiously at Dave.

"Inspector Chuck Williams was a troop mate of mine in basic training. He speaks highly of you. Staff is unaware that I assisted Chuck to quickly find you a suitable posting here without a lot of administrative delays. Chuck had mentioned the threats against you and added that there is more to you than meets the eye. Although I do not want to know the details, rest assured that we will keep your name out of the news. Please come to me if there is an issue."

Dave stared at him thoughtfully, as the staff sergeant returned.

"Thank you Corporal," said the superintendent. "Carry on. Staff, I believe we have time for lunch before we head back."

With that they left. Dave stared after them, it had been exactly one hour. He had probably said less than 20 words.

CHAPTER 12

JB was surprised, but pleased to see Dave come into the bar. Too bad he was no longer in his new uniform though—it suited him well. "How was the big meeting today?"

"Went well," said Dave. "This afternoon was another blitz on reports and filing so I decided I deserved a quiet beer. And I had to get out of that new uniform before it ripped my skin. It needs a dozen washings to soften up."

"You look good in it," she said. "Look, it's still nice and sunny on the veranda, and no wind. Have a seat and I'll bring your beer."

She looked around the bar—almost empty and the few people there looked good for now. She poured two cold drafts and carried them out onto the porch. She couldn't figure Dave out yet. He'd not turned into a keen do-gooder, which was nice, but he hadn't really turned into anything. He kept pretty well to himself, was polite enough to people the few times they saw him on the street, but wasn't really involved in the town. He acted like he was just putting in time.

"Here we are," she said. "I'll join you for a bit."

They sat quietly for a few minutes.

"Settling in okay?" she asked.

"Yes."

"Getting used to real winter?"

"It's definitely real," he said.

"Room okay?"

"Yes, it is, thanks."

She sat a bit longer. Small talk's not his thing, she thought. So much for getting to know him. "Well, I'll leave you with your beer—"

"No, that's all right," he said. "Stay a bit. Sorry, I'm just tired. I haven't slept well."

"In the executive suite?" she asked.

He shook his head. "No, it's not the room, you've a great place here. I'm just still adjusting I guess. Really busy too, as there's a lot involved in just the running of the detachment office, and managing staff. I'm used to being more of a loner. I'll be glad when my few things arrive from down south, and I can scatter them through that big house and settle in."

She reached over, touched his arm, and looked into his eyes. He was hiding something. "There's more to it than just new job jitters, isn't there. Come on, I can be a good listener."

"Well, it's just that I've been been having peculiar dreams," he said. "In them I'm lost, with animals, always animals, all sorts of them, watching me, chasing me. I keep running from them, rather than running to anything. And there's often something else there, something evil, behind me, watching me. It must be from all these woods around us. Guess I'm not used to so much nature. Or the quiet. So quiet it's boring at times—sorry, but I miss the city life."

She nodded. "It's a slower pace here. An interesting dream. Not the being chased part, but the fact that it's all animals. Plus that extra presence. When did this start?"

"Since I arrived," he said. "I've also had a lot of headaches too—just tired I guess."

"Let me talk to my grandfather about it," she said. "He has a knack for figuring out dreams. As for our laid-back pace—well, I love it. I was down in Ottawa for a year, taking some university courses, and I think the biggest thing I missed was the quiet up here. I finally started to adjust, then my dad disappeared and I had to rush back to try to find him."

"It's really too bad about your dad," he said. "Always rough to lose a parent." Dave's mother had died when he was young, and his father was away so much it seemed like he'd lost him too, years ago.

"It has been hard," she said. "Grandfather and the other elders have been a help, but we all miss him." She paused. "You know, the whole investigation was just too tidy for me, too quick. Not many people got interviewed during it either. I'm sure there are several others here you could talk to."

"Well, for now my focus is on the big funding visit," he said. "Maybe later on I can do more. Right now I don't want to cause any waves, as I've enough of a learning curve as it is."

JB glanced at him. She'd hoped for more.

"What about the office though, doesn't Sheila run that?"

"Yes, she does," he said. "At least some of it. At first she spent most of her time talking about her husband and town politics, but she's started taking on a bit more. She even ironed my uniform before all the brass showed up today, and tidied the office. She was surprised when I complimented her, but I figured she'd earned it."

"She could use the occasional boost," said JB. She suspected Sheila hadn't had many compliments in the past. "So are we the quiet town you expected?"

"Not sure what I expected," he said. "There are a lot of minor day-to-day things, like you'd see in any town. The bigger issues here are not things like the big drug problems I saw in Toronto, but more related to alcohol and poverty. And then there's the mill. I've heard lots of rumours, but I'm sure it's like any new operation with lots of funding—there are bound to be a few issues. Plus I'm not an accountant or a business analyst."

"Don't you have some sort of central group of fraud guys or something?" she asked.

"Sure, lots of expertise back at headquarters, but they usually rely on the field for leads and initial evidence."

"Can't you just bring them in on this?" she said.

He shook his head. "Maybe after this mill visit. But I can't promise that it will go anywhere."

"I know you've just arrived," she said, "but be warned that some people have high expectations of you. Some see the issues as very black and white, you're either with them or against them."

"I can't really take any sides," he said, "I have to be impartial here."

From what she'd seen so far, he already seemed to be on the mayor's side. "There's a lot under the surface here too. For example, my grandfather and some of the elders are concerned about some non-physical changes they've seen in our town lately. They see a darkness.

68

They feel the presence of unfriendly spirits."

Dave looked at her, and raised an eyebrow.

"I know," she said. "It may not sound like the logic a big city policeman is used to, but my people have a long history of customs and beliefs related to the spirit world, to our links with nature. And they don't like what they see coming now."

"Great, more good news," said Dave.

JB reached over and patted his shoulder. "Sorry, I didn't mean to bring you down even more. And sorry that I can't really help, other than listen. But you're welcome to drop by whenever and chat. Don't be a stranger." She heard someone calling her from inside. "Back to work for me, sounds like the pre-dinner drinkers are starting to file in."

She paused at the door and glanced back. Dave was still gazing out over the frozen lake, eyes squinting against the setting sun. She didn't see any darkness around him right now, just the glow from the sunset. She found herself attracted to him, which worried her. He was an intriguing person, but she sensed that there was a dangerous side to him.

CHAPTER 13

Dave sat at his desk and crossed off another big X on his calendar. Day Number Six. He wasn't looking forward to Staff Scully's next visit, especially if Dave suddenly 'discovered' there were problems at the mill. When he finally got connected to the intranet he realized that it would take at least an hour a day just to scan through all the announcements, news and messages from Staff and others. He really did need to get Sheila in the loop on this.

He did remember Staff's warning about major events, so he jotted off a quick e-mail to the district office advising them of the possibility of a protest during the Minister's visit. He also asked if Scully thought that this would require extra police officers to help out for the day. He didn't think so, but Scully had made it clear that Dave was only a small part of a larger team, and he thought that asking for his advice might just soften up the staff sergeant.

Dave was starting to feel like he fit into the routine—at least his uniform no longer chafed so much. All his things had arrived from Toronto too, so now he had his own place to retreat to. He thought fondly of the drug squad where he only had to look after himself.

He stared into space, trying to decide who to follow up with on those pollution issues, or if he even should bother. He could hear Sheila talking to someone by the front counter.

After several minutes of giggling and talking, she called, "Dave, it's the mayor!"

Mayor Palin bustled into his office, "Hi Dave, I just wanted to touch base with you again about the upcoming visit. It's a big honour for us to have the Minister make the announcement here in person. We're counting on you and your boys to make it all run smoothly for us."

"Don't worry sir, I won't be rocking any boats here, I'll just fade into the background."

"That's what we want here in Kirk's Landing," said the mayor. "Smooth sailing. We're just a quiet little town, a good place to settle in, to retire to, to vacation in. Glad you see it that way too. The visit should go well. Tony Barretto can help you with security of course, and Head Office for the mill has asked their people to stop chasing down all those vague rumours."

Dave wasn't sure what 'Tony helping' meant, but he'd have to find something important looking to keep him and the mayor happy, and out of the way.

"No problem," he said. "Focus will be on a smooth visit." He smiled at the mayor. "But, on the other hand, I'm sure the press already knows there are some allegations being made. We wouldn't want those big city reporters suspecting us of running any kind of cover-up, would we?"

"Oh, I wasn't suggesting anything like that, no, no," protested Palin. "Nothing to the rumours though, so would be a waste of your time to even look into them. We all want the same thing here, to see our town in a good light."

"I agree," said Dave. "We all want to ensure this visit is a success for the town."

"Thanks for the support," said the mayor. "When this is done we should see about getting you a nicer place. My brother owns a beautiful cottage—more of a year-round home really—right next to mine. It's been sitting empty since he left to be an MP. He wants to keep it, but I'm sure you could have it for the rest of the year. Free of course, just our way of showing out appreciation."

"Thanks, but as you know, the RCMP provides my residence, and I really need to be here next to the detachment," said Dave. Which he did, but he was even more worried that taking the offer would be too much like a bribe. Besides, living next to the mayor would be a little too close for his liking. Dave found he could only stand so much of him at one time.

71

"Well, let me know if you reconsider," said Palin.

Dave stood and opened the door. "Thanks for calling in. Now, if you'll excuse me, time to go for a walk down the main street."

"I'll join you," said the mayor.

"Maybe another time," said Dave. He didn't really want to look too friendly with the mayor. Or with anyone else, for that matter.

Dave grabbed his coat and headed for the door. "I'm heading out for a bit, Sheila, doing a tour of the main street. Radio will be on."

Hopefully it would not be a busy day in this backward little place, and he could walk in peace. When in doubt, he could always fade. It was a handy tool when investigating something, but it was also a nice way to keep his distance from people—not that there was anything wrong with the locals. The people he did meet were as friendly and happy as usual, so he didn't know what was this dark change in the town that JB had mentioned.

He walked past Rosie's, with its mid-morning coffee club, and the knitters in the corner. They all waved as he walked past the big window. He nodded back, but didn't go in.

"Dave, over here!" It was Mike, from the pub the other night, along with several other people. "Out working on your tan?"

"Time for a patrol," said Dave. "I was told your council prefers some foot patrol, instead of letting us drive. We'd cover more ground if we did, though."

"Actually, your predecessor began that," said Mike. "He liked to stop and chat, to get a feel for some of the issues. He said he got some good tips too." Mike introduced the others, then added, "We're part of a citizen's group here. We'd like to talk to you some time about the mill problems."

"It seems that's all I've heard about since I arrived," said Dave.

"Well, it's on our minds here," said Mike. "People are eager for some action."

Dave felt his headache quickly building, and his patience fading. "Easy for you to say. I wish you people would quit whining. Everybody complains about pollution and corruption, but nobody gives us evidence or anything we can work on. We aren't magic you know!" Mike looked startled, and was about to speak when Dave cut him off. "Come in and set up an appointment when you're ready. I have to get back on patrol here."

As Dave continued down the block he spotted another group of locals heading up the street, probably eager to greet him and pester about all their problems. He stepped behind a parked truck, then faded—wincing at a stab of pain in his head. He crossed over to the post-office, safe from discovery, and leaned against the front wall, taking in the bright sun. He tried to relax. It was nice to be left alone as he watched the locals bustle up and down the street, ignoring him. All except for JB's brother. The tall native was standing across the street, arms folded, glaring right at Dave.

Dave ducked into the post office, and eavesdropped for a while. The talk was of him, summer tourists, mill issues, and the upcoming visit. This was a certainly better way to gain information than face to face. He'd used it a few times already—in line at a store, walking down the street, up at the highway restaurant. And it worked, people talked as if he wasn't there. The only problem was Junior, acting as if he could still see Dave. Maybe it was because of the bright sun against the wall. When Dave stepped back out onto the sidewalk, Junior was still across the street.

Still watching.

***

Sheila smiled as Dave walked through the detachment door. "Good morning, and congratulations, Corporal."

"On what?"

"I was just talking to my hubby, and he tells me that he and council are very pleased at how well you're managing things over the past few weeks, what with the Minister's visit and all."

"Just trying to keep things stable," he said.

"Well, I'm glad to see you didn't believe all those rumours," she said. "Just a few troublemakers spreading lies about the mill. I think they're just too lazy to work hard and get some bonuses. They think they're owed something for nothing."

"There have been some official complaints made though," said Dave. "Especially in the past few days. So we do need to investigate."

"Nothing serious, right?" she said.

"Some of it could be," said Dave. "I don't know yet. And there is that disappearance of Jacques Bourbeau."

"Oh, that's nothing I'm sure," said Sheila. "He just got lost. Don't get me wrong, tragic for him and his people, but an accident. Just keep up the good work, you'll find the whole town's behind you."

It turned out by the whole town she meant mainly the mayor and his buddies. Dave tried to correct the pro-council bias people saw in him, but the mayor and others had done a good job of spreading their spin. His blow-up with Mike hadn't helped either. Now, whenever he'd meet up with people, some would be overly friendly, saying how glad they were he supported them, but most of them were barely polite. Some, including many from the reserve that used to help him, were almost rude at times. JB was distant too, treating him like a stranger. He missed their friendly chats. It had been relaxing just to sit with her and share for a bit.

He mentioned the town's attitude to Reese. "Is it just me, or are they like that with you now too?"

"Oh, very much like that for me," said the young constable. "Norris too. It's now become an 'us and them' world. Certainly makes it harder for us to do our jobs, so I hope this big funding visit is worth it."

"Well, it's easy to back off on mill issues with no cooperation," said Dave. "Not to worry. I've learned over the years that there are glitches on every posting. Sometimes you can take action, sometimes you just have to wait things out. You'll find you'll have some good ones, some terrible ones." He realized he sounded like one of the old guys he used to make fun of. He did envy Reese, just starting out.

"You just need to keep your eye on the big picture," said Dave. "On where your career might lead to."

"That doesn't sound like much fun," said Reese. "It's hard to think that far ahead and just ignore what's happening here. I'm a small town guy, I guess. I'm used to knowing most of the people on the street, and having them stop and chat. Or at least say hi."

"Wait until a few more postings," said Dave. "Look at me, I got into trouble down south, so I'm up here to serve my time. I don't really like the north, but I can tough it out, no big deal, it's only a year."

"At least my family is near, back in Kenora,' said Reese, "so I can get a break and visit them. What about you, any family?"

"Nope, no one really," said Dave. "My dad was a master sergeant in the army, so of course we kept moving around, just like me now in the RCMP I guess. He was a demanding person, of others and himself. Then my mom died and it was just the two of us, still moving. Eventually he and I just drifted apart. The rest of them are here and there—we were never a close family. Most of my friends are in the Force now, or back in Toronto. Unfortunately it's not very safe for me in Toronto now. Although lately I'm thinking I might try sneaking back there for a break and taking my chances."

Dave was surprised to be confiding all this in Reese. He was a nice kid, but pretty inexperienced. Dave really did miss JB.

"I think this Minister's visit is stressing us all out," said Reese. "I'm sure it will all go smoothly and then we can all get back to our quiet life. Look, it's Rosie's birthday today, a bunch of us are meeting at the pub after 9. Why don't you come down?"

CHAPTER 14

Dave paused at the bar entrance and unfaded. He'd decided to follow Reese's suggestion and check out the gang at the pub. Just for a beer or two, and if he didn't feel welcome, he'd just go back home and rest. At any rate, he'd been popping pain killers to help fight the headaches, and didn't think they would mix well with alcohol. He'd faded on his walk to the pub, just so people didn't stop him to chat—it was getting to be automatic now.

When he walked in he realized most of the town was there already. Every table was full, and a live band was playing at the other end. Nothing fancy, just classic rock and roll, but the small dance floor was packed. He glimpsed JB through the crowd at the bar, rushing back and forth as she served drinks. He tried to catch her eye but didn't succeed.

"Dave! Over here!" Reese waved from a table right in the middle of it all, birthday central, with streamers dangling down and helium balloons tied to the chair backs. Rosie had a silly hat on his head, a beer in each hand, and a big grin on his face. He looked slightly tipsy, but very happy. Dave recognized a few in the crowd around the table too, besides Rosie and Reese. Mike was there, from the mill, and that George guy he'd met the first day. And JB's grandfather, the chief.

He nodded to the others and held out his hand to Rosie. "Happy Birthday, sir."

"Sir?" said Rosie. "Now I do feel old, thanks. It's just Rosie, especially with you off duty. Relax, will you?"

"Sorry Rosie," said Dave. "Not used to relaxing lately, been pretty busy."

"Good to see you dropping by," said Rosie. "I think the mayor has been playing you lately, as well as putting his own spin on things. I've been trying to convince people to give you a chance. We'll fight back, and fight fire with alcohol. Have a seat, grab a beer. Oops, we're out again, how did that happen?"

"My treat," said Dave. Once he got to the bar people pulled back and let him through, acting as if he wasn't there.

JB nodded to him. "Haven't seen you in a while, you must be keeping busy."

"Yes, a lot to the job," he said. "But busy is good, keeps me from worrying too much."

She looked concerned. "Still have those headaches?"

"Yes, and the dreams." He paused. "I miss our talks too."

She smiled. "So do I. Nice to see you relaxing in here, especially when it's with Rosie and his crowd. Another pitcher for them?" She started pouring. "They're good people. We should talk some more, too. I'm concerned about some things. Things in town, things about you. I'm sorry, we're really busy tonight, but I will give you a call." She handed him the pitcher. "Here you go. Give the birthday boy a hug from me."

And with that she was off to the other end of the bar, chattering to all as she went. Dave carried the jug back, managed to find a chair, and poured beer all around. He passed on the birthday greetings, but not the hug. He sat and drank, watching the crowd, trying to ignore the increasing pressure in his head. It seemed everyone in there knew Rosie, and were making a point of dropping by to give him their best wishes. Many also had a few words with the group about town matters: jobs, schools, stores, tourist season, petty crimes. It looked like these were part of an informal town council. Dave got a few nods too, probably because he was sitting with Rosie, and a few even talked with him briefly. The two elders kept looking at Dave, and muttering to each other. He was about to ask them what was wrong, when he heard his name called.

"Corporal! Hey!" Barretto was sitting with a group a few tables over. Probably all from his security crew from the mill, as they all had that same sort of tough look. Dave poured himself a second glass before walking over.

This group had been celebrating for a while too, as their table was covered in empty quart bottles and shot glasses. Barretto smiled. "Guys. You all know my friend Corporal Browne, the new detachment chief. Corporal, some of my boys, Frank, Jake, Steve. The Corporal and I have been working closely to keep this town safe, right Dave?"

"Actually, the town is my turf," said Dave. "But I do appreciate the work you people do in the mill."

Frank Risso scowled at him. "We have real issues there," he said. "Not your petty little things, like speeding tickets and lost kittens. It's a big operation, complicated. We need to enforce the rules so nobody gets hurt, or killed."

"Now, now, calm down," said Barretto. He laid a hand of Frank's shoulder.

Dave just looked at Frank, wondering what triggered this off.

"Who's side are you on, anyway," said Frank. He shrugged Barretto's hand off. "This guy's up here for a year. Big guy from the big city, thinks he can come on here and show us what to do. Probably messed up somewhere else, and we're stuck with him because he's a loser."

Dave felt himself getting angry as Frank went on and on. He'd met lots of blow-hards like Risso before, but they were just annoying, like a fly. Usually he would just ignore them, but for some reason he felt a rage building inside, and had an urge to actually swat the little pest. He took a breath and tried to calm down, as he didn't want to lose his cool in front of everyone.

"I think maybe you've had a little too much buddy," said Tony. "Sit down and shut up." He gave Dave an embarrassed smile.

"Don't tell me what to do," said Risso. "You're always bossing me around. Just like this cop here. And the rest of his crew are just as useless —some young kid and a dumb broad—he's just here to babysit them."

Dave felt the rage building inside him again, his breath quickening, muscles tensing. He stepped closer to Frank. "Watch it," he said.

"Make me," said Frank, as he poked Dave in the chest with a finger.

That was it. With a surge of adrenaline and a growl Dave threw himself at Frank.

***

The next thing he knew, he was on the floor, shoulders pinned by

Junior, and with Mike and Barretto piled on too. Even JB had hold of him, grabbing one of his hands. Her touch felt soothing.

"Breathe, Dave," she said. "Slow down."

"Dave, can you hear me?" said Mike. "Can you hear me now?"

Dave nodded. "What happened?"

"You flipped out, that's what happened," said Mike. "Junior here had to wrestle you down. Are you all right now? Can we let you up?"

Dave nodded. As he stood he noticed the once noisy bar was hushed. The band was quiet, and everyone was looking at him. "Sorry Mike, that's never happened to me before. That Frank guy that was hassling me—where is he?"

"Over there," said Mike. "You let out an unearthly roar and then threw him right over that table. You're a lot stronger than you look. Took the three of us to wrestle you to the floor. Pretty scary."

Dave didn't remember that part, after Frank had prodded him in the chest everything was a blank. "How is he?"

"He'll survive," said Reese. "He landed on a couple of these flimsy chairs. Broke his fall, and some of them."

"We all saw him going after you," said Mike. "He's like that whenever he has a few drinks, gets in people's faces." Mike looked around. "Look, I know you guys are trained to stop bar fights, and we all know he deserved it, but ... I guess I was surprised. You moved so fast and you had this freaky look on your face. And then you tossed Frank like he was a 10 year-old. JB here was ready to phone the cops, but you were all here already."

"Except Norris," said Reese. "She's on call, but the call would have gone in through dispatch back at headquarters."

That was a relief. Dave didn't need yet another fight on his record. "Thanks Jim."

"I didn't think we need them involved," said Reese. "I think it was just those painkillers talking."

Dave had mixed painkillers and alcohol once before, when he'd hurt his back. That time it had just made him dozy, but this time it was the opposite—he'd felt edgy, irritable. He wasn't about to argue with Reese, though. He nodded, then smiled at the crowd, palms out. "Sorry folk, I apologize. I've been having some bad migraines, and I'm taking pain killers for them. Guess beer is not a good mixer. Don't try this at home, folks."

There were a few chuckles, but he noticed most people were still keeping their distance from him.

He turned to Rosie. "Sorry for busting up the party. It's been pretty busy lately. I've been working pretty solid. "

"No problem," said Rosie. "You just make sure to get some rest. At least take a day off, man." He slapped Dave across the shoulders. "We do have to work on your people skills, too. Come on, I'll drop you off home."

Rosie smiled at the crowd. "Thanks for a great party folks, had a great time, but I still have to open early tomorrow. Get back to your dancing. And free breakfast for any of you that can make it into my place before 7:00 a.m."

With that the band started up and conversation resumed. Dave felt drained, and was all too happy to get an escort home. He was worried—he'd never lost it like that before, never felt the rage take him over. In addition, he was having all these strange headaches and dreams. Nightmares really. Always with him being chased, sometimes as if he was being herded to go in a particular direction, but before he could see what the goal was, he woke up in a sweat, looking behind him. Maybe it was related to some change in his power since Toronto. He wished he had someone to talk to about all this. If he told his boss, he'd be sent for a psych evaluation. Once they found out about his power, they'd probably stuff him into some high tech super-secret lab—never to see the light of day again. As for JB, aside from the fact that they weren't really talking anymore, she'd think it was just crazy until he disappeared in front of her. Then she would likely run from him, screaming.''

CHAPTER 15

"Thanks for coming in to help," said JB. She was still tired from last night's party for Rosie.

"No problem, sis." Junior stacked the last of the chairs.

She put her feet up on a chair and sipped her water. "What was with Dave?" she said. "He can be a little reserved and distant at times, but I thought there was a nice guy hiding in there."

"I do see something hiding in there, but it doesn't seem nice to me," said Junior.

"His grandmother was First Nations," she said. "Anishinaabe, so he should have a strong spirit in him. Apparently he worked undercover in some gangs, so maybe some of that rubbed off onto him."

"I don't know," said Junior. "I've seen how the real world can affect your spirit, make it brighter or darker, but this is different."

Lately JB had been looking at Dave carefully, and sometimes thought she saw something, but it was faint. "You can see these things better than me—so what do you see in him?"

"It's like I can see two spirits at once, on top of each other," Junior explained. "I see a lighter one, that seems to be there all the time. But then there's a darker one, that comes and goes."

"Really? Have you seen that before, like in others?"

"Nope, but I've only learned how to do this a few years ago. Grandfather says he has seen it in others. Such as our cousin, just before he turned really bad."

Their cousin had initially just been an annoying pest before he began teasing the local dogs and then started being mean to the younger kids. From that it escalated to drugs, stealing from the band office, and getting into fights all the time. The band had tried healing circles, a sweat lodge, none of it worked. When he refused to let them help anymore their only choice had been to force him out, like cutting out a cancer.

"So that's it?" she said. "He's done for?"

"Not necessarily," said Junior. "I've been discussing it with the elders, we think it's like something has caught on to Dave, rather than developed within him. And like I said, it comes and goes."

"When exactly do you see it?" she said.

"I've seen it a few times in him as he's walking around the town. I definitely saw it last night, when I came into the pub, just as Dave was talking to Barretto and his pals. It was just sort of a dark haze, but it got much darker, almost black, just as he attacked that jerk Risso."

"Good thing you came in then," she said. "Nice take-down, just like you were right back on the wrestling team."

"Thanks," he said. "But it almost felt like I was wrestling with two people, one physical, and one spiritual. I had a good hold on his body, but then had to really push with my own spirit against whatever that dark thing was. It felt evil to me. Then Dave passed out for a moment and the darker one faded away."

She told her brother about Dave's dreams, and his other symptoms. "Grandfather is concerned, and so am I. Dave is really stressed. Good news is that he told Rosie last night he was going to take a day or so off to re-charge."

"Where's he going?" said Junior.

"Likely nowhere," she said. "Too dangerous to go to Toronto, and not a lot of links to his family." She sat and stared at the wall, deep in thought. "Any ideas, little bro?"

"Well, when I need a break I usually head for the woods," he said.

"This is a city boy," she said. "The idea of heading off into the woods is NOT going to calm him down."

"Why don't we ask him," said Junior. "Here he comes now."

***

"Hi guys," said Dave. He was glad to see JB again. "What—not working? JB, I think this is the first time I've seen you sitting still."

"Not for long," she said. She did have a lot to do today, but it

82

certainly could wait for a bit. "Good to see you again."

"Good to see you both," he said. "And thanks, Junior, for wrestling me down last night," said Dave. "I'm sorry for that, don't know what happened, never did that before."

"You mentioned pain killers with a beer chaser," said JB, "but you were acting really hyper. You really should get checked out, see why you got that interaction."

"Just headaches," said Dave. "Nothing to worry about. I went home and crashed. I slept like a log. Not even any weird dreams. Anyway, I just dropped by to grab a coffee and apologize again for last night."

"That's okay," said JB. "We managed to reassure people that you were fine, and then the band distracted them all with their standard version of Mustang Sally."

"What about taking a break?" said Junior. "Relax, forget about all your issues for a while."

"Already booked a few days off," said Dave. "My plan is to stay in and watch some satellite TV and rest up. I'm a little embarrassed right now to be walking around town.

"What about a real break from all this," said Junior. "Away from the town. As in out into the woods."

"What, in winter?" said Dave. "It's only February."

JB had to smile at the look on Dave's face. He obviously thought they were both crazy.

"Sure, it's easy," said JB. "You've already got warm enough clothes for walking around town. I'm sure there are snowshoes in your office, too. It'll be just like taking a walk, except you'll be walking away from your distractions."

"Is it safe?" asked Dave.

"Safer than walking in downtown Toronto," said Junior. "I need to go out tomorrow anyway, to check some snare lines. It will be a nice walk. I know when I get out there it always calms me right down."

"Snare lines?" said Dave.

"My friend and I set out snares for rabbits in the winter. Well, technically hares, but whatever they are, hopefully they'll take advantage of tonight's clear weather to get out and run their trails. Run right into the trap, and into my cooking pot. I'll cook them all up and do some extra for you."

JB could see that they were winning him over. "It's a good skill to add. Think of it as training, without the evaluation part."

She didn't mention that Junior would be watching him carefully, to see how he reacted to being alone out there, and to see if there was a difference in this spirit thing.

"Okay, I'm in," said Dave.

"I'll pick you up at seven," said Junior. "By the time we get to the trail it will be sunrise. Dress well, it will be plenty cold before the sun comes up."

Dave finished his coffee. "Looking forward to this, I think. Thanks guys, I appreciate the concern." He gave them a nod, and headed out the door.

***

"Junior," she said. "What about just now, did you see any darkness in him?"

"Just a bit, when you were pushing him about his problems. It seems to react to him being stressed. Almost like a defensive thing. I'll draw it out tomorrow—once he's out in the woods it's my turf and I can push him a bit."

"Carefully though,"" she said. "We've seen that he can get pretty violent."

***

Dave was dressed and waiting inside his door when he saw a lone set of lights coming down the dark and empty street. By the time the truck pulled into his driveway he was out and waiting, snowshoes under his arm, thermos of coffee in his hand.

"Ready for an adventure?" asked Junior.

"I am," said Dave. "I'm feeling better today, after a good sleep. I must have really been run down." He slammed the door, then held his hands over the heater vent. "Is it ever cold out—you sure we'll be all right?"

"Was only around minus 20 last night," said Junior. "A warm spell. Heading even lower tonight, though. Today is supposed to be a sunny day, so it'll be good for stomping around in the bush."

"Glad I have this parka," said Dave. "What sort of things do you

84

have in store for me today?"

Junior smiled. "Nice feeling for me to be in charge of you for a change. Your job is just to enjoy the day and nature, to calm down and chill out. No radio, right? And no more coffee today—sorry, doctor's orders." He grabbed Dave's thermos and put it in the back seat.

"That was my breakfast coffee," said Dave. "No matter. Lead on!"

They headed down Main Street to the lake, then turned left toward the reserve road. As they passed the mill Dave could see plumes of steam and smoke rising from all the stacks.

"Looks like there's not a lot of pollution control going on today," he said.

"We see a lot more from the stacks in winter," said Junior. "In this cold weather you're seeing mainly steam and hot air. The scrubbers are supposed to filter everything, but there's still a lot of pollution mixed in with that too, trust me. Luckily we're normally upwind, but if not—well, it can be like a fog of rotten eggs drifting through the town. Pretty gross. Most of the pollution is in the water though. We've seen the evidence in the lakes and rivers around here, and in the people's health. That was what my dad was looking into when he disappeared, the water pollution."

They followed the road further, glimpsing the river through the dark trees as it twisted its way west, into the heart of the reserve. The sky was just starting to show a rosy tint to the east as they drove into the reserve's village. A few houses had lights on in the kitchen and smoke rising from the chimney. The convenience store had a few trucks and ski-doos parked outside, and of course they were accompanied through town by a chorus of dogs. It was all very peaceful looking, yet Dave still felt keyed up, apprehensive for some reason.

The road cut back into the woods, past a frozen creek, through the blue tinged snow of the pre-dawn light. Junior turned up a small side road, and, after a few hundred yards, stopped.

"We'll walk now. Time to unwind."

CHAPTER 16

They had walked for a good twenty minutes, and all Dave could hear now was the crunch of their feet on the snow and a few birds calling in the distance. The racket from the dogs had faded, but he could still smell a whiff of wood smoke from the town. Junior got their snowshoes and a day pack out of the back and pointed up the road. "We'll be fine on the trail for now, but will soon need snowshoes when we head into the bush."

They followed the road—more of a ski-doo trail—for another 5 minutes, then Junior paused, just where some faint snowshoe tracks headed off to the right into the trees. "Time to head in to look for dinner."

Dave's snowshoes were oval, a metal frame with a flat plastic mesh in between and a harness in the middle. Junior's were a similar shape, but made of wood, with a web of rawhide lacing filling the middle. "I thought real snowshoes were more pointy," said Dave.

"These are a better style for getting around in the bush," said Junior. "The ones with a tail are more suited for walking in open country. They're a little narrower, and the tail helps them track straighter, and also keeps the tip up when you walk. Otherwise it catches in the snow and over you go." He showed Dave how to slip his feet into the harness, then put his own snowshoes on. "Let's go. You first, just follow my old tracks."

Dave took a few cautious steps, and almost tripped. He tried again, this time walking a little bowlegged to clear his ankles.

"That's it," said Junior. "It will become automatic, just let it happen. Don't be afraid to relax and enjoy the day. Just take it slow."

Although they'd had snow the day before, Dave could still see the markings of the trail, slanting up toward a small stand of aspens, with their yellow leaves quivering in the slight morning breeze. The sun was starting to come up, peeking over a hill and into Dave's face. He squinted into it, enjoyed the contrast between its warmth and the crisp feel of the air as he breathed in.

"This isn't so hard to walk in," he said. "Do we even need these things?" He turned back toward Junior as he spoke, and somehow ended up stepping on one shoe with the other. Before he knew it he'd fallen sideways, off the trail, with a face full of fluffy snow.

Junior said, "You were saying?"

"Shut up," said Dave, with a smile. His smile quickly changed to a frown, as he tried to push himself up and his arm promptly sank into the snow, right up to his armpit. He tried the other arm. Now both were stuck. "Give me a hand here, please."

Junior just gestured toward the trail. "Roll over to where it's packed down, then you'll be able to get up."

Dave untwisted his feet, pulled his hat back down over his ears, and rolled over onto the trail. After much twisting and puffing he eventually managed to get back onto his feet. He brushed off the snow and shuffled carefully around until he was pointed again toward the thicket ahead.

"Well done," said Junior, "maybe later we'll try a race. "

Dave turned and looked back at him, carefully. "Much later. I was just starting to look around and enjoy things—don't rush me."

The trail meandered through the aspens, into the shade and out of the warmth. Dave realized that the exercise was heating him up just fine, as he'd already loosened his collar a bit. After only a few more yards Junior called a halt and pointed off to the side. Dave noticed some stirred-up snow, then a fleck of red, then some white fur and a black eye came into focus. The rabbit's long body was twisted in death, eyes bulging, big back feet stretched out in one desperate attempt to run. A thin shiny wire stretched tautly from a small branch to a loop tight around the animal's neck. There was spot of blood on the corner of its mouth.

"Whoa," said Dave. He'd seen death before, but never like this. "Pretty gruesome."

"It's actually pretty quick, though," said Junior. He carefully stepped off the trail, reached over to the body and loosened the wire noose. As he bent over the rabbit he muttered a few words, then smiled back at Dave.

"When we kill something, we say a prayer asking for its forgiveness and giving thanks to the Creator."

Junior slipped the frozen body into his backpack. "This looks like a good trail. I think there will be some out tonight, so I'll set it again. I have a friend I share this area with; he'll come out tomorrow."

"What if it snows more?" said Dave. "How will he find his way around?"

"The same way you can navigate your way around a big city," said Junior. "We follow the landmarks, like a lone pine, or a stream, or a ridge, or particular clump of birch. Obvious to us."

"But this would be all different in the summer," said Dave.

"Some of it," said Junior. "No big deal. I'll show you later what I mean. Now we need to set another snare here."

Dave peered at the snow carefully, and could just make out the rabbit trail as it led further through the thicket, toward some spruce. Junior untied the wire from the branch, then moved a few feet along the rabbit run, keeping to the side so as to not disturb it. He carefully arranged the wire back into a small loop a few inches in diameter, and tied it to a sapling next to the trail, just under an overhanging branch. He plucked a few strands of grass from the snow behind him, and replanted them on either side of the noose. Finally, he picked up a small twig that had fallen from overhead, and placed it under the snare.

"What's all that for?" asked Dave.

"The grass will encourage our little friend to stay on the trail, and when he sees the twig he'll make sure to keep his head up, and right into the loop, before he even realizes how we've manipulated him. Or, maybe he'll be smart and not stick his head into the noose. Maybe he'll go around and break a new trail. There are always choices in life, even for a scared little rabbit."

They carried on, following Junior's previous trail, enjoying the warming day. Dave wasn't sure how Junior knew where to look, but there was a series of snares—some in the open, some in the bushes, some under a tree, and almost all with a rabbit in a noose. The third one had tracks that just went around it. Junior moved that one to another location. At the sixth place, the snow was disturbed, and there was a lot of blood, but no rabbit, just a loop with some fur in it.

"Did this one manage to get free?" said Dave.

Junior examined the ground. "Yes, from the snare at least. But I see a few drops of blood along the trail. And these tracks here, following behind? Fox. I think he escaped here but still was caught last night."

The trail led out into a small open area, with an outcrop of bare rock. Junior slipped his snowshoes off and sat on a log. "Time for a tea break," he said. He pointed under a nearby spruce. "Could you please duck in under the branches and bring me some dead twigs?"

Dave came back with a large handful. "They're all pretty small," he said.

"That's good enough," said Junior, "we're making tea, not cooking dinner." He pulled a strip of wispy white bark from the log he was sitting on and arranged it under a pile of twigs. He took a bundle of three sticks from his pack, all tied together at the top, and set them up as a little tripod. Junior reached into his pack again and pulled out a small blackened pot. He scooped some snow into it, hung it from the tripod, and took out a small butane lighter.

"What, no flint and steel?" asked Dave with a smile.

"Only when I'm trying to impress some pretty young tourist from the big city. You're neither pretty nor young."

As the snow melted, Junior added more to the pot, as well as more twigs to the small hot fire. Within a few minutes the water came to a boil, just as he used up the last of the twigs. He threw in a handful of tea and sat back. "No smoke break, Dave?"

"I'm trying to cut back," Dave said, "as well as eat a little better. I've been feeling run down and tired lately, maybe I've caught something."

"Or something has caught you," said Junior.

Dave froze and stared at Junior. "What are you talking about?"

"Relax, nothing serious," he said. "I've been talking to the elders. We think we can help you."

"Secret aboriginal remedies?" said Dave.

"Sort of," said Junior. "Just an idea they have."

"What kind of idea?" said Dave.

"Calm down," said Junior. "No big deal."

Dave felt anxious about where this conversation was going. "Come on, what's going on with you and JB and the elders. Stop jerking me around."

Junior shook his head. "Dave, we're not jerking you around. There's something about you but we don't know what it is. We suspect it's something aboriginal in nature, but an elder is going to have to explain it because I can't. For now, enjoy the day, please."

Dave forced himself to pause and take a deep breath. "Sorry, okay. Carry on."

Junior took some mugs out of the pack as well as a small bag of sugar. "Tea's ready," he said, and filled the mugs. "I brought some food too."

"Pemmican?" asked Dave.

"No, I find it too tough. We've some paté and a chunk of baguette my sister packed for us. Just enough for a snack, as we don't want to get you all filled up and sleepy. You may need your wits about you later on."

"Not today," said Dave. "I'm off, remember?"

Dave sat back against the warm rock and turned his face to the hot sun. "I'm feeling better already. My friends will never believe it when I tell them I've sat out in the woods, in the middle of winter, sipping on tea and munching a bit of baguette and paté. Hell, I'm not sure I believe it either."

He started idly pulling little pieces of something off the rock. It looked like pieces of dried up leather, dark green and brown, and was surprisingly hard to pick off.

"Don't do that, please," said Junior.

"Why not?" said Dave. "What is it."

"That is a living thing," said Junior, "called lichen. It and the rock belong together, they live off each other. Just like everything around us is interrelated. That little patch might just be something a hungry deer is looking for some cold day."

"Oh, sorry," said Dave, looking around. He could see more lichen, some moss, some grass stems, even a few little shrubs. "More here than meets the eye."

"You got it," said Junior. "We think we know what we see in front of us, but we sometimes get lazy and assume we know what it is, and don't really look. You need to learn to slow down and open your eyes and really see. Now, if you're finished your tea we'll loop around to check the last few snares and then we'll be almost back to the road."

After the last snare was done, they stopped to share a smoke.

"Just a puff or two," said Dave. "This has been a great day. Glad you suggested it."

"You were good company," said Junior. "Maybe next time you can set some traps too." He peered into his pack then shook his head. "I left my extra snares back a couple of stops. I don't want to lose them in a snowfall. I'll run back and get them and we'll continue on out to the road. Or you can go ahead on your own if you want."

"No problem," said Dave. "I'll just sit on this log and relax for a bit."

"Good, practice the art of seeing," said Junior. "And of slowing down."

Dave watched Junior disappear back along the trail, listening as the creak of his snowshoes slowly faded. He sat and gazed across the clearing. He realized he hadn't really thought at all about work issues— he'd just enjoyed the break. This final stop was on a bit of a rise, so was still in the sun, but he could already feel a bit of a chill and see shadows creeping toward him, like black fingers. He checked his watch. Junior had been gone for over twenty minutes. It wasn't even five o'clock, and already the sun was disappearing. He was getting tired, and cold, especially his butt. Dave tried to remember if Junior had said definitely to wait or to go on ahead. Dave didn't recall him pointing to the road either. He'd just sort of waved his arm back at Dave then disappeared down the trail. It definitely was getting colder, and darker. The trees seemed taller in the fading light, and every direction looked the same.

He called. "Junior? Junior?" He could hear just a few crows, cawing in the distance. Was this some kind of prank?

"Junior! Come on, this isn't funny!"

He started to panic, his breath coming a little faster. He really didn't know which way to turn, how to get out. Here he was, no GPS, no radio, no cell-phone, not even a compass. Not that a compass would help, as he had no idea which direction the road was. He supposed he could retrace the trail all the way back to the start, but it would be dark long before that. No way did he want to be out here alone after dark. Junior had said it would be even colder tonight—he could freeze out here. What was that kid up to?

"Junior!" His voice echoed through the trees.

There was that rage building in him again, a fury that just wanted to destroy. Damn that kid, leaving him all alone out here. Maybe this was to make him look stupid in front of the townspeople. Maybe Junior was working with the bikers. He had an urge to run.

"Junior, when I catch you you're dead meat!"

CHAPTER 17

In spite of his anger, Dave could also feel another part of him inside, shouting to be heard. Maybe Junior was in trouble. Maybe he'd sprained his ankle or fallen into a creek. His concern for Junior washed away some of the rage. Once again, he reminded himself to breath slowly, to focus. He forced his muscles to relax. He wasn't thinking straight—he'd been in worse situations before.

He took a slow breath. Junior had said it was just like landmarks in a city. So, what if this was a city he was lost in, without a map or signs. How would he solve that? He closed his eyes for a moment, took another deep breath, then thought back to the start. When they'd set out in the morning, the sun had been in their face. And they'd walked away from the road and looped around. Some twists and turns but he remembered more left turns than right. Definitely a loop, then. The long shadows were all pointing away from the setting sun, pointing toward the east. So the road was now to the west of him somewhere. They'd also walked on an uphill slope at first. Right now he was on a bit of a ridge, with the ground on one side sloping west. Just to confirm it, a sudden breeze brought a faint whiff of woodsmoke up the hill—likely from the reserve. Dave smiled, as he realized he wasn't really lost—he just wasn't sure where he was. Same as when wandering some of the back streets of a city. He'd know the lake was that way, or train tracks were somewhere to the right, and could soon orient himself. He checked his snowshoe harness, settled his pack on his back, and headed off through the trees toward where he was pretty sure the road would be.

Sure enough, after twenty minutes, he stepped out of the bush onto the road. The snow was smooth and unmarked, which confirmed that the truck would be to the left. A few minutes more and he topped a small rise in the road and spotted the truck, with Junior leaning against it. Hmm. So no broken leg.

"Fall asleep?" said Junior.

"What happened to you?" said Dave. "You just disappeared and left me."

"I had to circle back more than I thought," said Junior, "so I just continued out to the road. But you managed to figure it out, obviously."

"Yes, but what if I hadn't worked it out? I could have froze out there. You'd have come right back for me, right?"

"Well, we didn't need to get that far," said Junior. "Come on, let's hop in the truck and get warm."

They were both quiet as the truck bumped over the snow covered road back to town.

Dave woke to Junior shaking his shoulder.

"Here we are, back at your place," he said.

"Wow," said Dave. "Guess I was a bit tired. A good idea, going out."

"Anytime I'm feeling edgy I just head out into nature," said Junior. "It helps me to look at things from a bit of a distance, to put them in perspective, maybe figure out some solutions. I'd be glad to take you out again, or JB could."

Dave smiled. "Thanks, I may take one of you up on that offer. Just don't bail on me again. Maybe I do need to chill out a bit and figure out how to make the best of things for the year I'm here. Find some sort of balance." He laughed. "My plan was to mentor you, on things like youth issues, and here you are mentoring me."

"You're welcome," said Junior. "We all have our strengths, and in a small place like this we rely on each other more. Give us a chance. Get to know us, and let us get to know you. Enough now, I'd better get going, I still need to clean these rabbits for that stew. You done for the day?"

"Not sure," said Dave. "That little cat nap helped. I'll grab a shower and a bite and see how I feel. I might walk down to the Roost after."

***

As the cold air swirled in, JB turned to catch Dave standing at the door, watching her. She liked that. "Dave, how was your day?" He certainly seemed to be in better mood, as gone was the frown and hunched shoulders.

"Excellent," he said. "Who knew all that boring bush could actually be interesting." He peered around. "Quiet night?"

"A little," she said. "It was a nice day here with the sun out, but didn't take long after sunset for the temperature to plummet." She gestured at the tables. "Only a few people ventured out tonight, including my grandfather and his euchre buddies."

"What do they play for?" said Dave.

"It varies," she said. "Sometimes just for beer. Sometimes they keep a tally for a week, and pick a bigger prize, like a month's worth of driveway plowing. This one's big, for a pow-wow."

"With all that dancing and stuff?"

"It's a big gathering," she said. "Dance competitions, people showing off clothing and jewelry, lots of great food, and meetings between elders. It's our version of an Annual General Meeting."

"And the winner has to organize it?"

"He will coordinate but they'll all work on it," she said. "They all have done it several times, so it's not that hard for them."

"How come Junior is there playing—would he run it?"

"No, he's not in the pool for that yet," she said. "Although he does spend a lot of time with them, considering his youth."

"He seems pretty astute at times for his age," said Dave.

"And a goofy kid at other times," she said. "But they like that, just trying to work out a balance with him, he's like a junior elder right now." She smiled at Dave. "Let me grab my jacket and we can pop out on the veranda for a smoke. I'm eager to hear about your day."

She waved at the few tables of customers, and let Sid know she would be right back. Her grandfather smiled and raised an eyebrow, and George made some kissing noises on the back of his hand. She shook her head and smiled back at them, then   stepped outside into the cold. "Thanks for allowing our little smokers lounger here," she said. "I know that technically it is under a roof, but we keep to one end, and there's not a lot out here this time of year."

"I won't write you up," said Dave, as he sat and lit up. "I choose my battles."

JB sat back and gazed into the night. It was very quiet, and very cold. She could hear the distant barking of a dog, and the cracking of the lake ice, under its blanket of snow. The sky was clear, lit by a sliver of a moon and wall to wall stars. This was one of the many things she'd missed in Ottawa, just sitting outside on a quiet night, looking at the sky, and thinking. She could smell wood smoke from the many chimneys in the town, and a whiff of cologne from Dave.

"Nice after-shave," she said. "Is that just for us at the pub, or do you have a hot date?"

She liked the way he blushed.

"No, I just cleaned up after a quick frozen dinner," he said.

"You're not much of a cook I gather?" she said.

"I have a few recipes," he said. "Sometimes I just feel like taking the easy way out."

JB passed him a blanket, "For your legs." She'd noticed that he'd followed their advice and started dressing in layers. That big brown parka certainly helped, too. She reached over and helped him spread the blanket out over both their legs.

"This is nice," he said. "Right now my friends in Toronto will be sliding around in the slush with street shoes and a skimpy jacket, heading for the long lineup outside a bar and complaining about how unfair it is that it gets cold in winter. And here—is it minus 100 yet?"

JB laughed. "No, only about minus 40 tonight. Bit of a cold snap— just for you—but it is supposed to warm up to minus 10 by the day after tomorrow. You'll be fine, just don't underdress when you're driving. You never know when you'll be stranded. Your patrol cars always find at least one car a year up along the highway with a flat tire or no gas, a couple inside that are on their way to a party. Him in a suit, her in a gown and heels, and both close to freezing."

"I'll keep this parka on for a few weeks yet," he said, "as well as my big boots and mittens. It certainly sounded cold on the walk here. It's kind of neat, the way the snow crunches with every step."

"Did you notice the smoke?" she asked. When he shook his head she added, "Check it out, look back at the town and the chimney smoke."

He walked to the corner of the porch, paused, then came back.

"That's cool. It goes straight up and sort of all flattens out in a layer."

"It's a temperature inversion," she said, "and only happens when it's very cold and there's no breeze. Did you hear the hydro poles crack on your way down here?"

Dave looked at her. "You're putting me on, right?"

"No, honest, when it's this cold you can hear them—they don't break in half or anything, but there's a snapping sort of noise." She pointed to a flicker in the sky. "Northern lights. Like on the Discovery Channel, but better. Listen carefully, you can almost hear them hiss and crackle."

They sat quietly, enjoying the night.

Dave started to whistle, and before she knew it, she'd reached over and put her hand over his mouth.

"Hey," he said. "I don't sound that bad."

"Sorry, it's not that," she said. She hoped he didn't think it was silly, but it was part of her culture. "My grandfather told me that if you whistle at night, then the Northern Lights come closer, and a spirit will take away someone close to you. I know, might not seem logical to a city boy, but I've believed it."

"No problem," he said. "If it bothers you I'll stop."

"Thanks. Now tell me about the day," she said, settling back in her chair. She'd already talked to Junior, but wanted to hear from Dave.

His face was animated as he described the events of the day, the sights and sounds. "And at the end, I almost lost it," he said. "My panic started to get a hold of me, more than I'd expected it would. Definitely scary for a bit but I managed to calm down and use my eyes and brain to figure it out."

"Good for you," she said. What he didn't know was that he'd passed a very deliberate trial set up by the elders and Junior, to see if whatever was in him would cloud his judgement, to determine how much control he still had. Now that he'd passed that test, they could work on the next steps to deal with whatever was 'in' Dave. Junior hadn't given her any guarantees though, he'd admitted they were having to make some of it up as they went along.

"Any idea what's different in you?" she said. "Something that would cause a different sort of panic?"

"No, nothing different," he said. "Just a fluke—maybe I was tired." He seemed a little nervous as he answered, so she didn't push for more, just let him continue on, excited about his day yet looking more relaxed. He was complaining less about the details of his work and talking more about what he was doing up here, the town, the rest of the year.

"This place sort of grows on you," he said, "The city boy in me misses a lot of the action down south, but maybe a break is good too."

"How about the mill," she said. "Any thoughts on that?"

"I have been getting a lot of official requests to not go poking into things about the mill," he said, "but I've also been getting a lot of unofficial requests from people to do the opposite. For now, I'm thinking it would help if I at least knew a little more about the town and its history. I could maybe get some books from the library—any recommendations?"

"The library is basically one room in the town hall," she said, "so there's not much. I think there's one History of Kirk's Landing, about the initial settlers, mostly Scottish and Metis, but other than that it's light fiction. Stuff for the long winter nights, or lazy cottage days. You're better off just to talk to people. Maybe I could help."

"Thanks, that would be nice," he said. "Maybe over a coffee at Rosie's." He yawned. "Sorry, it was a busy day, I need to head home. I'll have a big day tomorrow catching up on things."

"Is one of them my dad's disappearance?" she asked.

"Yes, that's still on my list," said Dave. "I'm going to to follow up on a few threads that have been bothering me."

"Thanks," she said. "I do miss him. Last year, when we finally accepted that he was dead, not just missing, we had a wake for him. With my people it's more of a gathering than a mourning. We gather to honour the person, tell stories, eat lots of food, play cards, and enjoy each other's company. It helped, but I still feel really lonely without him, and frustrated that nobody seems to know anything about his disappearance, or even wants to find out more about it."

She sat quietly for a moment, and was surprised when Dave reached out and gave her a hug. Not so surprised that she didn't hug him back though. Just as she was starting to enjoy it, Sid popped his head out the door.

"Sorry, JB," he said, "we need your help in here."

Damn. With a shrug and smile at Dave, she followed Sid back inside. It was nice to see that Dave had a sensitive side to balance the tough guy. He'd need both of those in the battle to come.

CHAPTER 18

"Nice place," said Norris. "Looks like you're settling into your new house finally."

"Thanks," said Dave. "It's been a few weeks now. Certainly was good to get my stuff up from Toronto and spread it out." He'd even washed all the dishes and glasses before putting them away.

"Fancy stuff," said Reese, "but not a lot—it sure does spread out thin. I think you need a trip into Winnipeg. Maybe hit the IKEA there. Or the curling club garage sale here."

"Well, I never was much of a homebody," said Dave. "I don't mind this, but I suppose I could add more things eventually."

He'd managed to pick up a few nice pieces of chrome and leather as part of his undercover identity in Toronto, but this place was a lot bigger than his old apartment. It did look a little sparse to him, but he wasn't planning on entertaining. The place was just fine for him and Snowball. Somehow the cat had found his new place and moved right in.

"Now, let's have lunch," said Dave. "I've some juicy burgers the butcher made up for me."

He was gradually settling into the detachment, and getting used to having his own place again. He'd cooked a few meals and tested the smoke detectors. Nothing fancy, just making himself a quick lunch or heating up a frozen dinner. That and steaks on the BBQ—so rare they still dripped. Other than that, Rosie's had a great menu, including moose and rabbit—both local of course. This was Dave's first time with guests, for a combination lunch and status meeting.

"Burgers sound good for me," said Norris. "I'll see what you have to make a salad."

"Already found it," said Reese. "It's a bag from the Metro, marked Salad. Dave cooks like I do."

"I keep it simple," said Dave. He peered through the patio door at the BBQ, sitting on the snowy deck. "These may take a while in the cold."

"We did it all the time at home," said Reese. "Just need to keep your beer in an inside pocket if you're out there too long."

"Okay," said Dave. "Norris, anything new on the mill?"

She'd managed to cover a lot in a short time. She'd discovered that after the last round of mill financing there had been a big spike in new vehicle registrations, as well as sales of home theatres, new boats— mostly to a small group of people. Nothing good enough for a fraud case, but a start.

"Make sure Sheila is out of the loop," said Dave. "At least until we find out the mayor's involvement." He'd had a talk with their clerk to remind her about her confidentiality agreement, and the penalties associated with it. "She's getting better, though."" I wouldn't want to have to think about replacing her. She could be a good asset for us, if we could just get her loyalty. And a bit more enthusiasm at helping out in general, rather than just be on a few things."

"She was disappointed to not be joining us today," said Reese. "I told her it was just a staff meeting to discuss performance and training." He was playing with the TV remote. "Nice channel selection on this, and a huge screen."

"Thanks," said Dave. "Now, back to the mill. What are some other ways we can try to find out what's going on in there?" Dave had a few ideas but he wanted to see what the constables would come up with. "Do we know anybody who works in there?"

"We know lots of people who work there," said Norris, "but the second we start asking questions it will spread like wildfire and the evidence will disappear. It's a small town. I'm trying to think of somebody discreet who works there who'd also like to help." She and Dave looked at each other and together they turned toward Reese.

"What?" he said.

"So Reese," said Dave, "remember John from the mill? With the bags of dope?"

"Oh sure," he said. "That's working out really well. Like you suggested I talked to Winnipeg about Restorative Justice, about helping us set up a community consultative group. They were pretty excited about us doing aboriginal cases with a Healing Circle, but I'd told them, 'No, sorry, for now just a white guy and a bag of dope.' There's some paper work of course, but we can probably process John with community service, no court and no criminal record. I haven't actually processed it yet—sorry, I meant to tell you."

"So would you say that John is very grateful to you?" asked Dave.

"Sure." Reese was enthralled with the On-Demand option on the TV. "Wow, this is cool. Oh sorry, yes, John really wants to keep this discreet. He could lose his job at the mill over something like this."

"And what does he do at the mill?"

"Something in the main office, in engineering. He works with their systems I think."

Dave and Norris looked at each other. "Maybe we can explore this idea later when we're not all so distracted?" said Dave.

She smiled. "Hey Reese, he claimed he did this to impress some woman he met on-line. So how did that turn out?"

"Ha! Sweet!" Reese was now trying to connect the game modules to the TV. "What, John? Over before it started! Once he had no stuff, she stopped answering his calls. Just as well, he found out she's on parole from doing federal time in Regina. Guys really do stupid things to impress women! Hey, he's single! You could give him a try!"

Reese looked up mystified to see them both laughing at him. "What?"

"No way!" Norris said. "Not interested. I have a full-time job and a 6-year-old. I don't have enough energy to handle another dependent male wanting me to look after him. Relationships are on hold for now."

"No way for me either," said Reese. "I'm not ready for that sort of complication. First I want to concentrate on my career. I'm going to follow Dave's advice and not get attached, at least until I've seen a few more postings."

Norris stared at Dave. "YOUR advice?"

Dave looked embarrassed "Well yeah. I find it easier not to get involved. My life has been pretty hectic."

"Yeah, how's that working out for you?" said Norris. "It can be a pretty lonely life if all you have is the job. You've a nice place here, especially with that deck. I know that it's awkward for us—especially you —to be at the Roost very often. But you could invite friends over here for a game, nuke some snacks, do some PR work. Maybe even pick up a few leads on the issues here."

"That might work," he said. "I'm looking for a way to get people talking to me, rather than about me. Burgers and beer might help."

He also wanted to finish unpacking his boxes and invite JB over. She'd already had a quick tour and teased him about how bare his kitchen cupboards and fridge were. She claimed to be a good but simple cook, maybe he'd take her up on that. He did enjoy her company, and made a point of including a quick coffee at the Grande whenever he was out on foot patrol.

"How are you guys with the shifts, not too much?"

"The extra cash is good," said Norris. "Babysitting can be a challenge sometimes, but I'm managing."

He'd tried to adjust the work shifts as best he could for the three of them and arrange for some off days, but with only the three of them overtime was inevitable. Luckily the band police had things there under control, so other than keeping the reserve in the loop on the patrols, there was not a lot extra work there. Summer would get busier with the addition of more tourist traffic on the road and visitors to the park. He'd already been over to the local Park Conservation office too, and met the officers there.

"I've talked to the District NCO about getting a summer student," said Dave. "They were open to the idea. Would be someone uniformed, but not armed. Someone to work on some projects and take non-confrontational calls, working with whoever is on duty."

Reese spoke up. "But we need members who can take on shifts. I like the money, but I could use sleep once in a while."

"That's the best news," said Dave. "We're top of the list for getting a Reserve Program constable, and apparently there is one qualified in this area. Retired, but looking for a part-time contact. Nice part is he—or she —would be armed and could work shifts by themselves. The District

NCO didn't have many details, but was hopeful there would be something by summer. I've also talked to staffing at sub-district about adding an Auxiliary Constable. I think there are some people in town that might be suitable candidates for that, we'll have to talk about it later."

Dave was relieved that things were running smoothly. He was not used to having staff under him, and having to talk and work so closely with people, but he was trying to get to know his staff better. Norris was doing well, just needed help with managing paperwork, and some good projects to boost her confidence. Reese was eager, but in need of the occasional reminder to slow down and think, that quick reactions weren't always an advantage. He would learn it all eventually, just needed to be gradually given some small projects to work on. Norris had been Reese's Field Coach, and had done a good job of balancing the mentor and mother attitudes. Reese had ruffled a few feathers in town with his exuberance though, forcing Dave to get out and talk with people, and in the process find out more about their problems and concerns. Other than last year's disappearance, nothing big had happened, or likely ever would. The biggest influence on the town was of course the mill, with all its issues. People either loved it or hated it.

Dave hadn't really picked a side yet, but both groups were pressuring him to choose. He'd wait until after the Minister's visit, when things got back to normal.

***

Dave and JB had finally matched their schedules enough for a coffee at Rosie's. As they walked toward the cafe, Dave's ears picked up the rattle-rattle-rattle of a spray can just up ahead in an alleyway. When they reached the open space he could see that it was empty, with just a faint smell of paint and a partially done mural on the wall, colourful and intricate.

"Nice art," said Dave. "Is the owner doing it?"

"No, but he's okay with it," said JB. "The artist is really talented—we just might run into him."

"Depends who's definition of art it is I guess," said Dave. "I like this one, though, but not all would agree. The mayor's pushing a goal of zero graffiti in town—tagging or otherwise. I suspect that in a small town like this, I'll soon get to know exactly who the taggers are, but I'm not convinced the solution is to keep throwing them all in jail. I did assure him the issue was on my list, though. Didn't you do a mural wall last summer up here?"

"Yes, I did a whole event around one in the park," she said. "I saw some of them back in Ottawa, so decided to try it up here. We had some local DJ's, dancing, the Kiwanis club did burgers. It was pretty popular with not just the kids, even some of the townspeople and elders liked it. I know the elders would like to see our youth develop more of an interest in the arts, this was one way to make that happen."

A teenager appeared around the corner of the building ahead. He was tall, thin, First Nations, with a backpack on his shoulder, and the latest style in sneakers on his feet.

"Hey," said JB, "it's my brother."

"Hi Junior," said Dave. "Good to see you again. Thanks again for the trip into the woods, it was a big help. What are you up to today?"

"Nothing much," said Junior. Dave pretended to not notice the paint stains on Junior's hands as he shoved them into his pockets.

"JB tells me that among your many skills you're also an artist?" said Dave.

Junior looked surprised, then smiled. "Yes, I do some stuff," he said.

"He's pretty good," said JB. "He'd be a good choice to lead a mural program here."

"Whoa," said Dave. "I like the concept, but for now that's as far as I can go with this." He really didn't need a new community project. "What I can do is see if I can find some people that are into this and pass on their info to you."

Junior nodded, then stuck out a hand. "It's a deal."

As he walked away, JB turned to Dave. "Thanks for the discretion on the painted fingertips. He's pretty good about not tagging anymore. He's matured a lot in the last couple of years, might even be a link for you to some of the other kids. It's hard for them, especially those from the reserve. There used to be a lot of tensions between them and the town kids a few years ago. There was a big gang on the reserve too, years ago —my cousin was in that big time. I had my problems too, but was lucky enough to have had a supportive family. Some of the kids are even having to juggle school with looking after the family—because the parents won't."

"Guess there's no place for street kids here," said Dave.

"No, it's either stay at home or move away to the big city. Big step, and sometimes not with a good ending. A friend of Junior's is in that boat —great kid and responsible, but her parents have a lot of issues. The Children's Aid finally found a great home for her two siblings in the area, but she needs to get out too. She doesn't want to leave town, but can't afford to get a room either. She's doing some on-line studies for now, and acing everything. A smart kid, would hate to see her fall through the cracks."

Dave looked at her speculatively, an idea suddenly blossoming in his head. "Is she reliable? If you had kids would you hire her as a babysitter?"

JB looked at him quizzically. "Sure I would, and why are you asking me about kids already?" She grinned at Dave.

Dave felt himself blush. "Constable Norris," he said, "is having baby-sitter problems. She needs something a little more permanent. Maybe she could give this girl a place to stay in return for looking after her son. Give me this girl's info and I'll pass it on to Norris."

"Thanks," said JB. "Good solution. As for that mural idea, I'll work with Junior more on it."

CHAPTER 19

"Dave, sorry I'm late," said Norris. "Got stuck up at the grocery store. At least I don't have babysitter problems now—JB's friend Andrea started this week and is working out just fine—Bobby just loves her."

"That's okay," he said. "It's just after four. Glad that's working out. I was heading out for some fresh air before dinner at Rosie's," said Dave. "Take a walk with me, will you?"

He'd been getting more involved in staffing issues lately, not that he liked it but he realized he couldn't just ignore it. Norris had potential. She had great empathy with people and a clever mind. He'd checked her 1004's on file, the performance logs were generally favourable. Her main problem was that she was off and on as far paperwork went—nothing so drastic to put her on report, but she needed to be guided a bit. He wasn't sure how though, as he wasn't much better than her at that bane of their existence.

As they stepped out the door Dave blinked and reached for his sunglasses. "Wow, it sure turned nice today. That sun is still blinding off the snow. I guess the days are finally getting longer."

"So, what did you want to talk about?" said Norris.

"Nothing serious," said Dave. "You're doing a great job. We're lucky you were here to manage things before I came."

"It's been a challenge," she said. "Reese has been good too."

"You've been doing the important things," he said. "But now that I'm here to share the load, and before the summer rush — "

"Let me guess," she said. "Paperwork. I know, reports are late, and I miss diary dates sometimes."

"I understand," he said. "You've a lot to handle."

"I can manage," she said, "Don't be afraid to give me hell if I'm messing up—I don't want special treatment just because I'm a single mother."

"Understood," he said. "I can give you some shortcuts with your reports, though. Some quick ways to help make them look good for Staff up in Sub-division. I'm going to start assigning more specific work to Sheila too. I think she can handle it; just needs more of a challenge and responsibility."

He still wasn't sure what Sheila did on her three days, other than chat on the phone and bustle up to 'her' counter when anyone came in. Maybe getting more involved in some specific reports would give her a feeling of being part of the team.

They continued their walk down the main street, enjoying the sun while it lasted. The sidewalks were busier than usual, as it seemed like a lot of people had the same idea. With Norris by his side Dave couldn't very well fade, so he ended up talking to everyone they met. It wasn't that bad, maybe because he was more at ease with his job and the town, or maybe people were just warming up to him.

***

"What's today's special, Rosie?"

Dave settled onto a stool at the counter. In addition to the good coffee, the fries were exceptional too—not frozen, always fresh cut. Aside from the great dinners, Dave also enjoyed just sitting and talking with the owner. Well, it was more listening to Rosie, but he did have helpful comments to make, and seemed to know everything that was going on in the town.

Rosie smiled from the kitchen pass through. "You're early, I'm still prepping for supper. How about some soup and an omelet?"

"I'll take it," said Dave. "I just finished my shift and took a stroll with Norris as she started hers. Took a while because everyone wanted to stop and chat. They seem friendlier today."

"You can thank JB for some of that," said Rosie. "She's spreading the word about you. Telling people you really are an okay guy, if they just give you a chance. She does have some say here behind the scenes,

108

directly and through her grandfather. And of course, I have mentioned to people what a good group you all are."

"Thanks," said Dave. "It would help my investigations if I could get people to share more details with me."

"Anything new on Bourbeau's disappearance?" asked Rosie. "Or is all that classified."

"It's still open," said Dave. "Still working on it. Funny, when I mentioned it to Barretto and Klein they acted like the case was closed. They were quite worried that I'd keep going, wanted me to drop it."

"And will you?" said Rosie.

"Drop it? No. But maybe that's why my promised mill tour keeps getting delayed, maybe all my questions are making them nervous. I don't think there's any link between the two though."

"It can be an interesting tour," said Rosie. "It's pretty impressive in there at first glance."

"Well, I have had some complaints about pollution and the mill. Not really my jurisdiction, but I will try to keep my eyes open."

A few minutes later Rosie set a plate down in front of Dave. "Here you go, omelet and soup."

"This looks amazing," said Dave. "My omelets just look like scrambled eggs."

"Patience," said Rosie. "Now when you get to the mill, Tony Barretto will be giving you the standard Paper Mill for Dummies tour, but maybe you can read between the lines. Notice where he doesn't take you, as he can be sneaky. He's very much a loyal mill employee too, and likes to brag, so he may let something slip too. He's dumber than he looks."

"I'll push him a bit," said Dave. "Thanks for the tips. They never told me in training I'd have to be an industrial spy too."

***

"Thanks again for working on all those reports," said Dave. "You're doing a great job on them—you're a fast learner."

"Glad to help," said Sheila.

They'd had a few stormy winter days, so Dave had focused on getting Sheila more involved in the internal paperwork. He'd just opened the budget file when he heard a cheery voice at the desk, "Hi Sheila, is Dave in?"

"Yes, I'll let him know you're here —"

"No problem, I'll do it," JB interjected. Before Sheila could even unwedge herself from her chair, JB popped in the door and perched on the corner of his desk.

"How's your day?" she asked.

"Pretty good," he said. "We're all getting more used to each other in here. Sheila has taken over a bit more too—that's a help. My little trip into the bush was a good break to get me thinking about some of the benefits of up here too. People seem more open to me, which is nice, I think."

"Well, it's sometimes more work to be a loner up here," she said. "We are a friendly bunch. Might as well relax and enjoy us."

"I feel a bit better," he said. "Still having those weird dreams though, mostly with those animals in them. Nothing specific but I get the feeling they mean me harm."

"Hmm," she said, and looked at him thoughtfully. "You know, the clouds have cleared away, and it's a nice day out there. Why don't you let me take you for a walk."

He was tempted, but he was just beginning to get the hang of running a detachment—staffing reviews, schedules, reports to headquarters and the town, even a trip to the local school to give a talk to the kids.

"Sorry, I'm on a roll here, just about to tackle the budget figures."

"Budget?" JB laughed. "Whatever has possessed you? You used to hate paperwork."

"Dave, it will wait," said Sheila. "The top of your desk is in need of a cleanup again anyway. I've a pile of file folders and labels and am dying to tackle it."

Dave was pleased to see this new side to Sheila. He smiled and grabbed his parka. "Sounds like a win-win for me. Let's go."

***

JB took a deep breath as they stepped outside. The air was crisp, but clean. They headed down the street slowly, jackets open a bit, occasionally bumping into each other and quickly apologizing. Birds flitted from branch to branch down the street, chirping in the warm sun.

Dave pointed to a large black and white one. "What's that? It looks like a huge chickadee."

"That," she said, "is a Canada Jay. We call him Wisakedjak, or Whisky Jack."

"Reminds me of you," he said. "Always hopping around, never rests, seems to be interested in everything."

She was pleased that he had noticed. "Good call. The Whisky Jack is my totem animal, my spirit guide."

"What's that for?" he asked. "Is it like a guardian angel or something?"

JB smiled. "Or something. My people use animals and dreams a lot to help us in our lives. We believe the spirits speak to us through them. Often it's a particular animal for the person, and the meaning can be related to the kind of animal, or what happens in the dream."

He looked at her sideways. "And when did you become an annoying little bird?"

"Annoying?" she said. She gave him a poke in the arm. She could tell he was teasing, but didn't mind. "My mother said that while she was waiting for me to come into this life, she often saw the Wisakedjak outside her window, like he was keeping an eye on her."

"Well, I guess whatever works for you," Dave said, "I've always been a logical practical type, never into religion."

She suspected that was about to change, once they started to investigate whatever was in him. "Think of it as a spiritual thing, not a religion," she said. "I can tell you more if you're interested."

"That I am," he said. "Part of my aboriginal liaison studies."

Now it was her turn to look at him quizzically. If he wasn't serious about learning this she didn't want to waste her time.

"I admit, initially that was just something my boss put on my to-do list," he said. "That and stay out of trouble. But I'm not asking because I have to, now I really am interested."

"Okay then," she said. "It is part of our culture after all, and we're part of the community."

She smiled, then whistled at the bird. It squawked back at her and flew off. "Daylight whistling is fine, don't worry."

"Thanks," he said, "you had me worried for a minute, I was afraid some dark spirit was going to take you over."

She glanced quickly at Dave, but he seemed to just be joking. She didn't see any darkness now in him, here in the bright sun. As they walked he told her a bit about his other postings, and his latest one in Toronto, doing undercover work, and getting busted, when they saw through his disguise. When she pushed for details, there was that nervousness again, and a bit of a shadow around him. Interesting. She'd have to mention this to the elders; they needed every clue they could find on this.

"I overheard you practising your French on some locals," she said. "It was passable. Where'd you pick that up?"

"Here and there," he said. "Besides the Ojibwa there's some French and some Irish in me. My middle name is Bernard."

She laughed. "Bernard Browne? That's rich, especially with that big brown parka you arrived in town with. Still just here for the year?"

"Yes, only a year," said Dave. "Less if I can arrange it. Just making sure things go smoothly before I head on to more drug squad work, and hopefully a promotion. How about you, up here for good?"

"I might be," she said. "When I was down at Ottawa U, I wasn't sure what to take so settled for just a general arts program. It was interesting, but wasn't that inspiring. I've always been an artist, so when I met some kids down there doing graffiti murals I persuaded them to let me watch them and learn. I'd tagged up here as a kid—everyone does I think. And no, I won't tell you which are mine in the back alleys here." She smiled, as he held up a hand in protest.

"No problem," he said, "Let me guess, you got distracted and spent more time outside than in the classroom."

"You got it," she said. "I started priming walls, then graduated to small pieces on my own. Went to some clubs with the artists, met some DJ's, danced all night. After a while I was spending most of my time working on my art, even getting some pieces onto the top legal walls. I really liked it and the crowd."

"What sort of crowd?" said Dave.

"Some were students," she said. "Some worked in a pub or a shoe store or a bank. Some were street kids sleeping under a bridge. What tied us together was our passion for this art. I volunteered on some youth projects too, even helped start a program for some First Nations kids. It was great to see what changes can be made once you find the key, a way to reach kids."

"Sounds like you found your passion," he said, "both the art and working with youth. Why did you leave?"

"Well, aside from failing all my courses, my dad disappeared."

"Oh yeah," he said, "sorry. So, now what? I understand the Grande is yours, right?"

"Yes. It was my dad's, now is mine. I work at the pub, hang with some friends, talk to my grandfather and other elders. They can actually be quite interesting, especially when they start with the stories. Just don't expect the Reader's Digest condensed version; they do go on and on at times."

"Like George did my first night here," said Dave. "He knew I was already half asleep."

JB chuckled. "I think they enjoy the process of storytelling as much as the specific ending. They need to ensure our culture is being passed on. It used to be discouraged, especially in the old residential schools, but it's back out in the open now. Our culture is important to my people in many ways, and is even more in need as we try to deal with modern world issues. The elders and their stories are not only our historians and leaders, they are also our version of psychologists. They can guide us and help with our problems. Even more, sometimes it's used to pass on knowledge to the gifted, help them further on their path—maybe to being a leader some day."

She laughed and said "Don't get me going, I get very excited when I talk about this topic. I could go on forever."

Dave smiled back. "I don't mind, I enjoy listening to you. Your eyes really light up when you get excited. I like that."

Well, that was unexpected. "Thanks," she said.

There was a pause. "So, when do they have these story times?" said Dave.

"It used to be a regular winter thing," she said, "for the long dark evenings. Now it only happens at special occasions, like a pow-wow. And it's getting harder to find youth willing to listen, as all they seem to want to do is play video games or turn on the TV for some mindless American sit-com."

"I'd like to listen," said Dave. "Let me know when I can hear some."

"Just be sure to have a strong coffee first," she said.

"I will," he said. "Speaking of which, I need to drop in at Rosie's— join me?"

"What like a date?" she said. She was joking at first, but realized maybe it was time she got over Pete the jerk 'and tried again. Dave didn't seem like the jerk type.

Dave looked back at her, paused, then said, "Sure, a date, let's try that."

CHAPTER 20

Norris had done the initial investigation on Bourbeau's disappearance, so Dave asked her to help him review the file.

"Looks like it took a while to start the search," Dave said.

"They didn't realize right away that there might be a problem," said Norris. "He'd left early in the day, supposedly was good weather, a bit of an early thaw. Lots of snow in the bush still, and lakes still pretty solid, but witnesses said it was one of those days when you could feel spring around the corner. When he didn't return that night, people figured he got delayed in some wet snow, and had just decided to camp out."

"In the snow?" he asked.

"Oh yeah, was mild, easy for an experienced woodsman like him to put together a bit of shelter and light a fire. We used to all do it as kids just for fun. Anyway, by noon the next day he still hadn't returned, so Rosie showed up and wanted us to start a search."

Dave leafed through the pages. There was a statement by Barretto that he'd bumped into JB's dad as he was heading out, and he'd told Tony he was heading to Dexter Lake to do some sampling.

"Had Bourbeau left an itinerary or map of his trip?"

"Nope," said Norris. "There was just Tony's statement. Should have been easy to track him down anyway. Rosie wanted to get out and look right away, but Barretto talked us into waiting for a proper search party to be organized—mill people and all. But that meant we lost yet another day."

"Sounds like he was eager to help though," Dave said.

"It was a little unusual," she said, "seeing as they didn't like

Bourbeau poking around. Rosie did go out finally, but we'd lost several hours of daylight by then so he turned back. And it had already started to snow—not a lot, but enough to cover up any fresh tracks."

He looked through more of the file. There was documentation on the search too, of the areas covered, people involved. It was quite extensive, but focused in one area.

"All that effort on Dexter Lake," said Dave. "Yet nothing found, then or in the spring."

"Initially it was just there," she said. "JB didn't believe Tony, so she and most of the band expanded the search within a few days to other trails and lakes. However, by then it had snowed so there were no tracks to follow. They found nothing."

"So what's the connection to the mill?" he said.

"JB's sure the mill was involved in it somehow," said Norris, "but there wasn't anything to connect them, other than his interest in pollution. She's sure her father was close to something, too close. He was all excited about this huge collection of damning evidence, but just needed one quick trip before heading off to some conference."

"Maybe a fresh set of eyes looking at his disappearance will help," said Dave. "Just not any mill connections. That part will definitely have to wait until after the Minister's visit."

***

Dave drove over to the curling club in their not-so-new SUV. Reese had picked up a few scratches and Dave had managed to add an actual dent when he'd slid into a bridge railing his first week there. The dent was small, but he now knew that at minus 40 even snow tires can get hard and slick. The good-natured teasing from the townspeople was a positive sign, he supposed.

He headed down Main Street, nodding back as people waved to him, then turned left at the lake, toward the mill road. The rink sat along the lake shore, in between some cottages, just before the mill. It was a plain rectangular building with a long rounded steel roof, and a plume of steam rising from a small building tacked on one side. The parking lot was full of cars and trucks, and of course ski-doos.

Today almost everyone there was out on the ice: shouting, scrubbing away at something with their brooms, or sliding up and down the ice after those huge stones. He had no idea how they managed to push them, or guide them in a straight line for that matter. Many of the throws curved one way or the other too—seemingly at random. There were only a few people lined up along the gallery window, watching the action on the ice, drink in hand.

He noticed a couple of youth sitting together at the far end of the room. One he recognized as being someone he'd caught underage before, but today he was sitting there with nothing to drink in front of him. However, his older buddy next to him had two pints of draft, both half empty, in front of him. Dave shook his head and walked over to them. "Come with me guys, and you, carry both of your beers too." He didn't even listen to their pretended innocence. He walked them over to the bartender and pointed to the two. "Okay, what's wrong with this picture?"

"Damn it, kids," said the bartender. "I'm not losing a license from your tricks—you're both banned here until next week."

There were indignant protests then, as they complained about how unfair that was, and how they would miss their weekly league game.

"Too bad," said the bartender. "You'll have to find subs and explain what happened."

"Last warning for all of you." said Dave, "Next time it's charges all around." He walked over to the window and watched the players finish up their game. He had no idea who'd won, as the scoreboard was a mystery to him, just a row of numbers on pegs.

Rosie came in from the ice and waved to Dave. "Hey, buddy, did you catch that last end?"

"I suppose I did," said Dave, "whatever an end is. I have no idea what is going on. Or who won. There was a lot of yelling and hurrying, but I really don't have a clue."

"No problem," said Rosie,"you'll learn it all in the turkey bonspiel. It's on in March."

"Let me guess," said Dave. "You slide frozen turkeys down the ice. No, wait, you all dress like turkeys."

"Very funny. No, it's just a regular curling game, but a competition for turkeys as prizes," Rosie said. "There's four for the winning team, and more as door prizes. The local Metro usually has a bunch left over from

Christmas so we get a deal. My team won last year. Come to think of it mine is likely still in the old chest freezer in the back of my place. JB's dad left his there too, but he made me promise to give it to his daughter, before he headed out that last time. A weird sort of legacy I think. But that was a year ago, so I keep thinking I'll just stew them up or something. "

"Let me know when and I'll skip lunch," Dave said.

Rosie laughed, "No, not for the cafe, there's a woman on the outskirts of town that takes in stray cats. They wouldn't mind a bit of freezer burn with their supper. Anyway, back to this bonspiel, it is a lot of fun. We'd love to have you join in. We've still room if you want to put together a team from your office."

"I don't know," said Dave. "I'm not really into team sports. I've never curled before, plus I don't think a detachment team would even get close to winning."

"You never know," said Rosie, "You won't be the only rookie there. It would be good for your image too. It's a mixed event so you'll need two women and two men on the team, and hopefully have at least one person on your team that has actually curled. There are a few real keeners that sign up but you can just ignore them. Come on, the whole town goes, it will be fun."

Dave hated being told something would be fun, because usually it wasn't. On the other hand, it would help him connect better with the town. Sounded like everyone would be there, including JB.

"Sign me up," said Dave. "I suppose I could ask JB for my team."

Rosie shook his head, "Sorry, she's one of those keeners, she needs some stars. She does like you, but that doesn't count when she's gathering a team. Even when she was away at school she'd join a local rink and always make it back here for the bonspiels. She'll have her brother with her for sure, and will have already recruited two others. Why don't you do a detachment team? You, Reese, Norris and Sheila."

"Sheila? Really?" said Dave.

"Well, if you leave her out you know she'll likely just pout and slack off even more. And, she may not look very athletic, but I noticed last year she managed to make some amazing shots, in spite of her husband putting her down. Mind you, she also made some horrendous ones but that's up to your skip to manage."

"Skip?"

"That's the head of the team, they decide the strategy and call a lot of the shots. Norris looked pretty good on the ice last year, maybe she could do that for you. We usually have at least one practice session before, too. Lets the rookies learn enough so that they don't make complete fools of themselves. Maybe just partial fools."

"Well, it seems like a popular sport here in the north," said Dave. "We do see it down south once in a while on a sports channel—usually when the bar can't find anything else. But this looks like an expensive setup—how does a small town afford it?"

"We were creative," said Rosie. "The plans were done by a local retiree that used to be an architect. The band has timber rights on their reserve, and they also have a small sawmill, so they did the framing. We got a deal on the ice plant from another rink that had partially burned down. They couldn't afford to replace the rink—no insurance—so let us have the equipment cheap. And we found a local trucker that was willing to use his float to get it all here. We had some fundraisers, got a grant, and here it is. Curling is a big deal for the town and the area; we manage to keep the ice always busy with the several leagues we have running."

There was a shout from one of the tables. "Hey, Rosie, we need your wallet!" One of his team members was waving at him.

"Winners pay for the drinks," explained Rosie. "Let's join them. I'll buy you a Coke."

They walked over and Dave shook hands all around. He'd met most of them in town, or out on the reserve; many were from the same group at Rosie's birthday party. As they all talked they reinforced his impression of a sort of alternative town council.

"Don't hesitate to contact any of us if you need information or help on something," said Rosie. "We need to work together."

Dave was cautious about making any real commitments. While they seemed to be the real movers in the area, they also had a bias against the mayor and the mill management.

"I hear your frustration," he said, "but I can't take sides on this. I have to be impartial and follow the law. Of course if any of you do have anything specific let me know, as I'm always glad to hear your issues and concerns. The investigation is ongoing on the disappearance of Bourbeau last year, but that's all I can say on it at this time. As for irregularities with the installation at the paper mill, right now I'm leaving that with their own investigator. I'm helping him where needed, but making sure he stays within the law—this isn't a TV episode of Dave the Bounty Hunter. "

***

"This won't take long," said Dave. Sheila sat forward, steno pad at the ready. "No, that's okay Sheila, it's not about work."

He looked at his team. "I hear there's a turkey bonspiel next week, and people are pushing me to put in a detachment team. I have never curled, have rarely watched it, and have absolutely no idea how it works. But I agreed to try and would like you to go too. I'm asking you, not telling you. What do you say?"

Sheila asked, "Me too?"

"Yes, you're part of the team. Are you a curler?"

"Well, I have a few times, I'm told I'm not very good though."

"Well I've never done it ever," he said, "so I can guarantee I'll be the absolute worst on our team. How about you, Norris?"

"I used to curl in my last detachment, I'm not great but I'm okay."

Dave turned to Reese. "Still looking for a star here. How about you?"

"I may have curled a bit back in high school," said Jim with a smile.

"You weren't by any chance the—what is it—skip?"

"Yes I was," said Reese.

"Did your team do any good?" asked Dave.

"Provincial champions two years in a row," said Reese.

There was a collective 'Woo-hHoo' from the rest of them.

"Let's keep this quiet," said Dave. "Sheila, don't mention it to your husband. Maybe we can get an edge in the odds and actually have a chance of winning a turkey."

"My lips are sealed," she said, and made a gesture across her mouth.

"I'm pretty sure they get enough turkeys donated for almost everyone anyway," said Norris.

"But it still would be nice to win it," replied Dave. "Rosie tells me there are lots of interesting side bets too."

120

"JB's team lost to Rosie last year," said Norris, "and ended up having to paint his fence. What do you think, Reese, can you turn us into curlers?"

"It's do-able I suppose," said Reese. "Do we get any ice time to practice?"

"Just before the bonspiel starts, I think," said Dave.

"Better than nothing," said Reese. "If we get together here for a couple of sessions, I'll be able to explain the basics and maybe some strategy. We just need to remember not to look too good at practice."

"Not a problem for me," said Dave.

***

Dave had brought coffees for his team, and was debating whether he should have maybe added a shot of whiskey to each one. It was bonspiel day, and he was a little nervous as they all waited for the first game.

They had told dispatch what was going on so they'd hold all but the most urgent calls. If something did come up, Norris had her uniform in a bag and could take it. Her son Bobby was the official cheerleader and was busy arranging pretzels on the table in cryptic signs under the watchful eye of his new babysitter, Andrea.

JB walked over with Rosie, a big smile on her face. "Ready to lose?" she asked.

"As long as we don't fall down I figure we're ahead," said Dave. "We're definitely here for just the fun, as you can see from the long odds Rosie here gave us after our practice. I'm aiming us for the booby prize. Besides, I thought it was all in fun."

"Sure, but some of the teams compete a little harder, against each other, right Rosie?"

"Careful," said Rosie, "don't scare Dave and his newbies off. We need all the entry fees we can get. Although we haven't done too bad this year, we got a few teams from as far away as Winnipeg and Kenora. Some are just here for the fun, the good food in the buffet, and the cheap beer. We did a deal again with the motel up at the highway, and we shuttle people up there, so no one has to drive home after partying."

Dave was reluctantly starting to like this new sport, with all the party talk.

"Who's the Winnipeg team?" asked JB.

"They were here last year too," said Rosie. "Quite a mix. There's a lawyer, an accountant, a sports equipment salesman, and a priest."

"A priest?"

"Yes, said Rosie. "Pretty athletic too, he used to play hockey a lot—he may be a ringer. Good luck guys, come on JB."

As they walked away Dave turned to Reese and dropped his voice. "Speaking of ringers, won't the Kenora people know you?"

"Of course," said Reese, "but they've promised to keep quiet about it and not spoil my surprise."

"Probably too late anyway," said Norris. "We've already got long odds on all those little side bets. We've got chances at a catered dinner, a garage cleanup, a fishing trip, and a year's babysitting."

"Very well done," said Dave. "Nice negotiating skills." Dave looked around at a sudden commotion in the corner. He saw Barretto with three other men, as big and burly as him, all fist pumping and back slapping. Barretto waved and headed over toward them.

"Oh no," said Norris.

"Now, play nice," said Reese.

CHAPTER 21

"Tony," said Risso. "look who's here—the cops have a team too. We'll smear them out there. They better watch out—those rocks are pretty heavy."

Tony shook his head. Risso always had to be the tough guy.

"Frank, this is not a full contact sport. Behave yourself today. I'm working on them, especially Dave. He believes our spin so far, and soon he'll be toeing the party line."

"I bet it's that Shy Vi you really want to work on," said Risso.

He wasn't that far off the mark, but Tony just waved a hand at Risso. "Stay here and behave, I'm going over to psych them out a bit."

He hitched up his pants, slicked back his hair, and strutted over to Dave's team.

He nodded. "Dave, Jim. Ladies."

"We have names too, Carmine," said Norris.

Damn—why did she have to pull that out all the time. He smiled. "Sorry. Violet, Sheila. You guys ready for us to beat you?"

"Ha! Even if you're twice as good as last year," said Norris, "we'd still beat you."

He flushed. "We were robbed last year, we had bad ice, it was really slow."

"Really?" she said. "Are you sure it wasn't the beer that slowed you down?"

She was such a smart ass. "We've got a good team, "said Barretto. "Especially Risso. He even wanted to be skip, but that wouldn't look good, seeing as I'm his boss. We've got this made. This year we're going to just throw harder, right through any slow spots like a rocket."

"Care to make a small bet on it?" asked Norris. "Say if you lose you —hmm—what about you dig up Sheila's garden for her this spring."

"Sure," he said. "But if—when—we win, you go out for dinner with me." To his surprise she agreed without hesitation. Either she was really confident, or did like him after all. He suspected it was the latter.

He did a little dance as he walked back to his team.

"All right boys," he said. "Psyched them out, plus got me a little dinner date. Don't let me down now."

***

"Jerk," said Norris.

"Dinner?" said Sheila. "Ewww."

"No problem," said Norris. "His team's all bluster. And he's their chief loser."

"Well, as far as work goes he does seem cooperative," said Dave. He was still trying to be optimistic. "He's a little rough around the edges —okay, a lot rough—but I'm willing to give him the benefit of the doubt for now." Everybody at the table, including V's son, rolled their eyes in disbelief.

Dave's team eventually got their turn at a bit of practice time, as did the other rookie teams. Reese had coached them through some of the basics, but their sessions at the detachment didn't prepare Dave for the reality of stepping out on the ice. He immediately landed on his rear end.

"Remember—balance and calmness," said Reese. " Don't forget, this is forty pounds of granite, so don't try to lift with your arm—keep it on the ice. Use your whole body and gently swing."

They all threw a couple of rocks, and practised sweeping. While Reese was careful to pretend to be awkward, Dave didn't feel he needed to pretend at all, he definitely felt like a real rookie. They weren't the only rookie team though, the team from Winnipeg in particular was there mostly to have fun. Although they'd been the year before they still looked brand new at it. Reese thought they were probably a one game a year type of team. One of them, the lawyer Dave thought, was on his way to the other end when his feet slipped out from under him and he fell back onto his butt. As he reflexively swung his broom out beside him there was a resounding "'whack'" that got the attention of all the teams on the ice.

"I'm okay, I'm okay, " he said. He held up his beer bottle. "Beer's okay too!" His buddies cheered and helped him up, then they all shuffled to the far end of the ice together.

***

They'd decided that Reese would be skip, Norris vice-skip, Sheila second, and Dave lead. As lead he threw first, but his first throw just barrelled through the target at the far end. The second one was so light that it barely made it far enough to stay in play, but after a few ends he felt like he was getting the hang of it. Sheila, as second, threw after Dave, and managed to do quite well on most of her shots.

"Good throw, Sheila," said Reese. "You've got really good weight on your rocks, setting up some nice ones for the rest of the team to build on."

Dave noticed Sheila's confidence increasing even more. With her successes, she relaxed more and joked around with the rest of the team. Maybe this get-together would have some real benefits back at the office too. Norris, as vice-skip, was third to throw and showed some good consistency. But it was Reese who shone—after a slow start he began to let his skills show, but very gradually.

"Guys, I think it's time for us to get serious," said Reese.

Soon their team was moving up the competition ladder and people started watching carefully.

Rosie called Dave over as his team changed ends.

"What's with Reese?" he said.

"Must be a fast learner," said Dave.

"Yeah, right," said Rosie. "Good to see you here though, as part of us. I'll have to introduce you around to more people in between games."

Dave knew many people already by sight, but having Rosie introduce him again, in an off-duty environment, opened some of them up. Dave used the opportunity to try to get to know some people a little better, including many workers from the mill. However, although most were open with him at first, as soon as he pressed for details on the mill they would back away, sensing a cross-over from personal to business. Maybe it was too soon. As for using his fade, while this would be a good place to eavesdrop on a lot of casual conversations, it was really too crowded in the lounge for that to work. Besides, he was starting to like

125

some of these people, so didn't want to just eavesdrop.

He was waiting at the bar for a beer when Mike came up to him.

"Dave, got a minute? Here, let me buy."

Mike led the way over to a corner. "I can't talk too long, as I don't want anyone getting suspicious. You told us the other day to not just complain. You were a little harsh but you were right, so I've decided that I want to do more about these mill issues. I've been working there for ten years, and I've seen a lot of things there that weren't right, illegal things. A lot of us have, we're not as dumb as they like to treat us."

"But aren't these things you should just work with management to solve?'" said Dave.

"We don't trust them," said Mike. "They're part of the problem. We know they are cutting corners, fudging records, polluting way more than the official reports show, but most of us are afraid to speak up. It can be a dangerous place to work, especially if Barretto or his goons are out to get you. Accidents have been known to happen to the most careful of us. Plus, some of the pay, and indirectly our small pensions, is tied into profits. But I don't care now. I buried my wife last fall and have nothing left for me."

"I'm sorry to hear that," said Dave.

Mike paused. "Thanks. She died of cancer, likely from that damn mill polluting our air and poisoning our fish. I think I can trust you to do the right thing here, you seem to care about the town more now. I'm not afraid to help you get proof on what is happening at the mill and about what I think happened to JB's dad."

"Not sure how much I can do," said Dave, "Already it sounds like a big problem, more than a few months' project."

With that Mike started to turn away.

"Wait," said Dave. There might be something there, and if he delayed it would only look bad for him after. "We've had some complaints filed recently, and I did ask people to do more than talk. Drop by my office, bring whatever you have, and we'll talk. If there's something, I can at least start something rolling. Right now, Tony's watching us, and my team is is next, so get out of here."

The field was starting to narrow, and competition was heating up, Dave checked the board—Barretto was their next opponent. Risso glared over at Dave and his team, smacking his fist into his palm, but Dave just smiled back. What a dope. It only took a few ends for the others to admit defeat. The better Dave and his team did, the worse Barretto's played—missing shots completely, taking out their own rocks, even falling as they rushed to sweep their rocks in, all the while with Barretto yelling at them. The only thing they could do well was drink a lot of beer.

As Dave's team left the ice, JB and Rosie were both there, waiting for him. "Sly move," she said.

Dave spread his hands out, and gave an innocent look, "What?"

"You know what, Dave." Rosie shook his head. "I was just talking with the Kenora team after we beat them out, they admitted that in high school they had lost to Reese's team—skunked. And to think we were even suckered into giving you better odds. Well played my friend. Now let's get out on the ice."

The rest of the day went quickly. Dave and his team mates didn't make it to the final round, but both JB's and Rosie's teams had to put in some effort to beat them.

The Detachment team were certainly the surprise hit of the bonspiel, both during and after the game. Throughout dinner and the awards ceremony there was a steady stream of people dropping by their table to tease them about their success, and asking if they would also be entering a team the summer baseball tournament. No big prizes for them, but they did win the Ringer of the Year award. The four from Winnipeg won something called the Twinkle-toes Award, for the member that fell and yet managed to not lose his grip on his beer.

"Team," said Dave, "I want to thank you for being just that—a team. We had fun and we managed to even beat some of the others. We won the spring garden work for Sheila—make sure you've lots of manure ready for Tony. The babysitting, I think it's obvious. That should go to Norris so her regular can have a break once in a while. As for the free dinner, I'll be hosting Rosie's team over at my place. It will be the most action my kitchen has seen all year and a challenge for him to cook outside the comfort zone of his cafe. Reese, thanks for being a great skip, I'll be picking up your bar tab next time we're at the Roost." He stood and raised his glass. "To us!"

Dave really was quite pleased with them, as even Sheila was acting more like one of the group. They had just finished dinner when her husband came over.

"Congratulations to the team. Glad to see the wife managed to not hold you back."

"Not at all," said Dave. "Sheila had some very nice shots, she's good at this."

"That's a surprise," said the mayor.

"I hear Junior won a little side bet from your team," said Norris.

"Something about a sign on the side of Rosie's cafe," said the mayor. "Finally doing something useful. I said I'd buy the paint, but he'll first need to submit all the proper forms and fees in his request to council."

"I think he and his friends are doing a mural," said Norris. "Rosie had supported some kids doing that back in Toronto. From his description there's some lettering but it's mostly a blend of various images from First Nations culture. At any rate, I believe a mural does not need approval."

"What?" said the mayor. "I'm not letting him cover that wall with his tags, and I'm certainly not paying for it. Corporal, if he even goes near that wall I want him arrested."

"Sounds like it's legal," said Dave, "as long as Rosie's fine with it."

The mayor opened and closed his mouth a few times—seemingly at a loss for words—then turned to his wife.

"Come along dear, our table's over here."

"I think I'll stay with my team," said Sheila. "You have a good time with your council buddies, hun." And with that she gave a little smile at Norris and sat down. "Pass the wine please, V."

The mayor gaped at her—again speechless—then walked away.

"Wow, a mural wall paid for by the mayor," said Reese.

"Oh, he's going to be very grumpy the next few days," said Sheila. "Poor dear."

***

After dinner, Dave spent most of the evening on the dance floor, as he was in demand with not only the single women in town but a few of the married ones too. JB had somehow managed to sneak off and change out of her normal casual clothes and into a short skirt and blouse. She'd put her hair up too, and slipped into some heels. She looked different, she looked cute—more than cute. He told her so, and managed to squeeze in a few dances. He felt like a debutante with a full dance card.

"What a great day," he said. "We almost beat you that one game."

"Almost," said JB. "The next big tournament is baseball I think—people will be watching for you."

"Hmm, we might try that," he said. "Things are going pretty good. I've learned a true Canadian game, made some new connections, and am dancing with a pretty lady." He smiled at JB. "Let me know if you'd like a police escort home, I'm good to drive, my team all made sure to take it easy."

"Thanks," she said. "You were hard to track down most of the night, but I could see you were keeping busy. I guess in a small place like this you're never really off duty. I'd like a ride—just let me finish this beer. I'm tired, we had to work hard to beat you, you little bugger."

"Just trying to challenge you," he said.

"Did you get any good leads tonight?" she said.

"Yes, I did, surprisingly so. Several people dropped by to confide in me. Maybe I should become a priest."

JB poked him in the shoulder, "Just stick with your day job. You really are good at it you know."

"Thanks," said Dave. "How about you, what are your plans? You seem to be settling in just fine up here. Still going to stay until you retire on a pension from the pub?"

"No, no pension there," she said, "but I do seem to be getting comfortable here—just not sure what else I can do besides the hotel. I used to enjoy being an artist. In fact I spent too much time doing that in Ottawa and not enough on my university courses. That and the youth group. Some of the kids where I volunteered reminded me of myself when I was growing up here, as I had a lot of similar problems with school and just life in general. Standard teenager in a small town stuff I guess, with a sprinkling of reserve life on top."

"What about something like that up here?" said Dave. "Be a teacher."

"I don't know," she said. "Not sure I can face more years of University. Kind of nice up here." She paused and yawned. "Oops—that's it for me—too much thinking too late at night. Take me home."

***

It was a short drive to the Grande, but JB was already half asleep by the time Dave pulled up. He walked around to her side and opened the door.

"Time to wake up?" she said.

"Afraid so," he said. "I'll make sure you get to the door safely." She took his arm as he walked her up the step, then at the door turned and gave him a hug. He hugged back for a moment, then she tipped her head back, pulled his down, and kissed him. She hugged him closer, then pulled back a bit.

"That was nice," she said. "The day, the evening, the kiss. Glad I stayed awake enough to enjoy it." And with that she was gone.

CHAPTER 22

Dave stared out his small office window. He could see a bit of his backyard, and the bird feeder by his deck. The feeder had been a house warming present from JB, just a bother he thought at first, but he'd grown to like trudging out to fill it up, and sitting at his kitchen window watching all the different kinds of birds that came in. At first he thought there was no order to their gathering, but then he noticed a pattern, a hierarchy, as each waited their turn. Once in a while too many would arrive at once, and there would be some angry chirping and a quick flurry of wings before peace was restored. The sizes and colours varied every day, but usually there was a Whisky Jack there, acting like a supervisor. He found it very calming to just sit and watch, even if for only a few minutes. He could relax, sometimes get a fresh perspective on the day's problems, sometimes just let his mind drift.

Sheila popped her head in his office, "Staff Sergeant Scully from Sub-division on the line for you." She waited in the doorway.

"Thanks Sheila," he said. "Grab the door will you?"

She looked disappointed but closed the door as she left.

"Corporal, I've had another call from a Minister Gottman's aide in Ottawa, about the upcoming visit.."

"Yes, we're getting ready for it."

"She reminded me that they are very concerned about everything going smoothly. She had heard there was a mill investigation going on at the same time—please tell me she is mistaken."

"Staff, I wouldn't say it's an investigation. Before I came here the office had only two official complaints about pollution. One was

131

forwarded on to the Ministry of Environment for their follow-up. The other was from this First Nations elder who disappeared last year so the complaint was closed. But even before that I see that we had told him there was insufficient evidence to proceed. A number of people have talked about concerns over misused grant funds, or excessive pollution, but until recently it was just grumblings."

"And now?"

"Well, since I've arrived there have been a few more official complaints," he said, "but I'm sure it's just because they are hoping a new guy will come in and fix it all."

"But you aren't, are you Corporal?" said Staff. "No big-shot heroics, no hunches, no break the rules and apologize after, right? If there's no case, don't invent one."

"Don't worry Staff," he said, "I'm a by-the-book guy now." Which was true, so far. He had encouraged Mike to get some documentation, but that was only to ensure this either went further or stopped. "Nothing more definite on any environmental protest planned for that day either. The mayor seems very supportive of this award and new funding, as is most of the town. He's asked me a couple of times already if there is some investigation going on, though. Do you know of any investigation from Winnipeg HQ that maybe nobody told us about?"

There was a pause. "Good point," said Staff, "I'll check, just in case. I doubt it though, as we don't have a pollution section, and the Commercial Crime guys have a list of pending files long enough to keep them busy for five years."

"We do have that disappearance from last year," said Dave. "It might be linked to problems at the mill, but I can't tell yet. It's a pretty cold investigation, not really moving. I can't see that getting in the way of a VIP visit. There are just the three of us, so unless you can find us some extra staff members for a few off hours we won't have time to look at any other complaints that day anyway."

"I'm seeing what I can do for extra personnel, Dave. Not for that, but the summer. And I'll share a little background about the politics here, as it's a little complicated. The Minister has a lot of money for areas like yours, and she's a close friend of the new Justice Minister. And you know how he's been busting our chops lately. Every time the Toronto Star prints another story about us, or the opposition stands and waves their finger at him and spouts on about accountability and oversight and transparency—he starts up yet more investigations and cutbacks and reorganizations. Look, I'm not saying drop things, but it would help our case—and your profile—if you reassured them that this visit had your full attention. Back off on your native liaison too. I know you think you've some good connections there, but the police have to be impartial and we don't want it to appear you're already cozy to one side or the other. Got it?"

Dave was feeling torn. He had new friendships, growing local cooperation, plus new expectations of him and of the direction his investigations were taking. Yet he still had that goal to spend a quiet time up here and then get back into undercover work.

"Dave, still there?" Scully asked.

"Sorry, yes, I hear what you're saying Staff, I can do that."

"That's good," said the staff sergeant. "I don't want to hear about any of these issues until after the visit. Do you understand what I'm saying?"

"Yeah, yeah," said Dave. He shook his head.

"Play nice with that aide if she calls again too," said Staff. "That's it for now."

Dave hung up and stared out the window again, trying to recapture his earlier calm.

***

"What's up Dave, you look tired." Norris was concerned. "Too many hot dates?""

"Who me? No, JB and I are just friends,"

Norris wasn't sure that was how JB saw it but she decided to let that pass. She and that girl had to talk.

"I haven't been sleeping well, that's all," he said. "My headaches are back again—not enough to bother a doctor, just annoying."

"Have you been at least eating well?" she said. "How's your cooking skills?"

"Still next to nil," he said. "It's hard to cook for one, so I just grab something quick when I'm hungry. Or sear a steak on the BBQ."

He was looking pretty worn out lately, even more so since Staff had called him. "What did Staff want from you—something serious? Hopefully not a bad review already!"

"No, nothing like that," said Dave. "He was just confirming what the Minister's aide had said—to back off all the investigations until after the big visit and funding announcement."

Norris looked at him quizzically. "Remember last week, when you were helping me with interviewing the kid that was booby-trapping the bike trail? You said to watch his face when he's telling the story, especially at the critical bit. And to not just listen to what he's saying, think about why he's saying it and what he's leaving out. That's where the truth would be hiding."

It had been good advice, as she'd discovered the kid was being bullied and trying to deal with it himself. Not as big as a Toronto drug bust she supposed, but still pretty satisfying.

Dave smiled. "Yes, you did a good interview. But what does it have to do with this?"

"I wonder what somebody is not telling us about this case?" she said. "Since when does a political aide in Ottawa tell us what investigations to do or not do? Especially when the only open case is for one missing person that isn't even really related to the mill. Other than a pollution study for some conference he was going to. Maybe it's not about the time it will take away from the VIP visit, but that they have already decided to hand over the money and don't want some embarrassment to show up at the same time. Maybe they know something and think we have an investigation but we don't."

Dave looked at her and nodded. "It doesn't make sense to worry about the time we might spend, but it would make sense if there's an embarrassing secret they don't want uncovered. Good work Norris."

She smiled at the unexpected praise. "Didn't Staff also tell you to back off the investigations?"

Dave smiled back at her. "Actually he said he didn't want to hear about any investigations until after the visit."

Norris smiled. "I see a window of opportunity in that choice of words. We just have to keep it low-key and ensure he doesn't hear anything."

"I'll be so low-key people won't even know I'm there," said Dave.

***

"Sheila, I'm heading over to the curling club," he said. "Just checking it out."

"Enjoy the break," she said. "Grab some breakfast too, you need more than just a coffee. I'll take a bagel if you're buying. Oh, and Reese's out on patrol this morning, I'll let him know where you're going."

Dave was intrigued by a few issues. Not just Bourbeau's disappearance but also all the talk about the mill. However, since he'd agreed with HQ to back off he couldn't very well go around doing interviews, or spend the time to build links with people. Once the mill visit was over he'd have time to relax, to get to know more of the locals face to faceand start gearing up for summer. For now it was easier to just use his fade to spy on them. It wasn't as if he had to use this ability all the time, right now it was just something he chose to do.

It was an interesting group that Rosie had introduced him to at the bonspiel, an ad hoc collection of councillors, business people, town and reserve people. Most were key people in town, yet not included were people like the mayor and mill manager. He'd decided this alternate group might be a good target to "fade" with and find out more about what their views were on the town—maybe they knew more than they were sharing with him.

As he peeked through the doorway of the club he saw it was quite a large group—Rosie, a few of the councillors, Darlene from the post office, the manager of the Metro grocery, JB, her little brother, her grandfather. Even Reese was there. The constable was on duty of course, so had likely dropped in on his rounds. Dave paused before entering, and faded, enjoying the brief surge of power. This was getting to be a habit with him and easier to do each time. He was looking forward to finding out what the group was plotting. He walked closer and stood quietly, listening. Rosie sat across the table from him, looking right through Dave, or where the not-Dave was.

"I agree," said Rosie. "Dave did say he was going to help, but there are a lot of things he doesn't know much about yet, like the depth of the corruption at the mill, misused funds from the grants, bikers trying to run in drugs. I did think he'd decided to get involved, but now seems like he's just putting in time. He's full of excuses about how sensitive this

135

Minister's visit is. Sorry Reese, but I think he's no different than others we've seen. They come up for a year, keep their nose clean doing the minimum, get their little checkmark on their resume, then head off to a bigger and better job in the big city. Unfortunately, I think we're going to have to work things out somehow without his help."

Dave was waiting for Reese or maybe JB to jump in and defend him when he noticed that JB was staring right at him. Glaring at him, in fact.

And so was her grandfather.

And so was her brother.

The band chief stood abruptly. "We're done here, no more talking. You!" He looked right at Dave. "We will have nothing to do with whatever you are."

Dave started to panic. They could see him!

"Go! Get out of our way," said the chief.

The chief, JB, her brother, all three were walking toward the doorway—and Dave. He didn't know why, but his former friends were now enemies, all gathering to attack him. The others at the table were standing too. Probably waiting their chance to attack. The rage was building in him, like it had just before he fought Risso. It was quicker and stronger this time, though. Now there were drums too, a pounding in his ears. He glared back at his opponents. They had no right to defy his authority like that. He needed to stop them somehow. As he clenched his fists, there was a sudden sharp pain in his head, and then a feeling of power, of new strength, washed through him.

"Stop right there!" he said. "I'm in charge here, not you!" He gestured at the chief in anger, felt a tingle in his fingertips, and was surprised to see the elder stagger back. Whatever Dave had just done, it felt good, and his confidence rose. JB and her brother caught the chief as he fell back, concern on their faces. Dave could feel a tingling in the air, like before a thunderstorm, as the overhead lights flickered off then back on. He raised his hands once more, feeling the power build again, flowing down his arms. He pointed toward Junior this time. Just as Dave was about to gesture again, JB's grandfather straightened up and raised his arms.

"Now!" said the chief. All three of the Bourbeaus stepped forward, extending their own hands at Dave, while Junior stomped a foot and yelled. Dave felt a push on his chest He stumbled back, then tried to direct his power back at all three. There was a blinding flash, dizziness, then nothing.

CHAPTER 23

JB was the first to recover. She bent down to her grandfather, who had slumped to the floor again.

"Are you okay?" she asked.

He nodded, then pulled her head down. "This looks very bad," he whispered. "That was not the Dave we know, what I saw was something very evil. He has some force in him. We need to figure out a way to deal with it somehow, but in the meantime use your skills to calm everyone down, reassure them with some story."

Rosie was looking down at the body on the floor. "What the hell, where did he suddenly come from?" He looked at JB. "What was all that yelling? Is he all right? How about you guys?"

"We're fine," said JB. She looked around at the crowd and raised her hands. "Calm down folks. Dave walked in, looking really tired again, and then yelled something. We rushed to help him but he just crumpled. As for the lights—I think it was some kind of compressor overload—can you smell the ozone in the air?"

The others looked at her and nodded. She could almost feel the tension fading away.

"My grandfather's all right too, I think he just stood up too quickly. He needs to learn to slow down a bit." She avoided her grandfather's eye, as she was sure he'd be scowling at her.

"Let me check Dave." She knelt down by Dave and laid a finger on his neck. She tried to reach –very cautiously—for traces of whatever had driven him to that rage, but found nothing. "Pulse seems fine. I'm guessing he skipped breakfast again. Rosie, can you call the mill clinic?"

"Good idea," said Reese. "I think the doctor's in town today, get him over here. I'll call Sheila at the detachment office, tell her Dave just felt weak for a bit, nothing major, and that he'll be at the clinic for a checkup. Don't worry folks, he'll be fine."

"Are you sure he's okay?" said Rosie.

JB looked over at Junior, who nodded at her. "Yes, he is," she said. "I know he's been stretched pretty thin lately, I guess it just caught up with him."

***

Dave regained consciousness just as they reached the clinic, but the doctor insisted on booking him in anyway. After checking his vitals, the doctor gave him a mild sedative, put him on a glucose drip, and shooed everyone out. The doctor's diagnosis was fatigue and low blood sugar, his recommendation was to get some rest and eat better. He didn't seem very concerned, but Dave certainly was. What was happening to him? He remembered a lot of anger when JB and the others had challenged him, then some kind of battle, then pain and darkness. The pain was still here, right behind his eyes. These headaches could be serious too. Maybe he needed a brain scan or something. He'd been using his one skill, his superpower, yet JB and her family had looked right at him. What was wrong with his fade—why had it changed? Maybe he just had to learn how to manage it better, to control those rages. He needed his power right now for his work up here, plus would certainly need it for his undercover work. He couldn't very well just give it up. He'd end up with a mediocre review from his stint up here, and spend the rest of his career stuck in little places like this. He was looking for his cell phone to call JB, when there was a knock on the door.

"Hey buddy, it's Tony, how are ya?"

***

Tony Barretto had been delighted when he heard about the fight. His contact had described some sort of battle between Dave and those do-gooders—that chief and his friends. A lot of yelling and shoving, Dave being knocked out—it was perfect.

The clinic's doctor had thought the three natives in particular had been shaken up pretty bad, but he'd just sent everyone home with orders to rest. Dave had been sedated just after being admitted, but he was

139

starting to come around now.

"I should call his friends," said the doctor. "They had wanted to stay."

"Don't bother, I'll call them for you—in a minute," said Tony. "Just give me a bit with him."

He tapped on the door and poked his head in.

Dave looked up. "Hey Barretto, didn't expect to see you in here."

"Well, it's the mill's clinic too, so I heard right away about your little turn for the worse. Bit of a confrontation with those vigilantes?"

"Who do you mean," said Dave.

"I mean that gang that gets together at the curling club."

Dave just nodded—he didn't seem too happy about it all.

"I'm sure they think they are helping in some way," said Barretto, "but they're just going behind the back of our mayor and council and proper citizen groups. I was surprised you would be meeting with them, though. I don't know the details of what happened at the club, but it sounds like they got pretty aggressive."

"They definitely weren't delighted to see me," said Dave.

"That's them," he said. "Always worried about their own agenda. I heard that Reese just dropped you off here then left—the doctor didn't even see the others."

"None of them?" said Dave. "I thought they were here before."

"Nope. You were pretty groggy. Guess they didn't care what happened with you." He was glad to see Dave a little unsure about his supposed friends. "You won't get much cooperation from them. I've been working a lot with the mayor on local issues here, so between the two of us I'm sure we could give you some good leads. Plus there's that mill tour I owe you—then you can see for yourself."

"I do need more info," said Dave. "Thanks, that would be a help." He fumbled around in the drawer of the bedside table then looked up. "I can't seem to find my cell phone, I was going to call JB to see how she was."

"Don't bother," he said, "I saw her earlier. She was fine—they all were. Whatever happened at the club didn't affect them at all. You just rest."

On his way out Tony called the detachment office. Luckily he got

Sheila, so was able to plant the story that Dave was recovering fine, and looking forward to cooperating even more with the mayor and his team.

***

"Bye V," called Sheila from the door. "I'm off now." Norris was happy to finally see some clear spaces on the desks and counters. Ever since the bonspiel Sheila was acting more like part of the office team than just a link to the mayor. She was still only part time but had taken over a lot of the routine paperwork, and helped Norris get hers more organized. Norris was wondering if it was a good day for a lunch at Rosie's when Mike Donnelly walked in.

"Dave's not in until this evening," she said. "But I can page him if it's urgent."

"No, actually I'm here to see you," he said. "I decided to wait until the mayor's wife left so we'd have a bit of privacy."

"Couldn't we just meet for a coffee?" she asked. He was cute, but the office was for business.

"Oh, sorry," he said. "Not a personal call—not that I wouldn't mind meeting you sometime. It's about some issues here in town, at the mill."

He was even nicer when he got a bit flustered. "So why not tell Dave this?" she said.

"I was going to," he said. "But I think Barretto and the mayor are involved, and I know Dave meets with them sometimes. They claim it's all in aid of better cooperation but I suspect their motives. And, to be honest, some people see Dave as not being as dedicated as they'd like. I think I can trust you to be impartial, and at least hear me out. Then I'll leave the next steps up to you."

She didn't like where this was going, but decided to give Mike the benefit of the doubt.

"But you're on the town council too, aren't you?" she said.

"Yes," said Mike, "but I'm not sure if I'm doing any good there. The mayor and some of his close buddies try their hardest to run it all on their own. He was elected promising to cut the gravy in local government, but it's even worse now—he and his buddies are always at the trough. They keep things pretty close to themselves, leaving those of us that want to see some change stuck on the outside. As does the mill manager."

141

"Come on into Dave's office and fill me in," she said. "Sounds like you have a few things to get off your chest."

Mike settled into the chair, and cleared his throat. "Well, first off, the mill itself never ran the way it was designed to. Originally it was just a small sawmill, then they added a pulp and paper facility, then that expanded a lot over the years as various owners took over. It was scheduled to be shutdown several years ago, as it was just too old and unprofitable, but the government intervened with bags of money. Personally, I think they would have been better to tear it all down and start over, or pour the money into something else—like the growing tourist area here."

"And now?" said Norris.

"Sorry," he said. "So a few years ago this huge upgrade was planned, with the best high tech equipment." He explained how much of it was never installed, or was always shut down, so most of the mill was still polluting as badly as ever. "It's not that big of a secret, there's has always been talk in town about these issues, and that there's also a big cover-up going on, but it was always just that—talk. Nobody would take it further. Well, I want to now."

"Dave is going on a mill tour with your head of security, maybe he'll see something there."

"Not if he isn't that suspicious," said Mike. "Especially not if Tony wants to keep him in the dark—it will be a quick superficial tour."

"Is there any documentation to prove all this?" she said.

"Actually, there is," he said. "It's just that nobody knew where to look. Several years ago the mill's head office went on a big push to go on-line with all the paperwork. They even scanned in a lot of the old stuff: invoices, installation reports, maintenance records, production levels. Now the mill processes are all automatically monitored and measured, as are any possible pollutants, and all that data is fed into the system—including the bad readings. A lot of it isn't used though, as lately upper management here has been sanitizing the numbers, cleaning things up to look better."

"So there's no more proof left?" asked Norris.

"Yes, there is," said Mike, "and they don't realize it. Which is where I come in. The thing is, all that data needs to be backed up."

"And you're the backup guy?"

"I'm the backup guy."

"But didn't you say they'd cleaned it all up?"

"They did," said Mike, "but not the data itself. I was put in charge of backup years ago, just for a rest when I sprained an ankle. The process was very simple, all laid out in steps a monkey could follow. Which they assumed I was, I guess. I was bored, so studied up, learning all about computers, networks, and databases. Eventually I became head of their IT department—such as it is. When I looked further into the systems there I discovered that the managers were a bit lazy in their cleanup. They didn't actually delete invoices and repair records, they just took them out of the data directory, but still left the data there in the files. Plus, they never actually disconnected the pollution sensors, they just stopped including some of them in the reports. Bottom line is that all this data is still being collected and stored."

"But they could wise up to this any day and go back and delete it all, couldn't they?" said Norris.

"Yes, they could," Mike said. He smiled and added, "However, as a hard working backup guy I added to the process and made an extra copy. Kept off site of course. All done legally and with proper auditing controls. I'm sure they don't even know about it. Accessible with the proper warrants of course."

Norris looked at him with amazement. If this was true, there was a massive amount of evidence to support not only pollution charges, but fraud and mischief. "Good for you," she said. "It would also help if we had something on the actual pollution, though, before we escalated this further. Like you say, there's been a lot of talk and allegations, but that's it."

"JB's dad was supposed to be looking into that," said Norris, "but when he disappeared last year a lot of his data on the current pollution disappeared too."

"I'd like to unravel this further," said Norris. "More information would help us, if you can dig anything up. As for Dave, I trust him, I know what side he's on, in spite of appearances. I'm going to have to bring him into this, and soon. Especially if some of it implicates people like Barretto and the mayor."

"Just let me dig a bit further," said Mike. "Give me a few days to look on-line to see what happened in the mill the day Bourbeau disappeared, so you have more for Dave to work with."

"All right. Thanks for this," said Norris, "but please be careful. If what you say is true, there's a lot at stake here. Things could get violent."

CHAPTER 24

Dave was up at the highway restaurant, at yet another informal meeting with the mayor and the mill manager, when the call came in from Sheila.

"Dave, Minister Gottman's aide is on the line, calling from the airport. She's in town to set up for the big announcement, and wants to speak with you."

"Already? Okay, I can meet her at the detachment in ten minutes, I just need to finish up here."

"She was assuming that you would pick her up at the airport. She was pretty pushy about it, and not very patient with me, the mere office staff."

"Nope, not running a taxi service here. Wait, don't tell her that."

"No problem," said Sheila. "I told her the Office of the Federal Auditor is looking at improper use of official equipment and vehicles and I wouldn't want any misunderstandings to reflect poorly on the Government."

"They are?" he asked.

"Not that I know of," she said, "I just felt like messing with her. She's grabbing a cab."

Dave smiled, Sheila had come a long way since his arrival, no longer content to just be Mrs. Mayor.

He spread his hands. "Sorry gentlemen, I do appreciate getting together again, but I'll have to cut this meeting short. Seems the Minister's aide is in town."

"Oh yes," said Klein. "She'd mentioned she'd try to be here in person. Sorry, guess I should have mentioned it. Later, gentlemen?"

"No problem," said the mayor. "Always open to these little meet-ups, they're a great way to share information."

Dave didn't agree with the mayor's enthusiasm. He's hoped to use these two to supplement his regular contacts, but he didn't see much progress. Although they had met with him several times so far, they seemed mostly concerned with showing off their association with him in public. As soon as Dave probed for details on the mill, he was met with vague answers and promises of cooperation and information that never went any further. They might just need some time to open up more to him. If not, he wasn't sure what he would do. Maybe go back to keeping his head down and waiting the year out.

***

As Dave walked into the detachment, the woman standing by the counter held out her hand and beamed.

"Hello, you must be Corporal Brown. I'm Emily Grant, aide to Minister Gottman. We talked earlier this year."

Dave smiled back and tried not to stare. Emily was young, pretty, tall, slim, and dressed in the latest Montreal fashions. She didn't look like she'd just spent hours crammed into a little shuttle flight from Toronto.

"Let's go into my office," he said. "Can I get you a coffee?"

She reached out and squeezed his arm. "That's sweet of you, but your clerk already offered. I'm afraid my taste buds are spoiled by the big city brews. They're not really up for your office coffee."

Sheila was rolling her eyebrows behind Emily, so Dave tried not to smile as he helped himself to a cup.

"I've come to like it," he said.

They went into his tiny office, and Emily perched on the edge of his one guest chair, crossing her long legs as she did so.

"So nice of you to make time for me," she said, as she reached out and touched his arm again. She certainly was a touchy-feely person. Dave moved his chair back a bit.

"Ms. Grant, how can we help you."

"Oh, Emily, please," she said. "I was on my way to Winnipeg anyway, so decided to stop off and make sure everything was all set for the Minister. This is an important visit for her and the town, part of the great work she's been doing. You know Dave, I actually used to be socialist back in university. Can you believe it? Then I heard the Minister speak at a rally. I was supposed to be there to heckle her, and her dedication just moved me. When this job came open I grabbed it. Now I have a chance to actually help change the country—get us back on the right track."

"Sounds great for you," said Dave, "but the mayor has all the details of the meeting worked out I think," said Dave.

"Oh I'm sure he does. I'll see him next. No, I meant for security. Our office has become aware that there may be a few here with an issue over the latest funding initiative. Pollution concerns also. Just a few hotheads, I'm sure."

"Anything specific?" said Dave.

"Same old complaints: pollution, from a top of the line mill mind you; dissatisfaction with the kind of jobs the mill is good enough to hire them for; threats of a protest. Some are even threatening to not renew the leases on First Nations land that some cottage owners have. Our office has had some frantic calls on that for sure. We want this to go smoothly in the press. Our Economic Action Plan is all about jobs and support for the local economy, as well as a demonstration of our Government's on-going commitment to Green Initiatives, as part of the Transformative Technologies Program."

Dave could hear the capital letters as she talked. She certainly believed in her new-found religion. He managed to assure her that all would be under control, and that he even had supplementary RCMP arriving to assist his detachment. He would certainly take her concerns into account, but his read of the local situation was that in spite of some people's concerns and opinions, all was fine. There would be no protest.

"This is a lot quieter than Toronto," he said. "Not a lot of marches or such."

"Always was somebody protesting something," she said. "Messing up traffic so bad I could never get a cab. I lived downtown, by King and Spadina. Aren't you from down there?"

He tried to not show his concern over her prying into his other life. "I've visited Toronto a few times," he said.

She leaned toward Dave, "You look awfully familiar to me. Did you ever get to Circa, down on John? Always a huge line, had to sweet talk my way in." She chattered on a while longer, bragging on about where she'd been, in trendy bars, catching hot bands. He didn't mention that while she was in them clubbing and flirting, he'd been in them undercover—likely busting her friends for drugs.

"Sorry Ms Grant. like I said, visited there, but not a lot. I'm sure I would have remembered if I'd met you." He just wanted to discourage her from telling her friends he was up here, but she just beamed back and told him what a sweetie he was. As he walked her back out, she went on still about all the new little places that had opened in Toronto.

She put her hand on his arm. "You just have to look me up when you're in town. Now that I've moved up I can get into all sorts of places without waiting outside with the regular people. And my friends will just die when they see me with a real RCMP officer."

Dave glared at Reese, who was shaking his head and trying not to laugh at the situation. He reached for the door for her and smiled. "Sounds tempting, but I can't promise anything," he said. "Tell your boss all will be quiet here."

The aide smiled and gave him a quick hug. "Call me, we'll do lunch," she said. With that she rushed out the door, almost knocking down JB.

"Oops, sorry sweetie," said the aide.

"Sure," said JB. She raised an eyebrow as she looked at Dave. "Anyone you know, Corporal?"

"Not really," said Dave. "She's here about the big presentation next week. She's the Minister's aide."

"Seems very friendly for a business call, all dolled up, with that big hug and the 'call me.' If some old girlfriend has decided to come and hook up again, just don't feed me some story."

"She's not an old girlfriend —"

"Whatever," said JB.

"Anyway, how come you dropped by?" said Dave.

JB paused, "I just wanted to check that you were okay after, you know, that 'thing' at the club. But you seem to have recovered just fine."

"Sure," he said, "looks like nobody got hurt from whatever it was. Best we all just move on, I guess."

"Nobody?" she said. "It wasn't that simple. Grandfather was in bed for two days after—which you would have known if you'd bothered to call."

"But Barretto said —"

She snorted. "Barretto?! Yeah, there's a reliable source. Never mind, I shouldn't have come by."

With that she was gone, leaving Dave staring at the closed door. Why would Tony have told him that?

"What was that all about?" said Reese.

"I have no idea," said Dave. "Maybe it was Emily—Ms. Grant."

"Nice looking for a government worker," said Reese. "Very high energy, physical kind of person, non-stop talker. Sounds like a real party animal." He paused for a moment. "I wonder if she needs an escort to show her around town?"

Dave laughed. "I wouldn't think she was your type, but I'm sure she would appreciate some official attention."

"But why did she go to the trouble of a visit here?" Reese asked.

"Well, she seemed worried about some general concerns and reports, as well as complaints from concerned local citizens."

"What kind of concerns?" said Reese.

"Ongoing mill issues, plus she mentioned some talk of a big protest."

He expected Reese to dismiss that right away, but he went quiet for a bit. "Oh, that."

"What do you mean, 'oh that'," said Dave. "Have you heard about any planned protests? Because it sure is news to me."

"Well, I may have heard word over the last few days of a protest for when the Minister is here. Some of the younger guys on the reserve were all hyped up to do something really big, get lots of media attention. The elders convinced them to tone it down a bit. Still, there will be a gathering outside the gates, they'll make some speeches, hold up some signs."

"And you were going to tell me this when?" said Dave.

"I know, sorry," said Reese. "I mentioned it to Norris, I thought she had passed it on when she told you about Mike."

"Mike?" said Dave. "What did he want?"

"He had some information about the mill. You were out so he talked with Norris."

"Great," said Dave. "I'll have a talk with her about that, and about this mysterious protest."

Reese looked flustered. "Maybe that protest was what JB was here about. Maybe she was here to give you a heads-up so that you could do a good job of providing security."

"Like I can't do that on my own?" he asked.

"Sure you can," said Reese. "But I'm sure she wants to help you look good, rather than help you look bad."

"I hope it works out that way," said Dave. "Ever since whatever happened at the curling club, I'm getting less cooperation from people. Luckily there are still some people willing to help, such as Barretto and the mayor."

"Are you sure you can trust them?" said Reese. "Maybe they are involved."

"I've had a lot of experience reading people," said Dave. "I read this group as being all right to work with. On the other hand, I'm having a hard time trusting you, or any of the other people who meet secretly and tell each other not to tell me anything. I might remind you Constable, this is not how police operate. We watch each others' backs. And if we have a problem we work it out between us before somebody gets hurt. That's all for now."

Reese gulped and went white, but he said nothing and left.

***

Dave was standing outside the post office, faded from view, enjoying a bit of sun and eavesdropping. He'd got an update—and apology for the delay—from Norris and was just waiting for some of Mike's documentation to surface. In the meantime, he figured that it wouldn't hurt to get more information. He'd been worried he'd lost his fade, after the battle at the curling club, but it turned out it had just changed, was even stronger now, easier to turn on. It had taken him over a week to get his strength back, but now he was using his fade pretty regularly, ignoring any pain. He noticed one of the elders—George he thought—glaring at him from across the street. Dave smiled and waved. He wasn't sure why his power had changed, but it was evident that some of his First Nations friends could now see him. Not that it really mattered, as they weren't the main target for his investigations. And if they didn't like him anymore, well, he was leaving in a few months anyway.

Dave noticed Barretto and Klein, the mill manager, walking toward him. The security chief did seem to want to help, maybe he'd been right about Dave following the wrong groups for his answers. Dave stayed faded and tried to get closer to listen.

"I thought you told me everything was tidied up and done with," said Klein.

"Well, it was," said Barretto. "The locals are just taking advantage of someone new to drag out all their suspicions and allegations again."

"And is Dave buying any of it?" asked the manager.

"He was poking around a bit, but has backed off now. The Minister's aide has talked to him about not stirring things up too much, as have both the mayor and myself. We've got him under control, don't worry. He's only here for a year at the most."

"Good, now how about Risso. I'm counting on you to keep him in check?"

"He's a bit of a loose cannon," said Barretto. "But if the investigation gets to him, the database records will — "

Someone jostled Dave, then clapped him on the shoulder. He was so startled by the bump, as well as a tingle where the person touched him, that he unfaded.

"Oops, sorry Corporal." It was the same elder he'd seen across the street. George looked Dave right in the eyes. "What you're doing can be dangerous. Be careful, Little Bear," he said, then walked away.

Barretto and Klein looked at Dave, startled. "Dave, didn't see you," said Barretto. "How are you doing? Ah, we were just going to check the mail."

They hurried into the post office, leaving Dave standing by himself, rubbing his shoulder.

***

"Inspector Williams? Dave here."

He'd decided to call his old boss back in Toronto just to see how things were going. He missed his solitary life as an undercover agent, both the thrill of it and the isolation.

"Just calling to see what's new," Dave said.

"Same old," said Williams. "Guns and Gangs unit is expanding here, as is our group. Looking to double by next year, both here and in Ottawa."

"Hopefully still room for me," said Dave.

"Don't worry about that right now," said the Inspector. "Your job is to just lie low up there, and pick up some people skills. How's it going? Quiet I hope."

"Okay I guess," he said. "It's a whole different world from Toronto. I do have an interesting file now that might involve pollution and corruption in the local mill. It's too soon to tell."

"Enough there for a case?" said Williams.

"Might be, but there's a big visit happening too. The Minister of Northern Economic Development is due soon, to announce major funding for the mill."

"Jeez Dave," he said. "Be careful with that—you're up there to keep a low profile. Let someone from your staff look into it if you have to, but make it very low-key."

"Not much choice," said Dave. "I tried to do some undercover work, but that backfired when I got caught out by some of the locals."

"Busted again? You used to be able to sneak your way into pretty well any group, but now I think you're going to have to learn to not depend so much on that skill. Just be a plain ordinary cop, and while you're at it, think about where you want to go next."

"I'll be fine," said Dave. "Don't worry about me."

"We'll talk about next steps in a few months," said the Inspector. "How about the staff you have up there? A good bunch?"

"They are," said Dave. "I've got two constables and an office manager, the mayor's wife. We're working better now, after being in the bonspiel."

"Curling?" said the Inspector. "You took part in a team sport? With other people?"

"I know," said Dave. "Who knew? It did a lot for the office staff and relations with the town."

"Sounds like you're really settling in," said Williams.

"I guess so," said Dave. "But this is only a term thing, right? Just a few more months then I'm out of this backwater and into the mainstream again."

"You got it, Dave. Still some people looking for you here, though, especially that Badger guy. I'm not sure why he got so riled up, but I'm sure this will all blow over within a year or two. And stay away from TV cameras. We'll talk later."

Dave didn't like the sound of that year or two limit. He was already feeling stir-crazy.

CHAPTER 25

Dave was doing his rounds of the town and had dropped by the Grande to see JB.

"Hey Sid," said Dave. "JB around?"

"She's around here somewhere," said Sid. "Say, I was talking about you earlier, but she was acting kind of pissed off. What did you do?"

"I have no idea," said Dave. "She's been upset ever since the incident at the curling club."

"I heard about that," said Sid. "She came back and spent the next day in bed—must have had a few too many drinks there."

"Barretto had told me she was just fine after it," said Dave. "I found out later she wasn't."

"There's been a lot of rumours about whatever it was you did at the curling club," said Sid. "Would you like a list?"

Dave shook his head, embarrassed. There was just no escaping the talk in a small town.

"Unfortunately, most of it was a blank to me," he said. "I just let myself get too run down I guess. And there was some electrical malfunction there too, something with the compressor." He pointed out the patio doors. "What's with the car out on the ice? Somebody miss the parking lot last night?"

Sid laughed. "No, that's an annual event we have. We put an old car out on the ice while it's still solid, then people bet what day we'll see the big breakthrough. Winner gets the pot of money plus the car. We leave a cable on it so that we can pull it back out.. I've already picked a day and paid my five bucks."

"I wouldn't have a clue when to pick," said Dave.

"Well, spring break-up usually is mid-April, but it varies. The time slots are first come first served, but still some open ones. Want to take a chance and guess when there'll be a breakthrough?"

"Sure," said Dave, "how about this day. At 3 pm." He circled a date on the calendar and took out his wallet. He was just handing over his money when JB walked in.

She felt both pleased and upset to see him there. "Paying for your coffee now?" she said.

"No, betting on the breakup," he said. "Why, did you want me to pay?"

"No, never mind," she said.

"I should cut back anyway," he said. "Maybe it's what's giving me these terrible headaches and mood swings."

"Whatever," she said. And then she relented at the sight of his sad lost face. She really missed him, and it was likely that he didn't know any more than they did about the dark spirit swirling around him.

She touched his arm. "We are worried about you, Dave—me and the elders too. We're afraid you're in over your head in something."

"Don't be silly," said Dave. "I'm doing just fine. Listen JB, I'm really sorry about what happened. I really don't know what's going on with some things and I was wondering if you…"

She noticed Sid looking expectantly at them.

"Maybe later," said Dave. He smiled and headed for the door.

She sighed. "Thanks Sid."

***

Barretto met Dave at the mill gate the next morning. "Klein asked me to be your tour guide today. I used to work in main control before I took over security, so I got to know how this all works. We normally don't do tours, as there's a lot of state of the art equipment our competitors would love to see in action."

"Well, I'm not a techie, so will likely not know what I'm looking at anyway," said Dave. "But I do appreciate finally getting the tour."

"We'll start up these stairs, in the main control room," said Tony. "There's a good view from up there."

Three of the room's walls were covered with an array of screens, switches, dials, chart recorders and lights. From the rumble underfoot the mill was obviously in production, yet several sections of the controls looked to be shut down. A technician stood in front of one of the active panels, clipboard in hand, tapping one of the dials. He glanced over as they entered, then went back to his work.

"Carry on, ah, buddy," said Tony.

The fourth wall was one big window, looking out over the main mill floor. The view was of several hulking machines, surrounded by clouds of steam, all interconnected with snaking hoses, cables, and a rainbow of colour coded pipes. Dave could see a few workers – in bright yellow coveralls and hard hats—scattered around the mill floor and up on the catwalks.

"Here's a chart of the basic process," said Barretto, pointing to a wall panel. "Logs come in to a de-barker, here, then to a chipper where they are reduced to small pieces. That then goes into a huge tank, the digester. We add chemicals and water and heat it for several hours, until it breaks down into pulp. That gets rinsed, then dried out a bit, then bleached, then dried more, and finally passes through a roller and dryer process. Out the end comes rolls of paper."

"Like newsprint?" Dave asked.

"Some mills do that grade, ours is a higher quality. It's a more complicated process but sells for a lot more per pound. Which helps, since we still have to ship a fair distance from here."

"Aren't most factories and mills completely automated now?" Dave asked

"Not completely," said Barretto. "There's a lot going on here. We still need people on the floor at key points, to monitor things, to troubleshoot, and keep the logs up to date. Plus we have a crew doing ongoing maintenance."

He went on to describe the other parts of the process, outside of this building and not part of the tour, due to safety concerns. "All parts are under control from here, though," he said. "For example, from that panel we can monitor water levels both upstream and downstream, and control the dam spillway. We use a lot of water in our processes, so much of the new equipment is designed to release it as clean as when it came in. We do generate a bit of electrical power at the dam, but the main function is to regulate the flow downstream, limiting flooding from spring run-off, keeping enough flow to dilute our effluent properly, and not leaving cottages on the lake high and dry. The whole system is very complicated, so we have a whole network of remote controlled cameras and sensors to knit it all together."

"Knit, I like that,"said Dave, "Looking down on the mill floor at all these components and cables it does look like something that's been knit together. But I've seen my mother unravel things too. Does this all come apart if you pull on a thread?"

Barretto seemed a little nervous at that suggestion. "Don't worry, we have safeguards on top of safeguards here. The control systems are all interconnected, and they react before we even notice a problem developing. Not that we have problems."

Dave pointed to the walls of panels and displays. "If there are so many systems all connected together, why are some of the screens blank, and all the lights off around them?"

"Not to worry," said Tony. "Some of those are for sections we've shut down for now, as we run them depending on what we produce. We target maximum flow with managed pollution. Everything is redundancy risk plans and, uh, fail-safe networked program modules. If you come another day you'd see those systems on now and some of the others off. Not that you'd need another visit—nothing exciting to see here."

It sounded like Tony was trying to recite from some memorized talking points. Dave noticed the technician look over with a smirk and then turn back to the panels. "Why don't we carry on, what's next?"

"That's it," said Barretto. "This room gives a good overview of the whole operation. Sorry, but we can't let you down on the main floor—insurance. We can go down to my office now and I'll show you some numbers on our security issues here—all minor of course."

Dave was still hoping to see some of the equipment close up. Not that he'd recognize any of it, he admitted, but Norris had tried to explain to him what sort of things to look for. However, after a twisted path through several corridors they ended up right in Barretto's office, just off the main mill floor. They passed a number of workers along the way, none of whom looked particularly happy to see Barretto. Or Dave for that matter.

"Not a happy bunch," said Dave,

"We have a lot of morale problems," said Barretto. "You'd think they'd be grateful for these jobs, but they are always complaining and skipping work. I think they may even sometimes sabotage equipment to get time off. Here's my office."

Dave looked back out onto the main floor. This might be worth another visit, maybe on a more casual basis, maybe by someone who knew what to look for. He pointed across the floor, up at the control room windows. "Couldn't we just have cut quickly through?" said Dave. "I would have liked to see some stuff up close."

"Sorry, no," said Barretto."Too dangerous. Noisy too. And nothing to see, really. Thanks for coming by, Dave, I'll just sign you out now."

***

Tony had made sure to hustle Dave out before he started looking too carefully out the office window. Even from here Tony could see several darkened control panels, and a couple of partially disassembled machines, surrounded by tools and parts. He should have had that cleaned up better before the visit.

"Barretto, busy?"

Tony looked up from his desk. "Not for my boss—what's up?"

"I saw that cop in here just now," said Klein. "Is there anything wrong?"

"No, he just wanted a tour. Sorry, I should have let you know. It went okay though. He didn't see anything he shouldn't have, and wouldn't know a faked record if he tripped over it."

"Do try to keep this quiet," said Klein. He turned and closed the office door. "We don't want anyone looking too closely at things here. We've got a good thing going for us."

"Don't worry boss. The records are all clean. And I've kept the 'in crowd' to a minimum. Nobody will blab."

"How about that guy last year, Bourbeau? He got a little too close to comfort."

"Well, we don't need to worry about him, do we?" said Barretto. "He disappeared."

Klein looked at Barretto. "Yes he did. Lucky for us. Hopefully we weren't involved."

Barretto smiled. "Just a coincidence. Don't worry. We're in the clear."

At least nobody could prove they were involved—same thing. His boss had no sooner left than Risso was at Barretto's door. Tony scowled at him. "What do you want now, Frank?"

"I seen that cop in here, and then Klein showed up. Problems?"

"Nothing to worry about, Frank. Just keep on with what you're doing, and you'll keep seeing those overtime bonuses in your weekly pay."

"That's what I was thinking about, Tony. I figure I'm the one doing all the dirty work, I've been keeping my mouth shut here. Maybe it's time for a raise."

"You should be happy you've got a job at all," said Barretto. "Especially after all that time off last year."

"Wasn't my fault," said Risso. "My old lady gets pissed off, makes up some story about me hitting on her, and I end up putting in three months dead time waiting for a trial. Then she shows up and changes her story and I get off. Stupid woman—I showed her." He slammed a fist into the side of a cabinet.

"Calm down Frank," said Tony. "You were lucky to beat that charge. I know, you lost your woman, your apartment, and your dog. You're like a bad country song. You're lucky I put up with you at all." He came around his desk and gave Frank a shove. "Out of here, you little weasel. Be grateful I don't fire your sorry ass."

He glared at Frank's back as he shuffled across the plant floor, shoulders hunched, head down. Frank could be a problem, he was a bitter man, and unpredictable. Good thing Tony had already set up something to use as leverage against the loser.

CHAPTER 26

JB was starting to feel sorry for Dave, in spite of being angry with him for caving in to outside pressures. She was frightened too, at whatever had taken him over at the curling club. They had all reacted instinctively, drawing on the spirit world to help protect them, but her grandfather was sure it wasn't over yet. He could somehow sense that the problem, the thing, was still within Dave.

She so wanted to trust her first impressions with him. He did seem a nice guy and she was sure he meant well, he just needed to figure out what he really wanted. Well, and get rid of whatever had possessed him. She wanted to confront Dave about it and see if he really knew what he was doing, but her grandfather had told her to wait for a sign.

She was sure she'd been given one last night, in a dream. She'd seen the bear, Makwa. He had been just waking up after a winter sleep, and looked like he was searching for something. She had been taught well on how to use dreams to solve problems, and was pretty sure this one was showing her the way. Still, she wanted to run it past her grandfather.

"Do you not trust yourself?" he said.

"Sort of," she said. "This is really important though, I want to get it right for Dave. More coffee?"

Her grandfather settled back into the corner of the booth. "No, I'm good now. If Rosie brings me any more, I'll start hopping around like you do, my little Wisakedjak. What was the dream?"

"The bear looked like he had just awakened from its long winter sleep, and was standing still, outside the den, fur hanging loose on him after his long winter fast. He stood up on his hind legs, sniffing the air,

160

then fell back down onto all four feet, making those deep 'chuff chuff' sounds and looking back and forth. It was a warm spring day, with the sun shining, patches of bare ground already showing here and there, and a brook gurgling nearby, like it was glad to be free of winter's icy grip. Flocks of birds were flitting from tree to tree. They were no longer huddling in the shelter of the spruce, but now high in the birches, enjoying the start of another year, chattering to each other happily."

"But what about this bear?" said her grandfather.

She smiled. "Grandfather, you taught me the telling is as important as the ending."

He nodded and gestured to her to continue.

"Okay," she said, "so this bear still just stood there, looking back into the darkness of the cave, then out across the bright snow, around the clearing, then back at the cave. He was acting unfocused, like he was half asleep. The chickadees flew around his head, back and forth, every which way. That got some response from the bear, but it was just to snap irritatingly at them. There was a rustling from a nearby thicket. A small hare came out and hopped in front of the bear, then off into the bushes again. Its wet feet left a path of prints on the warm rocks, but they evaporated even as I watched. And still the bear stood there, head down, gazing at the ground."

"How did you feel?" said her grandfather.

"I was starting to get angry with him," she said, "for not just getting out of there. The bear looked up and above him was a Wisakedjak. It fluffed its wings out and squawked at Makwa. No response. The bird took off then, and flew lower, over the bear, calling to it, and the bear began to change, right there, into a big black shape. Like a vulture, but with bright red eyes. It croaked angrily at the Whisky Jack, and flapped its wings threateningly, but was too big and awkward to actually fly up after it. The smaller bird held its ground, swooping at the black shape, yelling at it, ripping off little pieces with its claws, pieces that disappeared like melting ice. Still it kept attacking, until the thing—whatever it was—changed back into the brown bear."

She paused and hugged herself. Even now, in daylight, she could feel the wrongness of that shape.

"I think what you saw was evil itself," said her grandfather. "But it was just in the dream world, you are safe now. Keep going. I know your spirit will protect you."

She wasn't sure. She hoped it would be strong enough for this.

"The Whisky Jack was very persistent," she said. "She kept pestering the bear, swooping close to his head, actually hitting it with her wing tips. That worked, as the bear seemed to focus, and growled as he raised its head to follow the bird's short flight. The bird then flew off a few feet, toward the brook, stopped, tipped her head to one side, and squawked again. The bear moved a few paces toward the bird, crunching through the spring snow, then stopped. Again the bird squawked and flew ahead, again the bear followed and stopped. I watched as the two headed down the slope, toward the brook. I could hear the calls of the guide, the crunches of the follower as they headed off together. That was it. Then I woke up."

"That was a good dream," he said. "But you don't really need me to tell you what it means, do you?"

"No, I guess not, my path is pretty clear," she said. "I can't fix things for him though. I think all I can do is get Dave to focus on his problem. Somehow. And then there's this black thing. I recognize it now, it's that same sense of wrongness I used to feel around my cousin."

"You're smart," he said. "You'll think of a way to help your friend. He'll focus on his problem when he is ready. But he should not wait too long though, as I fear this can get a lot worse for him. The other elders are concerned too. We think this darkness in him may be the spirit of the Wendigo."

"Wendigo?" she cried. "The eater of people? Here? In Dave?" She leaped to her feet.

"Yes," he said. He motioned her back down. "Calm down, we need to go carefully with this. This is the first time we have seen this spirit in someone that is not one of us."

"But why Dave?" she said. "We were out walking one night and he started whistling. Could that be it?"

"No, it takes more than whistling at night," he said. "Maybe it's linked to the bloodline from his First Nations grandmother, maybe even the other side, the Irish blood. This is different too, as while we know the spirit guides are usually invisible, we have never seen anyone with the ability to make themselves invisible too. But it's the Wendigo that concerns us most, as it is a carnivore, a consumer of human flesh."

"Well then, I have to warn him," she said. "And we need to get it out of him."

"We don't know for sure why it picked Dave," he said. "And we don't know how closely it's interwoven. Getting it out might not be easy, and we can't show our hand too soon. If whatever is in him feels threatened it could attack even you."

***

"I'm off on patrol, Sheila. It's after six—close up and go home."

"I will, Dave," she said. "Didn't realize the time, got caught up in these last few reports."

"Won't your husband be looking for his supper?"

"No, it's his turn tonight to cook," she said. "I'm re-training him, slowly. Oh, I forgot, he was asking the other day if you had cut back on patrols. He said people were complaining they hadn't seen you out and about as much lately. I told him not that I knew."

"Nope, still out there," he said. "Just keeping it quiet. Good night."

He was still walking the Main Street, just not as noticeable as before. Initially these mini-patrols had been to give more visibility for the mayor and council, but now he just used them to get out for a break. It was getting harder to resist using his fade, as it really was a help with his unofficial investigations. It gave him the ability to watch people unobserved, to eavesdrop on them, to keep some distance from them. The rush from it was like enjoying a fine cigar or an expensive cognac, and left him feeling stronger, more aware of the world, above it all for just a while. He knew he could cut back on it if he wanted to, maybe after this investigation.

***

Dave was enjoying a quiet walk. When he spotted the mayor. He unfaded and waved. "Mr. Mayor!" he called.

"Dave, glad to see you out on the street. I was just telling the wife yesterday that I didn't see you out much."

"I'm out here often," said Dave. "Just keeping things low-key."

"You need to work it, Dave," said the mayor. "It's all about selling yourself. People feel safer when they see you on the street. I know some

163

aren't as friendly as they used to be—that's small towns for you. Don't worry. You've got the ear and support of those who count. Take care, buddy."

With that he slapped Dave on the back and headed down the street, glad-handing people as he went.

Dave stepped into a doorway, then faded again. The street was fairly quiet, so he'd enjoy the rest of his stroll in peace and quiet. He didn't really need to chat with people that much. He liked his solitude. His new place was comfortable now, with the wide-screen TV, freezer meals, comfy for just him and Snowball. Funny though, lately the cat had stopped dropping by so often, and would often stare at him and suddenly hiss. Weird. Birds had stopped visiting his feeder too—they must have found better food elsewhere. Even the Whiskey Jack would venture only to the fence line, then sit and watch him, its head tipped to one side like it had a question or something. He figured he'd just have to wait out his penance for the year, or whatever time line was imposed on him. He did miss JB—maybe it would take her a while to get over that arena incident.

CHAPTER 27

"Glad you could make it, Dave. Not in uniform today?" Dave slid into the restaurant booth and nodded back at Barretto and the mayor. "Can't stay long up here. This is supposed to be my day off. I have to do things like laundry and grocery shopping."

"Running low on frozen dinners?" said the mayor.

"Yes, but I do have a few basic recipes. Sheila and Norris even bring in the occasional casserole for me. And then there's dinner at Rosie's."

"Good to see you up here at the highway restaurant for a change," said the mayor. "We serve plain food, but good, and no foreign stuff. My team often uses this back corner for our meetings. Sara makes sure we get good service and privacy."

"Definitely quieter than the front," said Dave. He'd passed a group of truckers on the way in, all very loud and very large, crammed around a table full of food and beer.

"They've been here a while," said Barretto. "They'll be gone soon, then we'll have quiet for our meeting, away from Rosie and Mike and the rest of that crowd of busybodies."

"I've been digging around a bit," said the mayor, "and found some interesting things."

"Related to the mill problems?" said Dave.

"Sort of. As part of the initial start-up package, the mill and government gave money to the Chief and his people—over a hundred thousand. It was supposed to be for education, but I don't know where it went. We still get natives showing up at work their first day without a clue, and we have to waste a lot of time and money getting them up to speed. That's where you should be looking—ask them where they got the cash for all their new ski-doos."

"Thanks," said Dave. "I wasn't aware of that." He was interrupted by a loud crash by the front.

"Sorry folks, my bad, just clumsy." One of the truckers had knocked over a chair, and was now heading for the cash. Dave watched him weave a bit as he fumbled for his wallet.

Dave slid out of the booth. "Be right back," he said. "Order me a coffee when Sara comes by."

He walked up to the front, eyeing the very large driver, who was still trying to find his wallet.

"Excuse me sir," he said. "Are you all right?"

The man turned, and scowled down at Dave. "Sure buddy, no problem, just need to pay up and I'll be out of your way. I've got to get rolling before that storm hits Dryden. Don't bug me, okay?"

Dave felt a surge of annoyance, but took a breath, then paused for a moment. He took in the red eyes and slur in the trucker's speech. "Actually, they've just downgraded that storm, so should be an easy drive. Why don't you take an hour in your bunk and sleep off some of this beer. You look a little over the limit."

The trucker turned, and gave Dave a shove. "Piss off! Do you think you're a cop or something?"

Dave pause, but he could feel his annoyance turning to anger. Maybe he needed to teach this guy a lesson. The trucker might be big, but he didn't know the powers Dave could call upon. Dave stepped closer, almost toe to toe.

"Yes, I am," he said. "And in this town, what I say goes. So if I say sleep it off, then you sleep it off."

He'd no sooner finished talking when the trucker growled and punched Dave in the gut. Dave doubled over for a second, then straightened. Again, he felt that rush of anger, like he'd felt with Risso and at the curling rink. This time it was even more intense, faster to build. A welcome surge of power washed over him, making him feel invincible. He smiled as he watched himself reach out, grab the trucker by the shoulders, and shake him. Something within him flowed down his arms, out his fingers, and pushed. The driver, all 300 pounds of him, flew across the room like a rag doll and crashed into his friends.

Dave glared around the room. "Anyone else need a lesson?" As he moved toward the other truckers he felt Barretto and the mayor trying to pull him back.

"Hey Dave," said Tony. "It's all right, you made your point. Sara already called this in. Reese is just pulling into the parking lot. Let him look after this. Calm down, man, you scared the hell out of everybody."

"Yeah, calm down," said the mayor. "What the hell was that all about? You were acting like another person."

Dave shook his head, his vision gradually clearing. The pain was back, worse than ever.

"I'm good now, thanks." He walked over to the fallen trucker. "You okay, buddy?"

The man looked up at Dave, rubbing his arm. "What the hell did you do? Taser me? I'm fine, just stay away! I won't cause any trouble."

Dave turned, as Reese came in and stared at the damage. "Just a misunder-standing, Constable. These guys are just leaving."

Reese walked over next to Dave. "What happened here?"

"He was a little drunk, so I told him to go sleep it off. He got lippy and poked me so I taught him a lesson."

"Just badging him didn't work?" said Reese.

"No time for that," said Dave. "Then things just sort of took off."

"Do you think?" said Reese.

Dave looked around the restaurant. Luckily it had been fairly empty, with just a family sitting in a far booth—now very quiet and wide-eyed. Sara was peering through the kitchen doorway, with the cook, a large man, trying to hide behind her.

Reese came back from the group of truckers. "They say the other guy started it," he said. "They seem pretty eager to leave now, and were all good to drive. Do you want any charges? Assault PO for your buddy on the floor there?"

"No, I think we'll just drop everything and call it square," said Dave. "I'm off-duty and not in uniform. Listen, can you finish this off? I have a splitting headache and I can't think straight. Tell Sara I'll give her some cash for the damages tomorrow."

Reese gave him a worried look, then went over to talk to the truckers again.

The mayor came over to him. "You need to get a hold of yourself. That's bad for business. You shook us all up. I'm heading back to work, and I think Tony's heading off for a drink. He said he needed to calm down."

***

Dave and Reese spent almost an hour going over the trucks. They found a number of violations, and were just going over the last driver's papers when the call came in.

"Getting rowdy at The Roost," said Reese. "JB wants someone to just pop in. I'll take it. Why don't you just head home? You look pretty tired."

Dave wasn't sure if Reese was concerned for his health, or worried what he might do next.

"No, I'm good," he said. "I'll follow you down. Don't worry, I'll just be there with you for moral support."

***

"Another round of shooters," said Barretto. "One for you too, JB."

Tony had just dropped in for one drink after that weird thing with Browne, but had found his friends already there so stayed on. They were now all lined up on the bar stools, baseball caps firmly set in reverse, eyes on the TV above the bar, yelling for their team. Winnipeg was beating the Leafs, and had scored yet another goal. He'd just ordered another round when Risso climbed down off his stool and stumbled into him.

"Watch it, Risso, you jerk." Barretto couldn't stand him, but he was handy to have around to do the dirty work.

"Sorry Buddy," said Risso. "Just have to get to the can before I have an accident. Save my shot for me, will you?"

"No worries there," said Barretto. "Taking JB forever to serve this one." He snapped his finger. "Hey, bartender, some service here."

She glared back at him. "Calm down Carmine! I'm busy. I'll get there eventually. Here, have a round of waters for now."

He didn't want water, and she'd just lost her tip.

Risso sniggered. "Carmine!"

"Piss off Frank," he said, then glared at the rest of the crew. They all were sipping their drinks, avoiding his eye. He turned and looked the rest

168

of the bar over. It was a busy night for a change, packed with locals. The band at the end had finished with an Elvis tune, and was starting into what sounded like Hank Williams. A few women had jumped up, and were trying to encourage a man—theirs or someone else's—to get up for a dance. None of them asked him, which was just as well. From what he could see tonight's crew were all losers, with sad faces and saggy bodies. He was just turning back to the bar when that busy-body Rosie walked up to him.

"What do you want?" said Barretto.

"Good evening to you too," said Rosie. "Just here to grab a beer. JB, another Blue please?"

Barretto watched in amazement as she served Rosie.

"Hey, what about our round?"

"I think you boys have had enough for now," she said. "Slow down a bit."

"Fine, we'll drive over to the curling club and drink there," he said.

"Hey, what's this?" said Risso. "A new toy?" He was just back from the bathroom, and grabbed clumsily at Barretto's utility belt. There was a sudden smell of pepper spray and Risso stumbled back.

"What the hell?" said Barretto. He rubbed at his eyes and gave Risso a shove into the other bar stools. "You're such an idiot." The two others in his crew tumbled from their stools, scrambled to their feet and started swinging at each other. Rosie stepped back as Risso grabbed an empty bottle and came at Barretto. Tony just had time to raise an arm to deflect the blow, shaking his head to get the rest of the pepper spray away. He swung blindly and connected with someone, but the yelp of pain sounded more like a woman. As his eyes cleared he focused on Risso, and was about to swing again when there was a shout behind him.

***

As Dave followed Reese into the bar he saw that a fight was just starting to build. Barretto and Risso were right in the middle of it, with Norris trying to pull them apart. The band was still playing and most of the patrons were still watching them, but that could change with a few wild punches or thrown chairs. Dave felt the now familiar anger building in him as he crossed over to the bar, ready to knock some heads together. He got a whiff of pepper spray, from Barretto's crowded utility belt he assumed.

JB looked to be wading into it too. "Calm down guys," she yelled, just as Barretto swung blindly and caught her back-handed.

Dave stepped forward, a growl building in his throat, his eyes focusing on his enemy.

He grabbed Barretto, expecting to feel a surge of energy helping him, but there was nothing. Now that he really needed his power, to help JB, it was gone. Tony easily shook him off, pushing Dave back into someone.

"Hey, take it easy Dave," said Rosie. "You look a little shaky. Let your constables handle this."

Within a few moments, Tony and his friends realized they were all just fighting each other. Reese pulled Tony to one side, while Norris managed to wrestle Risso to the ground, then knelt on his back. She reached for her cuffs and looked up at Dave. "You okay, boss?"

Dave nodded then looked around. The rest had either stopped fighting on their own, or been grabbed by some of the patrons.

"All right. Thanks folks," he said. "Everybody just calm down and stay put until we sort this out."

Norris pulled Dave aside.

"Dave," she said. "You're looking pretty pale. Something's taken a lot out of you. This mess is all thanks to Barretto and Risso I think, especially Risso. I'll take them in. I'll check what other toys Barretto has on that belt too while I'm at it. You just catch your breath for a minute."

Dave nodded. "It did hit me suddenly whatever it was. I feel a little shaky on my feet, but I'll be okay, just give me a sec. How's JB?"

"She just got a bit of a bump," said Norris. "You just sit and supervise. I'll send her over."

In a few minutes she was gone with the two troublemakers and everything was back to normal in the bar. JB walked over, an ice pack on her cheek, and a glass of water in her hand.

"Here," she said, "have a sip. Thanks for being my knight in shining armour. Although I heard you already had one battle today."

"Oh, that," he said. "Word spreads fast here. Let me guess. Tony was spouting off about it. No big deal, just some trucker that needed a firm hand. He was a big guy though. I had to use a fancy judo throw to subdue him."

"Seems like you're developing a bit of a temper. Maybe you need another trip with Junior to mellow out a bit. Are you sure you're okay?"

"Oh yeah, I'm all right," he said. "This after-effect has happened a couple of times now, though. I hope I haven't caught some sort of infection. I just need a bit of rest." He finished the water, then stood up. He didn't need to waste time wandering around the bush again, he just needed to get a few nights good sleep and focus on his job. And figure out what was wrong with his powers. "All better now, thanks. I'll head back up to the office."

Dave paused outside the door, pulled his fur hat on, and headed slowly into the night. He was just passing some parked cars when two men stepped out in front of him.

"Not very nice what you did to our friend Frank," said one.

"I think it's time you were taught to stop snooping around," said another.

Dave tried once more to summon some of his power, but felt nothing there. This was not going to be easy. He was deciding which of the two looked weaker when he heard—sensed—something behind him. Before he could turn he felt a blow to his back, then his head, then nothing.

CHAPTER 28

"Dave, are you all right? Dave?" JB shook him again, then sighed with relief as he opened his eyes and looked around at the crowd. This was getting to be a habit for her.

"Hey, JB. Why am I sitting here in the snow?"

"Some of Risso's buddies tried to beat you up," she said. "Junior and some of his friends just happened by and broke it up. Broke a few noses too I think, as there was a lot of blood. Frank's buddies are going to look pretty bruised at work tomorrow."

"Did you catch any of them?" he said.

"No, they all took off," said Rosie. "But everyone knows who they are. How about you? Anything feel broken?"

Dave tried to get up. "Ouch." He grabbed his side. "And ouch again." He put his hand to his head. "Somebody really whacked me with something."

"Maybe this?" said JB. She held up an axe handle in her gloved hand.

"Yes, like that," said Dave. "Careful, might be some good fingerprints on it."

He tried again, and this time she managed to get him to his feet.

"Good thing you were all bundled up," she said. "I think that big winter parka and your fur hat helped." She touched his head carefully. "No blood, just a bump." She felt for any of that other spirit, but there was nothing at all. Maybe it was still weakened by his last battle. The elders would have to act quickly, before this thing became even stronger.

"We already called Norris," said Rosie. "She was in the middle of locking up those two jerks. We told her all was fine here, and we'd drive you back up to the detachment." He held up his hand. "No, don't say anything, you're not walking."

JB walked Dave over to the car. "Dave, you're a mess. We need to talk. Not now, tomorrow."

He looked up, "Sure, whatever."

"Don't whatever me, buddy," she said. She gave him a careful hug." I may not agree with some of the things you've done, but I'm still your friend and am concerned with whatever has changed you. At the very least I can give you a kick in the pants, a hug, and a sympathetic shoulder. Not necessarily in that order."

She was determined to get to the bottom of this and find out what was wrong. Dave seemed worried about it now, and maybe a little weaker. She hated to take advantage of him while he was so tired, but it might be their only chance. "We will talk. Meet me tomorrow. After five on the porch of the Grande. Be there."

Dave smiled back. "Yes ma'am."

***

"Leaving early?" said Norris.

"Yes, I'm meeting up with JB," said Dave. "She says she needs to talk to me. Somehow I think it will be to give me a hard time."

"We all are concerned about you," said Norris. "Not just because you're the Detachment Commander here. People still like you as a person in spite of what's happened lately. JB's a smart one, a keeper. Good luck with your rendez-vous."

As Dave walked down Main to the Grande, enjoying the sun on his face, he found he was looking forward to both a kick in the pants and a hug. He'd missed JB. Maybe she could help with his problem. He needed someone to talk to about the headaches, the dreams, maybe even his power to fade. It used to be something he just turned on and used, but now it had changed and was changing him. Changing him in ways he didn't like.

There was still snow on the ground, and it was cool in the shade, but the sheltered front porch looked toasty in the afternoon sun. There were two chairs set up, and between them a table with a frosty pitcher of draft, an empty glass, and an ashtray. JB was already sitting in one of two chairs, feet up on the rail, cigarette in one hand, glass of beer in the other, basking in the sun, with sleeves and pant legs rolled up. The setting sun looked nice on her dark skin. Dave was amazed that she was still trying to help him even though he'd been such a jerk. He had no clue what was causing his rages and or what was really behind his ability to fade, or if they were related. He figured if anybody was even close to understanding, it would likely be her or her grandfather. Dave had decided that it was about time to come clean and tell her everything—that is if she'd let him. He really didn't deserve her. He was still thinking about what Norris had said the other week, too. Yeah, he supposed he was still philosophically against commitment. It always hampered his style, and often ended in somebody being hurt. So far his strategy had been avoidance, but maybe he needed a Plan B.

CHAPTER 29

J B was lost in thought when she heard someone approaching.

"Dave, have a seat," she said.

He shrugged off his coat, and poured himself a beer. "I was worried that you didn't want to talk to me anymore."

"I was upset for a while," said JB. "But I've been worried about some things about you. A number of us have. And then a few nights ago I had a dream."

"About me?" Dave said.

"Actually, you sort of were there," she admitted, "just not as you. My people have a culture that is full of symbolism, of clans, of special animals called dodems, or totems. These spirits are all through our creation stories, and also explain much that happens in the world. And they can appear to us in dreams, to help us solve a problem, to teach us something."

She described her dream: the bear, awake but lost, the other animals trying to help, what she thought it all symbolized.

"I was pretty sure I knew what it meant, that I needed to be your guide and help you figure some things out. But I went to my grandfather for guidance just in case."

"Does he help you out a lot on things?" asked Dave.

"Well, he's an elder of our tribe, a spiritual leader, so we usually consult with him on things like this. He agreed with what my dream was saying, so here I am, ready to help. Like it or not."

She reached over and touched his arm. "Dave, tell me what

happened? What's got into you?"

He looked over the lake, started to talk a few times, stopped, then finally said, "I've sort of got this thing."

JB turned her head, tilted it, and raised an eyebrow—he laughed.

"Okay, that does sound a little open-ended," he admitted.

"A little?" she said.

Dave took a sip of beer and paused a minute.

"Look, just don't laugh at me. This may sound hard to believe but it's true. I've never told anyone all the details, but I feel I can trust you."

He described his early years as a shy quiet kid, just trying to avoid attention. How he'd developed a skill in reading people, so that he could see if they were going to give him a hard time.

"It was easiest just to avoid being noticed in the first place," he said, "either by the bullies in the schoolyard, or by my teachers. Even from my father, as he was sometimes pretty hard on me. I was managing okay, until the summer that I visited my grandmother."

"The First Nations one?" she said. Maybe there was some sort of link through his blood, but why him?

Dave nodded. "I hadn't seen her much, but with my mom gone and my dad always busy I needed more than babysitters and day camps in the summer."

He described how loving she had been, how accepting of him just the way he was. She lived in a retirement home now, but had been able to take him out into the woods a few times when he was young. She'd taught him how to sit quietly, not moving, feeling a part of nature, until the birds and animals didn't notice he was there anymore.

"Some of my people are quite good at that," said JB.

"She said I was a quick learner, that I took it on like a second skin, an invisibility skin. Things changed that year for me."

He went on about that first day back at school, how he was sitting quietly at one end of a table, trying to be ignored, by himself as usual, when some kids sat with him. Kids that would normally avoided him. They just seemed to ignore him, but not so much that anybody sat in his chair on top of him.

"So what did you do?" she said. "Poke them?"

"No, I just focused on being seen," he said. "Then suddenly the kid next to me turned and stared—eyes wide—and told me to get lost, this was their table. So I did, but I started experimenting with it and found I could pretty well fade and unfade at will."

"No way," she said. She folded her arms and sat back. "Show me." As she watched, he became less distinct—fading was a good word for it —until he was still there, but just not as clear, covered by a dark haze. Whatever it was, she got a feeling of discomfort from it, but reached out anyway where Dave had been. She touched his arm, and he was suddenly there again.

"Hey," he said, "that tingled."

She tried to describe what she had seen—the haze that covered him. She left out the impression of something being wrong with it.

"Really?" he said. "So you could still sort of see me? And at the curling club too?"

"We all could," she said. "Well, just the First Nations people that were there, the rest couldn't. But let me get this straight. This is some power that you can switch on and off at will? Can you also run faster than a speeding bullet?"

"No, no other powers," he said, "although avoiding bullets might have enabled me to stay in Toronto a bit longer. It's just this ability to disappear from people's notice, to fade from their perception."

"Any side effects?" she asked.

"Not until recently. It's always felt good to do it, as it gave me a bit of heightened perception, made me more in tune with things around me. Lately there's also been a bit of a rush when I use it too, a bit of a high, which is nice. Unfortunately, another new feature is the headaches. My temper gets out of hand more often, too, and I just lose control. Like with Risso. After those sessions I'm exhausted for a few days. But it's not a problem, really. Just some minor changes in how it works. It's okay, don't worry about it."

Dave had pulled away from her, and she could see the faint haze starting to darken around him again.

"Do you want to talk about something else?" she said. "Is this bothering you?"

He took a deep breath and the shadow faded again. "No, I'm good. Just felt a little antsy there."

"No problem," she said. "So, why don't you just not use this fade thing?" Seemed pretty simple to her.

Dave shook his head. "Overall it's still worth the benefits I think. I started using my ability a lot more a few years ago, as it was obviously a great tool for eavesdropping, for undercover work. I just had to avoid any cameras, as they could still see me. Then one day, back in Toronto, sitting in the midst of a local gang meeting, I lost it."

"What, your fadey thing?" she asked. "You lost your mojo?"

"Yes. I was tired from too many late nights, then someone saw me on their cell phone camera. Their yell startled me and I unfaded. Then everyone saw me." He described his flight out the window, through the garbage, and into a streetcar.

JB laughed. "Sorry," she said, "Sushi! Then a face-plant on a streetcar. And I can just imagine the look on their faces in that room as you suddenly materialized in front of them. They must have been pissed, though."

"Oh they were," he said. "I managed to escape okay. They still thought I was from a rival gang, but by the next day there was a price on my head. It was decided it was best if I left town for a few months before heading back south for reassignment, Ottawa I think. And here I am. " He sipped his beer, then lit up a cigarette.

"Wow," she said. "I wouldn't have believed it if I hadn't seen it. So you've been using it up here too? Spying on us?"

Dave looked embarrassed. "I was just using it to eavesdrop—mainly on the mayor and his buddies—trying to find out more about some of the issues in town."

"And me and my friends too?" she asked.

"Yes," he said. "Sorry. But nobody was talking to me, and I couldn't just let all this drop. I think it's related. But now I'm using it just to avoid people in the street, and there's all these outbursts. I don't know what is happening."

JB felt like she and her people had been somehow betrayed, violated. Like discovering a neighbour is a peeping Tom. He did seem worried though. And they couldn't just ignore him. The elders were worried this might grow into something evil.

"Fine," she said. "I don't like what you've been doing, but let's move ahead and see what we can do about this. So this has happened three times so far up here, right? Risso in the pub, and at the arena, and with that trucker?"

Dave nodded. "Each time I felt a rage take me over, stronger each time. And the second and third times—the arena and the trucker—I felt like there was a power flowing down my arms and into my hands. And out. Sorry again for attacking you guys."

"We're good for now," she said. "Tell me more about each event."

"Risso was more like just I lost my temper," he said. "But that time at the rink was weird, and scary. I was feeling frustrated. I'd started to build some good relationships for work, then this Minister's visit came up and I had pressure to back off things, yet wanted to keep looking into some stuff. And then everybody clammed up on me like I had a disease or something."

"Yes, or something," said JB. "Like a change of heart and direction. Leave that for now," she said, holding her hand up, "just tell me about what you think happened at the arena."

"I was feeling left out in the cold," he said. "Out of the loop for info. So I decided to use my power, my thing, and sit in hidden on some talk. I just wanted to get something to help me do my job, honest. I wasn't really spying, not in a bad way. But when I tried it at the rink it didn't work, and you guys just stared right at me. When you caught me I felt this rage. I don't know what came over me. I just wanted to attack. It was more than just a self defence kind of thing. I'm really sorry what happened, you've got to believe this isn't a part of me I like. I do like this ability I have, but not this way. But if you can see me, is my ability gone?"

JB reached out and squeezed his hand.

"Not sure if it's lost so much as changing," she said. "I do want to help you Dave. The spirits I'd talked about are not always helpful, not always friendly. Some are troublemakers, some are evil. We often have a specific spirit associated to us—we as in the First Nations people, not your people. Although you have some First Nations blood in you too."

"How about you," he said, "Do you have any super powers?"

She laughed, "No, I don't think so. I am good at calming a crowd it seems, but that's just a skill, handy for a bartender."

"How come your touch felt so calming when I was in one of those rages? Have you something magic there?"

"Not that I know of," she said. "I care about you and was concerned, that's all." She had been surprised how quickly she'd been able to calm him. She usually didn't have that strong an effect on people. But, then, Dave was the first person—other than her family—that she'd felt this strongly about.

"So how do some of you see me," he said, "even when others can't?"

She described as best she could how many people in her family had a heightened perception of the spirit associated with a person.

"It's like an aura?" Dave said.

"Yes," she said, "sort of like an aura. Hard to describe, sort of a blend between a ghostly image surrounding a person, and a 'feeling' about them, about the kind of spirit it is."

"So what's that got to do with me, do I have one of these things?"

"Yes, but different. At the arena we saw you come in, and pause, then suddenly there was a sort of shimmer and then you had this very faint thing around you, this dark cloud. What concerned us was what the spirit resembled in terms of the feeling we got."

"What was that?" he asked.

"It felt to us like the Wendigo, a particularly evil spirit. Grandfather realized we needed to leave right away. I wanted to stay and help, but he said it was too dangerous. Then when you attacked, we had to call on our own spirit world links just to fend you off."

"Can you see it now?" said Dave.

"Sometimes," she said. "It's strong when that rage takes you over. But we realized, grandfather and me, that this has probably been a faint shadow over you for a while, and now seems to be getting darker every day."

She had noticed as she talked about this that Dave was pulling back again, seeming less open to her. The shadow was back too, faintly. She would have to be careful not to push too hard, as they needed it to stay weak for what they had planned. She wondered if this spirit had gained access into him through his strange power to fade away. If so, the more he used it, the stronger the grip the spirit had on him would become. Even worse, they might not be able to separate the two. As she leaned toward him he turned away.

"It's not that bad," he said. "I can stop anytime. I can handle this okay. Just leave me alone."

JB laid her hand on his shoulder, and focused on calming him.

"Sorry," he said. "Got carried away again. But I would hate to lose this ability. Can you just teach me how to manage this?"

"We're not sure how much these new feelings are linked with your initial ability. It was there on its own for years, and it's possible this spirit just used it as a way to get access. Maybe it's to do with being up here, close to our culture. We've asked other elders about it, but we're still trying to work out a plan."

"So if I did want to get this thing out of me—are we talking some sort of exorcism?"

He sounded anxious to her again. "Calm down, Dave. We might not need that. It might be easier. Don't worry, we're not sure yet what to do. Give us some time." She didn't want to alarm whatever it was that was in him—better to appear that they were without a definite solution. Although she was pretty sure her grandfather did have one.

"Maybe I can just stop 'fading' - he made little quote signs - "and it will go away on its own."

"Maybe," she said. "We'll talk later. Right now you need to relax. You've been working pretty hard, pushing long hours. When was the last time you sat and looked at your bird-feeder behind your place?"

"Weeks," he said, "although there have been fewer out there lately. I guess it's empty anyway."

"Don't worry," she said, "Reese has been doing it for you. But they don't really need it, there's lots of food for them in the forest all around here, they were here long before the town was."

"So why do they come?" he asked.

"Maybe they can sense that it brings you happiness and calmness to watch them."

He smiled and nodded, as if he believed her.

"I'm glad you told me this," she said. "Once we know what the problem is, hopefully we can help you redirect that flow within you in a good way."

"Hopefully? So this might not work?" Dave lit a cigarette, then picked up his beer with a shaking hand.

"We're dealing with the spirit world, and some things here we've never seen." said JB. "Worst case, you just stop turning on your fading ability, never use it again."

"But I've sort of gotten used to having this thing in me," said Dave, "it's part of who I am, part of my job. Maybe it's used to being in there and won't want to leave. Maybe we should just leave it alone."

"For now, you just need to relax a bit," she said. "It's supposed to be a beautiful day tomorrow. I checked. You're booked off, so Junior will take you for another walk in the bush."

"He's not going to try lose me again, is he?" said Dave.

JB laughed. "No, not again, quite the opposite in fact."

"I don't know. Maybe if I just go back to Toronto it will start to work properly again," he said. "Although that Badger would probably stick a knife in me."

She sat up. "Badger?" That had been her cousin's nickname.

"Yeah, some native guy – sorry – First Nations – from down in the States. Big guy, really mean-looking, complete with a scar right through the middle of his left eyebrow. What's wrong—do you know him?"

She calmed her breathing and forced a little smile. "No, just startled me that it was one of my people. He doesn't like you?"

"Yeah, he glared right at me, even when I was supposed to be invisible. A nasty character."

He described the chase to her, Badger's gesture, and the dizziness. This was worse than she'd thought. "Go on home and get some rest," she said. "Sleep in a bit. Junior will throw a late breakfast."

After Dave left she sipped her beer and lit another cigarette to calm her nerves. It almost sounded like Badger had thrown some kind of curse at Dave. She'd never heard of that but maybe her grandfather would know about it. He definitely would want to know her cousin was involved. The scar clinched it. When he'd tried years ago to force himself on JB, her little brother had come to her rescue with a canoe paddle—right to her cousin's face. She picked up her phone and dialled Junior. They were going to have to change their plans for tomorrow. This could get very ugly.

CHAPTER 30

"Hey, where's this breakfast?" said Dave. "I was hoping for more than a tin can of tea over an open fire. It must be eleven by now."

They'd been walking for a while in the woods, but from the smells and sounds Dave thought they might be nearing the reserve, and hopefully some food.

Just when they saw the first houses, Junior turned away, up a narrow trail, with the snow packed down by many feet.

"Now what, more traps?" said Dave.

"Just showing you a new path," said Junior.

The trail wandered through some trees—birch and spruce Dave thought—with the sounds of the village still nearby. They finally stopped at the edge of a small clearing, surrounded by brush and snow drifts, bright under overhead sun. In the middle was a low domed tent, covered in canvas, about ten feet across and four feet high. In front of the door, to the east, was a fire pit, smelling of pine and cedar, with large round stones sitting in the hot embers. JB stood by the fire, smiling.

"What is this?" Dave asked.

"It's a sweat lodge," she said.

"Oh, like a sauna?" he said. "I like those, I used to go to them to unwind. I don't have to roll naked in the snow, do I?"

She raised an eyebrow. "Sounds like you had some interesting ways to unwind. No, this is more a healing thing, good for both body and spirit."

"Wait a minute," he said, "this isn't anything to do with that windy thing is it?"

"The Wendigo? No, of course not, just think of it like a sauna. It's very relaxing, feels great."

Dave felt a sudden flush of anger, and an urge to run. "I'm fine, maybe another time," he said, then turned away.

Junior, her big little brother, stood solidly in his path, arms folded. "Dave, what's your problem? Calm down, will you? If you decide you don't like it, we'll leave and go for that late breakfast. At Rosie's—my treat."

"I don't like surprises," said Dave. "And I certainly don't need any of your voodoo stuff." He went to push past Junior, then JB laid her hand on his arm.

"Trust me, Dave," she said. "It can be very relaxing, if you just let it happen. We use this all the time, it's a good cleansing."

He paused. She did look very sincere about this sweat thing, at least it would give him a good story to tell when he returned to Toronto. He felt his rage fade. "Okay," he said, "what do I do?"

"Well, it will be hot in there, so first you'd better strip down a bit," said JB. "We'll try not to get too upset at all that white skin."

He took off his parka and hat, then his boots and wind pants. It was actually not that cold, with the fire pit heat and the warm sun.

"Wait, who else is doing this?" he said.

"Just some of the elders," she said. "The heat is good for their aches and pains in the winter. My grandfather is in there."

"Is this some sort of special ceremony?" he said.

"It's a traditional thing," she said. "We find that while everyone is relaxing together, it's an opportunity to talk, share experiences, get to know each other better. They might even have some ways to help make your life here go smoother."

She lit a small bundle of twigs, which smoldered and gave off a familiar herb-like smell. "This is a smudge," she said. "We'll use it to cleanse you before you go into the sweat lodge." She moved around him, letting the smoke surround his body.

"There's a bit of ceremony that has to be followed as you go in," she said. She handed him a small packet. "When you crawl in you'll see my grandfather sitting just to the right. Offer him this tobacco, say you are there for guidance. There will be three other elders in there already, one just to my grandfather's right, one across from the doorway, one to the left. You've probably seen them around town, but don't greet them other than with a respectful nod. Initially you will take your place next to the one facing the door. Then just follow along with the cues my grandfather gives you."

She led him over to the door of the low tent.

"Oh, you'd better lose the t-shirt and pants too. Don't worry, I won't look."

He looked at her and raised an eyebrow.

"She's serious, " said Junior. "It really is like sauna once we heat it up. "

As Dave pulled off his shirt Junior whistled. "Nice tatoos. I like that protector bear. OK, get in there, the elders are waiting for you."

***

Dave crawled through the door. It was dark, and not that much warmer than outside. He turned to JB's grandfather, handed him the packet, and said that he was here for guidance. The elder smiled, then gestured for him to enter. Dave nodded to the others—he recognized George—then crawled to the other side.

JB stooped in the opening, with a small shovel in her hands, and passed in a large, round, hot rock, faintly glowing in the dim interior. One of the elders took the shovel from her, and placed the rock into a hollow in the centre. Three more times she did that, until there was a rock in each of the compass directions. Her grandfather then picked up a small bowl, and sprinkled something from it on the hot rocks. A sweet smell of cedar and sage rose into the air as a faint cloud. Dave fought the urge to sneeze. JB then passed in a number of smaller rocks, several at a time, which were added to the hollow by the same elder. Once the space was full, he signalled to JB and she closed the door flap. It very dark, and quickly getting a lot hotter. The small bowl was then passed around the circle, with each of them sprinkling some herbs on the fire. Dave paused when it came to him, dimly saw a tiny nod from his coach, and sprinkled some on too.

He heard the sound of a small drum, four gentle taps. There was a pause. Then someone sprinkled some water on the rocks; there was a burst of steam and a smell of more sage and cedar. A voice then asked him. "Who are you, why are you here with us?"

He paused, confused. "I'm Corporal Dave Browne, and I'm here to run the RCMP detachment. And have a sauna."

The voice asked again, "Who are you, why are you here with us?"

He realized there was a little more depth expected. "Well, I'm a cop, and a southerner, and I've been told I'm a loner. I'm someone people look up to and I'm good at solving problems, especially with some unique powers I have."

Another voice, JB's grandfather this time, prompted, "Why are you here in this sweat lodge, this town, this life?"

Dave paused. "I thought this was just a sauna?"

"We are here to help you to choose a path, and hopefully to combat that which is consuming you from within. Don't worry, you can talk in here, our medicine is strong, stronger than that which hides within you."

Dave felt a stirring inside himself, again that urge to flee, and was just starting to rise when there was a single beat of the drum and then a short, sharp shout from all the elders. Startled, he sat back. Whatever had been bothering him was quiet. He felt calm again.

The questions continued, gentle, guiding, persistent. He tried giving the shortened version of his life, but the elders patiently worked at drawing out things he hadn't even realized were inside. He told them about being a shy kid, a loner, and of finding this power with the help of his grandmother. When he talked about the gang in Toronto they were very interested in this Badger character. He spoke about using his power to manipulate others, the balance between the rush of pleasure and the increasing pain, and his increasing isolation. As they talked he realized his use of this power and his rejection of others was hurting both him and his friends, and that it had become more than a way of life, it had spiralled out of control into an addiction.

"And yet," said one of the elders, "your work in Toronto was using your skills to help fight against addictions in others."

Still the elders continued, delving into his concerns, his fears, his dreams. Every so often yet more water would be sprinkled on the rocks and it would get even more humid. Twice more the flap was raised and more hot stones passed through the doorway, but he felt no urge to flee— he felt safe. He remembered sipping on a cup filled with some cedar flavoured water—like a weak tea but refreshing. As the heat increased, he began to feel light-headed, and his thoughts wandered.

"What do you see?" said JB's grandfather. "Close your eyes."

"I see a wide plain," he said, "surrounded by mountains, empty, covered in brown grass, with a haze of dust above it."

"Tell us about this plain, is it truly empty?"

Dave felt drawn into the image, as the dust swirled, then coalesced gradually into a huge herd of bison. He could hear the shuffle of their feet as they slowly circled, like a sluggish whirlpool. In the middle of the herd stood a clump of trees, dead, covered in black leaves. As he watched, some of the leaves rose above the tree, and flitted above it like birds. The bison crowded in around the tree even more, drawn to the dark cloud.

He could smell the sweat from a thousand animals, hear the rumble of their hooves, feel the sun hot on his fur, the buzz of flies around him. He was a bison, too, and a huge one, bigger than any in the herd. He felt somehow possessive of them, as if they were in his care. He stood on a path, looking down at his herd. The path led behind him too, twisting and turning down the other side of the ridge, through rocks and canyons to another valley, far in the distance. He felt his fur starting to stand on end, and realized a storm was brewing overhead, with dark storm clouds full of lightning and rain.

He didn't have much time left to make a choice. He turned back toward the herd, calling to them.

"Come, my brothers and sisters, come with me. There is danger here for you. We must leave this place and find a new home."

As he called, the black shapes on the tree started to fly up, and race toward him. As they neared, he saw they were still just shapes, bits of blackness torn from something larger. They were formless—without mouths or eyes—yet gave off an evil chill. They swirled around him, but he held his ground, bellowing, tearing them apart with his horns, stomping them into dust with his sharp hooves.

There was a cry, and a flurry of sparks. He felt sudden heat on one arm, then an icy grip around his neck. He tried to grapple with whatever it was, but there were several people all fighting at the same time, trying to pull it away from him. He gave a mighty shove and a yell, then fell back, exhausted. The bison, the dark shapes, the storm—all blended into a grey mist.

He suddenly woke up with a jerk, confused, falling …

***

The elder next to him, George, caught him as he fell sideways. It was a little cooler now. The stones had lost their glow and the door was open a little bit, letting in a breath of fresh air. Also letting out all the smoke. He felt his head start to clear.

George chuckled. "How was your sleep?"

"Sorry," he said, "it was very hot and very relaxing. Until the end that is." He sat up and brushed some ashes off his arm. "Did I get burnt?" He looked around. The other elders no longer looked so composed, they too had smudges of ashes on them, clothes askew, and one now had a split lip. "What happened in here? Did I cause any trouble?"

"It's nothing," said Charlie. "We're all fine. You just got a little excited when you fell into the fire pit. But did you dream?"

"Oh sorry," said Dave. "Did I dream? Did I ever, and a powerful one. Animals—I think I was one—some sort of battle, a storm—"

Dave told them about the bison, the black forces, his choice, the battle. All the while the elders kept nodding at him, none seeming surprised at the events he recounted.

"Have you heard this story before?" Dave asked.

"Not exactly," said Charlie. "We are all different, as are our paths. Many of the things you describe are common in our stories. And the buffalo, special for you of course. But how do you feel after your battle?"

Dave noticed that his headache was gone, finally. And he felt different inside, somehow, as if something had left.

"Did you get rid of whatever my bad mojo was?" he asked.

"Yes, we did," said Charlie. "It was a spirit we call Wendigo. In our legends, it would turn someone into a cannibal—not what was happening to you though. In your case it was possessing you and taking over your ability, making you fight everyone."

"Why me?" said Dave.

"Just because it could. It's part of its evil nature."

"But it's gone now, right? It won't come back, will it? Tell me you've destroyed it?"

The chief shook his head. "It can't be destroyed, but it's gone, at least from you. That was part of your battle. You cast it out of you. I don't think it will come back to you again. You're safe."

"That's a relief," said Dave. "Whatever I did or you did—thanks. I feel different, but better. I guess it was time for me to make a choice. I know this ability of mine has been a part of me for a long time, but lately the side effects haven't been worth it. It was the correct decision, right?"

Charlie smiled, "What is right or wrong needs to come from within you. I think your body is already telling you it feels right. Maybe this power was given to you as a gift, and it's up to you to decide how to use that gift."

"I guess now I'll just have to learn to live without it," said Dave, "and do my job anyway."

"Maybe it's not gone though," said Charlie. "Maybe it's just back to what it used to be, in its purer form."

"I don't know," said Dave. "I don't think I can trust it anymore."

"Let's try something," said Charlie, "while you're under protection here in the lodge. Try to do that fading thing."

Dave looked at him, "Are you sure it's safe?"

"Yes, go ahead."

Dave closed his eyes and concentrated. He felt something change. It was like the same feeling he used to have when using his secret power back as a kid. There was no rush to it now, but also no pain. He just had a feeling that he was somehow more focused on his surroundings, more aware of them. He opened his eyes.

The elder smiled and gave him a thumbs up. "Looks good, you can stop now."

"Did it work?" asked Dave.

"Yes, I think so. I could still see you, just as we could before, but before when you would do it there would be a dark cloud around you. This time it was just a faint glow. This is good, I am pleased. Also, I'm relieved that we didn't have to do anything drastic."

"Drastic?" said Dave. "I don't think I want to know any more details now."

He looked around the interior of the tent. "I'm not sure what just happened in here, but I do want to thank you all for whatever you did. And I'm sorry for being such a jerk lately, I hope you'll give me another chance."

"We did it for you, but also for the safety of the community," said Charlie. "We're glad it worked out well after all. It's even better that the special power you had is still within you. You just need to develop some positive ways to use your link to the spirit world. We can help you with that, later. For now, you need to rest, let your body and mind recover from the encounter with the Wendigo. We're done here for today, we can leave now." He held the tent flap open. "You first."

Dave crawled into the bright light, shivering a bit already with the cold.

CHAPTER 31

It was almost evening and definitely cooler as Junior helped Dave into his clothes, "Here, I warmed them up by the fire."

"Thanks," said Dave. He wrinkled his nose. "A little smoky-smelling though."

"A good reminder of today," said JB.

Dave quickly dressed, and looked over at JB. "I thought you said this was just a sauna. It was like a battle in there."

She smiled. "So I lied a bit. We were concerned if you knew what we had planned you'd try to get out of it. But we were all really worried about you. Luckily it seems to have worked."

Dave paused. "You didn't know if it was really going to work or not, did you? Was there a plan B?"

"We were fairly confident," she said. "It did help, didn't it?"

"Yes, thanks," he said. He walked over and gave her a big hug, then, when he saw Junior looking at him, gave him a hug too. "Let's get to that meal now, I'm starving. I could eat a horse."

He stooped to pull on his boots. "Yikes!" he said. "One of these has fresh snow in it."

JB smiled innocently. "Thought you might need some cooling down after that." She shrieked as he scooped a handful of snow and tossed it at her.

Dave was about to chase her when he noticed the elders all standing outside the tent, wrapped in their robes. Dave stopped and nodded awkwardly in their direction.

"Thanks again, I really appreciate this. I won't let you down again."

Dave bounded up the steps to the office. After the sweat lodge yesterday he'd had a huge supper, then fallen asleep minutes after getting home. It had been a good sleep too, with none of those weird dreams. Plus, no more headaches, not even when he'd tried his fade again this morning. Granted, he also didn't get that same quick rush when he used it, but he could live with that.

He'd made a big breakfast today, and was sitting by the window to watch the birds while he ate. There were only a few sitting in the bushes, near the empty feeder.

"Sorry guys." He lifted Snowball down off his lap, pulled on his boots and stomped outside to fill it up. The snow was clean and white, but just under the feeder he found a large feather, much too large for any of the birds he'd seen so far. He tucked it in his jacket. JB would know what it was.

As he pushed through the office door Reese looked up. "You seem perky again today, your day off to relax must have gone well."

"Not sure how relaxing it was," he said. "It was different. Went out a walk with Junior, then almost cooked to death in a sweat lodge."

"I've been to one of those back in Kenora," said Reese. "More of a sweat for me, but my native friends would use it to resolve some issues. The spirit world was mostly an elders thing, but some of the young people were interested too."

Dave had a feeling his sweat lodge experience had not been the same as the ones Reese had been to. "This was pretty intense, Jim, but I'm not quite sure what was real and what was imagined."

"Well, something did you good yesterday," said Reese. "You look a different man. Did you and JB …?"

"No," he said. "We're just good friends. Nice to just get together and talk. Now leave me alone, I've got a pile of reports to work on."

***

As JB saw Dave approaching, she furtively put her cigarette out and slipped it back into the pack.

"Hiding the evidence?" he said.

She shook her head. "No, still trying to quit, or at least cut back. It's hard."

"Seems a little weird too, for you," he said. "You're so into health food and yet—"

"I know," she said. "Enough about me." She took in his smile, bouncy step, sparkling eyes—he was looking recovered. And handsome as ever, even if he was clothed much more than last time she'd seen him. She felt herself blush.

"Glad you dropped by," she said. "It's warmed up nicely this morning."

"We got some new leaflets on shoplifting today," he said. "Just some tips for the local merchants, before the summer crowd. Thought I'd hand them out, and perhaps accidentally meet you to chat."

JB smiled. "Always glad to chat and see how the new Dave is doing. The news is already spreading among my people. They've heard about your vision, and your choice of a new direction. But we are cautious, so many are still waiting to see if your actions match all your good words. The townspeople, especially, are going to still assume you'll be backing the mayor and the mill."

"That's no longer a given," he said. "Ever since that session I've been re-thinking a lot of things. I've made some good links here with people, and don't like to see them get shafted by others. There is a lot going on beneath the surface here."

"We'll be watching you," she said. "And look at you. You're already looking better. How do you feel?"

"Much better," he said. "Made a big breakfast, even filled the bird feeder. And found this under it."

She felt a rush as he pulled the eagle feather out. That was a very good omen for him. "Wow, that's an eagle feather," she said. "Very important to us, this can symbolize courage, and a new start in life."

"It was just there," he said.

"Nothing happens without a reason," she said. "Please, when you go back home, leave a pinch of tobacco out where you found this." She stroked the feather. "How about your fadey thing? Does that still work?"

"Sort of," he said. "It's still there, inside me, but not in the same way. Don't really feel the same urge as before to use it. Maybe I'm a little afraid of it too."

"I can ask grandfather to help," she said.

"Thanks," he said, "but no big rush. I'm hoping I can start over again with people here. I'm not sure what happened in that tent, maybe I saw some things, or maybe just fell asleep and dreamed. Your grandfather and the other elders asked a lot of questions of me, and were really interested in the dream or vision or hallucination I had—whatever it was. It felt like I made some important choices at the time, but some of the details are fading already."

"You do seem to have changed," she said. "Maybe that negative spirit has transformed into some sort of positive power now. Or maybe it's just that you're more comfortable with yourself and your direction."

She continued on. "What you saw in the sweat ceremony was important. We believe that our lives are all interwoven with nature, with the seasons, the weather, all the animals and birds and fish, the sun, the moon, the stars, all linked together. Our clans are intertwined with various spirits, spirits that protect and teach us through our ceremonies and visions and dreams. How we do in life, our success, depends in part on the assistance we get from the spirits. That wheel you saw in my art is our medicine wheel, full of symbolism and used in our teachings. The four colours—yellow, red, black, and white—represent the Four Sacred Directions. There was blue above, for Father Sky, and green below, for Mother Earth. Purple in the middle for the self, your spirit that is in this physical world."

She smiled, she could see his eyes start to glaze over. "Too much detail?"

"No," he said. "but it's a lot to take in right now, along with all that's happened to me. I do find this fascinating though, or even just chatting with you."

She smiled at Dave. He really was a sweet guy. Maybe they could move beyond chatting.

***

It felt good to be off duty. Dave had just finished another long day filled with all the tiny details of running a detachment. It was nice to see it running relatively smoothly. Over the past week he'd felt so much more relaxed, after battling his inner demons and winning. He hadn't had to give up his internal power, his fade; it was now a tool he could choose to use, or not. More of the locals were now not just looking for him to solve

194

their various problems for them, but seeing him as part of the town.

Right now he was looking forward to a cold pint at the bar and a chat with JB. As he walked up the steps of the Roost the door burst open and Barretto rushed out, almost hitting him.

"Whoa, slow down Tony," said Dave.

"Oh sorry man. Listen, still sorry for what happened the other day. I was totally out of line in the bar. You were right in what you did. And those guys outside were crazy. Glad to hear you tracked them down and charged them."

Dave paused. These words sounded like all the right things to say, but this was Barretto. What was his angle, and why was he saying this?

"I saw in your statement that you'd already left when I was attacked. Didn't take you long to get out of there—seemed to be pretty quick of you," said Dave.

"Oh yeah, the fight was over pretty fast, before I could even get back to help you. I sobered up pretty quick and just wanted to get home."

"Driving?" asked Dave,

"Oh no, on foot, figured I'd walk it off. Good to see you back on your feet, everything okay?"

"Sure, I'm good," said Dave.

"Haven't seen you at a lot of council meetings, or the businessman's lunches. I'd hate to see you wasting time with those other groups of busybodies in town."

"All part of how I do my job," said Dave.

Barretto jutted out his chin, trying to look tough. "Just saying, be careful where you start poking around, there could be consequences."

"I'm always careful. Thanks for the concern," said Dave. "It was just concern, right?"

"You're still new here," said Tony, "but you should know that when people start looking where they shouldn't, they might get hurt—accidents can happen."

"Is that what happened to Bourbeau last year?" said Dave. "Did you find him looking where he shouldn't be?"

"Whatever happened to him he brought on himself," said Tony. "Just a tragic accident. But the mill is important to this town, and you might not like what happens if you push people."

Dave didn't take kindly to threats, or being told how to do his job. He clenched his fists as he felt a surge of anger, an urge to poke that arrogant chin. He paused, and took a calming breath.

"I think we all should remember that there are consequences for our actions. Now, if you'll excuse me, I've business in here."

Dave pushed open the door to the bar. He was glad he'd not poked Barretto, and relieved that all he'd felt was a surge of old fashioned anger —nothing like those black rages that used to take control of him.

CHAPTER 32

Dave dropped by the cafe to grab an early dinner and to see how Rosie felt about him now. There was the normal afternoon group there—some workers off shift, a table full of high school kids, and crowded around the table in the end, the local knitting club. Needles clicked and flashed as the ladies worked—some young and chattering, some older, a little deaf, a little self-absorbed. Aware of Dave, they all paused and some even waved to him or smiled.

He sat at the counter end and motioned Rosie over. "Are we okay now?"

Rosie poured Dave a coffee. "Yes, we're okay. I talked to JB, and she said you'd been in a sweat lodge ceremony. She couldn't tell me any of the details, but she assured me that whatever had been bothering you was gone. Her grandfather has been spreading the word too."

Dave nodded. He was realizing which people had the real power in this town, and how being a loner hadn't really helped him.

"There's a lot of political pressure and attention around this big grant," said Rosie. "It's a big thing for the town, so people don't want to jeopardize it."

"I realize that," said Dave, "I'll keep a low official profile on it, but I've heard enough to know there are problems here. Plus I see people driving cars and boats much more expensive than they should be able to afford."

"When I ask, people are saying they just saved up," said Rosie. "Or that they like to blow their money on toys."

"I need more information," said Dave, "before I pass it on up the line, to my subdivision. They're the ones that will assign the right people to it then. Actually Mike did tell me he wanted to talk, then never did drop by. I'll try him again."

Rosie paused. "You know, we're all glad to see whatever was wrong with you is gone. Hopefully for good."

"No problem, I'm better now," said Dave with a smile.

He hoped that was true, that the occasional changes in his power were just him getting used to using it again.

"I've steaks on special tonight," said Rosie. "Tempt you?"

"Nope, I feel like a change from that," said Dave. "How about one of your stir-fries?"

***

"Come in Mike," said Dave. "Thanks for dropping by the detachment. And thanks for sending that file, Constable Norris is looking at it right now. How about the mill records around the date of the disappearance? Any luck?"

"Yes," said Mike, "I did find some peculiar things in it. The same day Bourbeau went missing there were some unusual settings at the spillway."

"Oh yeah, Tony talked about that thing on my tour."

"It normally is only changed a bit at a time," said Mike, "but that day the levels were wild, full flow, then minimum, then back to normal."

"What would that do to the river?" said Dave.

"Not much harm in the summer, but in winter there's ice cover to contend with. It had been a very sunny week, so the already soft ice surface would start to flex and crack, all the way down the river and into Loon Lake."

"So you would just stay off the ice then, right?" said Dave.

"For the river, yes," said Mike. "You'd just need to take bush trails —doable but a lot slower. And the lake would be affected, but still safe," said Mike. "There might be a few more puddles where the water was seeping through, but people just avoid those."

"Sounds like more than an annoyance than anything," said Dave.

"Exactly," said Mike. "Not sure what was behind it. Would mostly just be a delay, but supposedly Bourbeau was elsewhere, out on Dexter Lake. I'll keep looking."

Mike was just getting up to leave when Dave noticed the door was slightly open.

"Sheila, you there?"

"Oh, sorry Dave. Just bringing some papers in. Problem at the mill?"

"No, just some routine matters," said Dave.

He wondered how long she'd been listening there.

***

"Norris?" said Dave. "Can I see you for a minute?"

Dave was impressed by the change in Norris since he'd arrived in Kirk's Landing only two months before. Her paperwork was in on time, and she was more cheerful. As Dave admitted to himself, it might be because he wasn't being so moody himself. There was more to it than that though. She was really getting into this file and coming up with some insightful ideas.

"I'm quite pleased with the work you've done on this file so far," he said. "Good work. And thanks for getting Mike to come in and talk to me directly. I think we've got enough potential evidence here to put a case together. How did you convince him to come in?"

Dave was surprised to see Norris turn a bright pink and start shuffling papers around on his desk. Well that was interesting, and something to file away for a future conversation.

He filled her in on what Mike had covered with him, then added, "I really would like to look around inside the plant more, but their head of security is already a little suspicious, so he isn't going to invite me for a proper tour. Last time, even though he'd had time to clean up his act, I was pretty well restricted to the control room view. I tried to look for some of the things you'd mentioned, but he wasn't letting me anywhere near the mill floor. Any ideas how we can get in there?"

"Maybe if it was just me that went," she said, "I might get a little further. I know Barretto sees me mainly as another dumb woman, but sometimes being underestimated can work to your advantage. Plus—and he doesn't know this—one of my summer jobs was working in a big sawmill back home, so I do know a bit about machines and control systems."

"I like it," said Dave. "But what would you use as an excuse to have

199

to go in? Would you run it as a big drug bust? I would guess that we would be guaranteed to find something. But we'd need to obtain a warrant first."

"What if we already had an outstanding warrant? That would give us access," said Norris. "And rather than search the records for one, we could just get an employee list from Mike, run it through CPIC and see what pops out."

Dave was impressed, she was showing some good initiative. "That's creative," he said. "Have Mike email it to your own address, as I'd still prefer to keep Sheila out of the loop on this. Especially if her husband is somewhere in the middle of it."

"I'm not convinced our mayor is smart enough for that," said Norris, "but we'll see. Let me give Mike a call."

After a short conversation she turned back to Dave. "He can do it, all sorted by management or non-management, as well as job classification, so we can zero on to someone likely to be on the mill floor. He said that once we find some likely targets, he can even check the shifts to see when they are working."

Dave smiled. "The hunt is on."

CHAPTER 33

Norris was just closing up for the day when JB walked into the office. "Sorry, JB, you just missed him."

"Actually, I wanted to talk to you," said JB. "About Dave." She hesitated, not sure where to start. "This is kinda silly," she said, "I feel like I'm in high school."

"Let me guess," said Norris. "You like him but need me to find out if he likes you?"

JB laughed. "Okay, now it sounds even worse." She leaned on the counter. "But it's true I guess. I do like him, we're becoming good friends …"

"But you'd like more?" said Norris.

"Yes." A sudden thought hit her. "Wait you and Dave aren't …"

Norris laughed. "Us? No worry. The field's clear."

JB thought about his former life down south. "What about all his girlfriends in the clubs? Or that Emily person that works for the Minister?"

"All those girlfriends were just part of the life of Dave the undercover guy," said Norris. "From what he's let slip, no relationships there. And this Emily is way too forward for him, not his style—too much style."

JB looked down at her plaid shirt and jeans. "No style at all here. I don't know, I've been hinting but maybe he's not interested."

"No, you're fine," said Norris. "You're a beautiful woman even dressed like that. Trust me, he's a casual type of guy. And JB, thanks a lot for lining me up with Andrea. She moved in to my spare room and it's working out great, Bobby just loves her. You can't believe what a difference having reliable babysitting has made. Now I can concentrate on my work and I don't have to worry about working late at night or unexpected delays." She laughed. "I keep telling her to go ahead and have some friends come over, but I suspect they're a little shy about coming to a 'cop house'."

"Probably just as well," said JB, "as she doesn't have many nice friends. When she was living at home with her alcoholic parents the house was always full of losers and addicts. She was heading for a terrible future and you just may have saved her."

Norris smiled again, "It's a win-win I hope." She paused. Normally she didn't share her story with people but JB was a very good listener. "I can sympathize a little with Andrea because I was still in high school when I got pregnant with Bobby. It was hard juggling school work and childcare. His dad and I got married but we were way too young. Fortunately I had great parents and moved back home when it fell apart and Bobby's dad left. My folks looked after my son too when I got into the RCMP and had to go to basic training in Regina for six months. I don't know how I could have done it without them."

JB looked at her curiously "So why did you pick such a difficult career?

Norris replied, "Basically I needed a job that paid well enough not to depend on some guy to support me, and I really wanted to get out of my hometown and all the gossips who were whispering and pointing at Bobby. But it's not really a difficult job. It's often like babysitting a bunch of adolescents. Most people mean well, but they don't always make the right choices. We just sort things out and hopefully steer them in the right direction so that they can try again."

Norris gave a sigh. "But what to do with you two? Let's slap Dave upside the head and get him on the right path. I'm pretty sure he's interested. He just needs a nudge. You know how guys can sometimes miss subtlety." She scribbled on a Post-it and handed it to JB. "Here, put this on his desk calendar for tomorrow."

***

Dave walked back out of his office, morning coffee in hand. "Norris, what's this?" He held up a yellow note. "TBD – ask JB to

202

dinner? Really?"

"Yes, go for it," said Norris. "Trust my female intuition."

He shook his head, then pointed to her computer screen. "Any luck in CPIC?"

"I think we have a winner here," she said. "It's a quote unquote friend of yours, someone who's always writing in to the weekly paper, pestering councillors, calling here. He's always complaining about every little infraction, about every dollar the council spends, even on youth programs. Thinks we need to build a bigger jail for them all. Yet, for all his talk, he doesn't seem eager to talk face to face or actually do anything himself. Ring any bells?"

Dave leaned over and looked at the screen "You mean —?"

Norris pointed at a name. "Yes, the one and only Risso."

"I think I'll enjoy this," said Dave. "Couldn't happen to a nicer guy."

Dave looked at the file. Stalking a former girlfriend back in Winnipeg, Prevention Order against him a month ago. Apparently he violated the conditions last week, as he followed her out around the city, then back to her house.

"Chased her in his big shiny new truck," said Norris. "Right up on the lawn. Not his first offense either, some other things in there—assault on somebody in a bar, theft, probation violation, DUI. He's done a few months here and there."

"Sure sounds like a good target. Where does he work in the mill?" asked Dave.

"Out on the main floor. He's also one of the quality supervisors there, and according to Mike likely part of the cover-ups on pollution issues."

"Not a good choice for a quality supervisor you'd think, "said Dave, "unless you want to do some under-handed things."

"He's on the four to midnight tomorrow," said Norris. "We might not see anything helpful, but you never can tell. I talked to Mike again. He coached me as to what to look for in there. I think we should go ahead in. I'm off then but will ensure my sitter is available. I'd like to be in on this."

"By all means," said Dave. "This is yours. We might not find anything too incriminating, but this might just stir things up a bit. Maybe Risso will get scared and talk a deal. You mentioned a shiny new truck didn't you?"

"Yup. I don't think the Act lets the judge confiscate it, but he could get a licence suspension. I also found out he has a nice new boat to pull behind it too. Looks like he came into some extra money rather suddenly."

Dave walked away, then turned. "Anyone else pop up that I should know about?"

"Nothing significant from the mill," she said. "I checked a few other names from the town and found a few we might want to follow up on later. Nothing pressing though, mostly fraud and finance-related, but still interesting."

"Is the mayor one of them?"

"Yes," said Norris. "Years ago. Before he married Sheila. I checked her too, and she's clean."

"This will be fun," said Dave. "See you tomorrow for your first bust."

***

It was just after five. Mike had called to confirm that Frank was working the late shift, and was out on the mill floor. Norris had gone over her plan with Dave. She felt a little nervous but was eager to get going. As they stopped by the front gate, she rolled down the window and nodded to the guard.

"Official business," she said, "we have a warrant for someone and we believe he's currently in here."

"Who is it?" said the guard. "I'll call Barretto."

"Please just ask Barretto to meet us at the door. We'll go ahead and park over there."

The flustered guard waved them through the gate as he picked up his phone. By the time they had parked Barretto came bustling out the door, still strapping on his belt of toys.

"Evening Mr. Barretto," said Norris. She held up a piece of paper. "I've a warrant for Frank Risso, violation of conditions of a Protection Order. I have reason to believe he's working here tonight."

"Oh, okay, umm, let me check first." He reached for his radio, but

Dave put a hand on his arm.

"We'll just go ahead in. Do you know what area he's assigned in?"

"Yes," said Barretto, "it's right through here, main digester area."

Barretto led them onto the mill floor and pointed to the far side. "He's over there, working one of the monitor panels. I'll get him." He started to walk ahead.

"Wait a sec," said Dave. "I'd like Norris to go over herself on this. Just hang back a bit here with me. I'm sure she'll do all right."

"Okay," said Tony. "She's a little small to be confronting a big guy like that, but, you know, once he notices me here he'll fold pretty easily."

Norris looked at Dave with a smile then walked ahead into the mill. Frank looked up as she came over.

"This is a treat, I guess you got tired of being the little woman in charge of making coffee. Have you come to talk about those complaints I've got on file?"

She smiled. "No. I'm here because of a little woman of yours, or former one. Last week you were in Winnipeg and violated the conditions of the Prevention Order she has against you, so we're here to take you into custody."

"That bitch!" Frank threw his clipboard down. "She says she wants me to come and see her, but when I showed up she changed her mind. I'm not putting up with this crap!" He tried to push past Norris. They scuffled for a moment but she grabbed at his hand, discreetly but firmly. Frank gasped at the sudden pain in his fingers, and looked down at her in astonishment.

She smiled at him. "Be careful when you push a woman aside—she may surprise you. Now that I have your attention, Frankie, you're going to calm down. I'm sure you don't want to make a scene in front of your buddies and force me to take you down to the floor, and believe me, I can." She looked him in the eye. "We're just going to walk over to Tony and Dave, right?"

Frank looked over at Tony, who was glaring at him, and nodded. "Okay, I'm good."

"You see," said Tony, as they approached. "He just needed a look from me to calm him down. It's an alpha male sort of thing."

"Whatever," said Norris. "Frank, you lean against the wall here, hands out. And legs spread. That's it. You've done this before I think. Dave, would you do the honours?"

Dave pulled on some surgical gloves, "I'm going to check your pockets now. Nothing sharp in there is there?"

Frank looked ready to snap something back, then glanced over at Norris. "No sir."

Dave pulled out a wallet, some change, keys, cigarettes, and from an inside jacket pocket—a bag of white powder.

"Not good Frank," said Dave, as he took out his handcuffs. "Tony, know anything about this?"

"Nope, we've a clean plant here, zero tolerance. Didn't see anything like this in here before, must be Frank's doing, right?" He glared at Frank.

"Let's not get into this here," said Dave. "I'll talk to Frank back at the office, if we need you we'll give you a call, Tony."

"I know everything that's going on here," Tony said. "Nothing slips past me. You know, I applied for the RCMP few years ago, was overqualified if anything, went in for a few interviews, then they said no. Just like that."

Norris suddenly slapped at her pocket. "Damn," she said, "Corporal, I dropped my cell phone back there in the scuffle—won't be a minute."

She hadn't, but it was a good excuse to get back in to the work area. Risso's replacement hadn't shown up, and most of the other workers had turned back to their own jobs, so she used the few minutes to her advantage. She was glad that Mike had prepped her on what to look for. When she returned, Tony was still going on about his rejection by the RCMP. She held up her phone. "Found it, had slipped under one of those cabinet thingies so I had to dig for it."

"Didn't break a nail, did you?" Tony sneered at her.

She looked at her hand. "Nope, all good, sharp as ever."

Dave looked at her, and mouthed the words 'Cabinet thingies?'.

She smiled and shrugged.

***

After they'd brought Frank back to the detachment and booked him in, Dave turned to Norris. "Well that certainly was an interesting ride back. Frank certainly couldn't wait to talk. Even as I got him into the cell he was still going on how the plant might say zero tolerance but is in fact the best place in town to score, soft or hard drugs. He says lots of easy money came with the mill upgrade, and some of it is disappearing up people's noses. Even started name-dropping."

"It was as if he thought he could just talk us out of booking him," she said, "right up to that final click of the lock. What a goof."

"How was your little trip back in to find your phone?" said Dave. "I assumed it was just an excuse."

"Went well," she said. "Some of the equipment there was familiar to me, from my summer job, so I knew what should have been there. It looked like someone had tried to do a big cleanup, but I could tell a lot was still not connected. Lights were on at panels, but meters dead, recorders without paper. In behind were unconnected cables and piles of spare parts." She held up her phone. "It was easy to grab some photos. Unofficial of course. I don't think anyone saw me do it either, as I just have to press one button."

"Great job," said Dave. "It will take a little time to get our information together, especially since we're so busy getting ready for that big announcement for the mill. I think we should ask John the coffee guy to contribute some explanation about the meters—apparently he works with those systems. Get Reese to help with that. If there is fraud involved it should go to our Commercial Crime section, but depending on the evidence, it might be better going to a Federal agency. When we see what we have I'll call the District NCO to see which section is best to continue this investigation."

"He won't be upset with us stirring things up, will he?" she said.

"I don't think so," Dave said. "He definitely doesn't want any cover-ups, but he also doesn't want any grandstanding from us. Well, from me." He smiled. "This is good. We'll have some solid info for him now." Dave had just turned to go into his office when Mike Donnelly came in the front door.

"Hear you grabbed that jerk Risso."

"Yes, on some domestic issues," said Dave. "Thanks again for the help. We'll be sending him to Winnipeg to see a judge. Hopefully he'll be out of our hair for a while."

"That would be nice," said Mike. "Got a minute?"

"Sure, step into my tiny little office. Well, slightly larger now—we moved a wall. So, what's up?"

Mike settled into a chair and pulled out some papers. "You'd asked me to follow up on those water level anomalies the day Bourbeau disappeared, remember?"

"Yes," said Dave, "find anything?"

"Well sort of, but didn't think it was a big deal. Then I heard today you'd been to the mill and arrested Risso."

"Bad news travels fast," said Dave. "It was thanks to that employee file you did for us. But what's the link to him?"

Mike had a series of data logs, showing who was on duty and where. Dave didn't follow all the terms, but it looked like Risso had been there, then someone used his account to make changes.

"I checked the security log, as well as the audit trail," Mike said. "It seems somebody—as in Barretto—logged him out, made the spillway changes, then logged him back in. Happened both times the levels were changed."

Looked like Risso was being set up. Not that hard to do, as everyone would believe it was him, given his reputation. Dave still didn't see why it was done though.

"And you found the proof online?" said Dave.

"Yup. Local logs were changed, but the originals are still in the backups, safe from meddling."

"That's great," said Dave. "We're getting close now, just need to uncover a link with Bourbeau's disappearance."

CHAPTER 34

Dave walked into the Roost Sunday night at 5. It was almost empty, with Sid working the bar.

"Here to pick up your money for the spring car?" Sid asked. "It dropped through the ice this afternoon, after a week of teasing us. You were closest, at 3. I had something next week. The cash is yours, and the car of course, once we pull it out. "

"Not sure I need a soggy car," said Dave.

"You can donate it to the party we hold on the long weekend in May," said Sid. "We charge people a tooney for a swing at it with a sledgehammer. As for the prize money, you two could always use it for your hot date."

"Jeez," said Dave," are there no secrets here?"

"Not really," said Sid. "JB said you two have been out before, sort of, although maybe not all dressed up in a suit."

"I know," said Dave. "And it's not a red one either."

"She ran upstairs an hour ago, to get ready for you. Never seen her spend that much time—must be serious." He grinned at Dave. "Want a beer while you wait?"

"Thanks," said Dave, "but I'll just have a Coke or something. I'll sit out front and enjoy the warm evening."

"It's pretty nice out there," said Sid, "for April. Was almost 20 today, and sunset not until eight. Enjoy."

Dave was sipping his pop when he heard the click of high heels, an unusual sound around the Raven's Roost. He turned, paused, and whistled. "Wow".

JB had her black hair up, baring her slender neck. She wore a slim, and short, black dress, and heels. Around her neck and one wrist she wore simple red and white beaded jewelry.

"You look fantastic," said Dave. "So glad I wore a suit."

"Thank you," said JB, with a little pirouette. She took his arm, "Are we walking?"

"It is a nice night for a walk, but us parading all the way up Main Street to my place might attract too much attention, especially with us all decked out like this. We might get mobbed."

"Too late for any secrets now," she said, "lead on."

***

JB smiled out the window. Dave had been right—half the town just happened to be out on the sidewalk, beaming as they drove by. When they pulled up to Dave's he rushed around to open her door for her. It was nice to have someone spoil her.

Dave ushered her onto his front porch, opened the door, and swept his arm back. "Welcome to my Casa."

It was surprisingly tidy, with a few pieces of art on the walls and some avant-garde furniture in leather and chrome. "Nice things," she said. "Not quite the man-cave I expected."

"I managed to acquire these when I was in Toronto," he said. "Part of my cover. But man-cave? What did you expect? Mirrors and black velvet art? Dogs playing poker?"

She laughed. "Thanks, I needed that. Today has been a killer." She followed Dave out onto the deck, where he'd set up two lounge chairs and a small table.

"Oh, this is nice," she said. "Still a bit of sun, no breeze. Even a warm blanket on each chair." She sank down into the closest chair, kicked off her shoes, and closed her eyes. "Sorry, I do need to relax."

"No problem," he said, "your waiter will be with you shortly."

She sat quietly for a few minutes, enjoying the warm sun on her face. When Dave returned, it was with cheese, paté, crackers, and a pitcher of margaritas.

"Mmm, I like this," said JB. "Please pour me a tall one. Was just one of those days. First off, trying to calm down some band members with issues over the mill, mostly the younger guys."

Dave passed her a drink and settled down with his in the other chair.

"Thanks," she said. "Then the normal drama at the pub—customers arguing, shipments late—I know, seems trivial at times. I was talking to my little brother Junior today, too. He's almost finished high school, and we think he will pass, but I'm trying to convince him to keep at it. It has been a struggle for him, he buses to high school, along with the kids from town. That can be a problem sometimes. I mean they're not all bad. Most are tolerant, but still some of the kids—as well as teachers—can be surprisingly racist."

"Up here?" said Dave.

"Oh yes," she said. "Up here. I even see it in my own people, back the other way. And there's the whole culture bit." She took a sip of her drink. "Ours is not suppressed anymore, but it's not in the curriculum either. We try to promote it, but just like any other minority groups— Jewish, Russian, Chinese, whatever—if you want to teach the culture to the kids it's going to be an after school thing. Even harder up here, after a long bus ride from school too, I should add."

She sat back and shook her head. "Jeez, calm down JB. I'm sorry Dave, here you set up such a nice evening and I'm just bitching."

"No, that's all right," he said. He realized that back in Toronto he would likely have already tuned out what his date was going on about. This was different—he was interested in what JB had to say.

"If you care about someone," he said, "then you care about how they are feeling. So if venting a bit will help you feel better, then so be it. I also believe if there are things bothering us in life, we should change them. And if we can't change them—then learn to live with them and move on. There's some sort of saying for that, isn't there? "

"Yes there is," said JB, "something like 'Grant me the serenity to accept the things I cannot change, the courage to change the things I can, and the wisdom to hide the bodies of those people I had to kill because they pissed me off.' Right?"

Dave gave her an alarmed look. "Yes, sort of like that. Let me get some more margaritas and turn on the BBQ to preheat, then we can carry on. I'm wondering if you have any suggestions for adding culture to the local native youth experience—no, wait until I come back with the drinks."

It sounded like JB had a real passion about this, and maybe could help him deal with the local kids and their issues. He brought in the new batch of drinks and settled into his chair. "Okay, carry on."

"The problem many of these kids have is too many other demands on their time," said JB. "They have after school sports, friends, chores, part-time jobs to help pay the bills, even siblings to look after. It's hard for us to compete with that, especially when they see it all as just old guys telling stories. Yes, long stories, but the point is to listen, learn a lesson from the story, and practice being patient. That's not sinking in with the kids."

"You need some sort of hook to grab them," said Dave. "You'd talked about working with some youth groups back in Ottawa—instead of going to university classes—what got to them?"

"Well for those kids it was painting," said JB. "Not canvases, but murals. They started with tags as a way to express themselves. Eventually they got caught, but rather than fines and jail many were redirected into a mural program."

JB described the program the city had run, where local kids painted walls with permission, doing designs that had a bit of an edge but were acceptable to the community. Walls looked nice, it got the kids involved, and they didn't get tagged over.

"So you don't just pay a company to do a mural?" asked Dave.

"You can," said JB, "but the wall gets even more respect when it's local youth that do it. Especially if they are part of the hip-hop community."

Dave got up to put on the steaks. "These will be good, nice cuts," he said. "Medium rare?"

She nodded.

"So this is more than just tagging," he said.

"These are kids that have moved beyond that," she said. "They are real artists with a spray can. This approach helps not only in terms of respect but also for mentoring and community involvement. Soft skills too, like communication and negotiating, contracts, design."

"And the city backed this?"

"It was winning them over as it spread," she said. "The groups in Ottawa were setting it up so that the kids could be helped by other graffiti artists and learn some art skills, and learn that there are other ways to express themselves. Anyway, that's my spiel, sorry, I'm running on again. I'll sit quietly and drink my margarita. Your turn."

"No, that's fine," said Dave. "Sounds like a passion for you, nice to have one. You should keep it up somehow," said Dave.

"I could," she said. "Maybe Junior could get involved too. He had a great time doing that mural on Rosie's. Especially since the mayor hated it so much."

"I saw that," said Dave. "Nice images, especially that big bison. Just like in my dream. He must have been talking to your grandfather."

She smiled. "Just a coincidence I'm sure. But please, your turn, anything you need to unload on?"

"Actually, I had something specific," said Dave, "but it's too serious for now, better over a cognac after supper."

JB tried to get Dave to tell her more, but he refused. He stuck to a steady stream of anecdotes about his career so far, and soon had her giggling and wiping tears from her eyes. Once the steaks were done he carried them inside. "Let's eat in here, the sun's going down and it's getting a little chilly. I've set the table and lit the fireplace. What do you think?"

"I think I like this," said JB. "Shall I pour the wine?"

"Please do."

Once dinner was done they sat by the fireplace. "Wow, I know I kept saying so during the meal," said JB, "but once more—this is pretty amazing."

"And good company," said Dave. "I feel better, more relaxed."

"Yes, I do too." JB reached over and touched his arm. "So, what was this serious topic that you wanted to talk to me about?''

"I had another peculiar dream," said Dave. "Probably means nothing, but you were pretty helpful with the last one."

"I'll try," said JB. "Do you dream a lot?"

"Normal, I guess," he said. "Usually just a vague memory when I wake up. Although they seem to be getting more vivid since the sweat lodge, and staying with me longer. Sometimes I'm struggling against someone, or something, but always with animals involved too."

"Was that what this one was?"

"No, different, but still weird."

"Our dreams can be messages from our subconscious," she said, "trying to tell us something. However, all it has to work with is symbols. My people believe dreams are a way for the inhabitants of the spirit world to speak to us. Tell me what it was about—just tell it as a story."

Dave took a sip of his cognac.

"In this dream I was not being chased—for a change. I was just standing on a rocky cliff, above a lake. There was a big scraggly pine behind me—alone and windswept, like something out of a Group of Seven painting." He held up his hand, "I know, hard to believe, but I do have a bit of culture in me."

"No, I don't doubt it," said JB, "but that tree sounded familiar to me. Carry on."

"So, there was this pine behind me, and a frozen lake in front of me. It was a sunny winter day, with the sun low in the sky across the lake. There was a hole in the ice too, out from the shore a ways, black against the white snow. It was quiet, except for this deep coughing sound. I peered over the edge, and down at the foot of the cliff there was a big brown bear. He was making that noise. I could hear a loon too, in the distance. But in reality the bear should have been asleep and the loon down south, right?"

"It's the dream world," said JB. "Keep going."

"So I was up there on the cliff listening to this loon calling, then suddenly I was somehow down on the ice, and now I was the bear. I was trying to walk toward the big hole in the ice, but it was out a ways from shore. I kept walking, but couldn't seem to get there. You know, that dream thing, where everything is slowed down in a dream, where you can't act? My feet—my paws I guess—wouldn't move. They were stuck in the snow, and getting cold."

"Then what?"

"Then I woke up and discovered that I'd kicked all the blankets off my feet and they were cold. I covered up again and just stared at the ceiling until my alarm we went off. So, was this dream trying to tell me something?"

JB sat and stared into the fire for a moment. "There's always a message in our dreams. I think I recognize that cliff facing the sun, I've seen it. It faces east, and is one of many sacred places around here, places the elders talk about as being associated with the Manitous, the spirits. Also, my father was of the Crane Clan, but his totem was the loon. I think we can assume that was Loon Lake. It's not far, maybe 50 miles down river from the mill, close enough for a day trip. It's one of the lakes my father was interested in when he was collecting his data."

"But he didn't head there that day, did he?" said Dave.

"Supposedly not," she said, "at least not according to the mill. I wondered a bit why he went to Dexter Lake for those final pollution readings. It's not directly downstream from the mill, in terms of waterflow. It's to the east, downwind from the mill, but whenever he talked about his work he was more concerned about the water pollution than air pollution from the stacks. And it was strange that the mill was pushing that one lake so strongly."

"Which way is Loon Lake?"asked Dave.

"Basically northwest of the mill, definitely not to the east so the search wouldn't even come close, said JB. "Not too far, just a quick day trip by ski-doo, following the river."

"This sounds like it ties in with something Mike found out," said Dave. As he told JB about the mysterious orders to change the water levels up and down, she got more and more agitated.

"WHAT! This is incredible! They knew all along!" JB jumped up, spilling the rest of her drink. "They deliberately weakened the ice. They killed my father, they knew he was going to rat them out and they killed him."

Dave got up and grabbed her arms, "Whoa, don't worry, we'll sort this out. Calm down! I'm not sure yet why they played with the water level. It's a long shot to assume that would drown somebody. But if the river ice was unsafe, then the trip in and out would take longer, right?"

She nodded, reluctantly. "Well, yes. That would have delayed him enough to miss his flight, and the conference, and those damning results."

"Exactly," said Dave. "So there's a bit of a connection there, and maybe we'll find more. As a friend, I'll say they look guilty of something to me, but as Chief Constable here, I have to work carefully to determine what's happened and who's responsible."

JB sagged against him. "Sorry Dave, it's just been so stressful for the last year. It's still sinking in that he's dead, and I'll never see him again."

Dave wrapped his arms around her. He hadn't meant to but she was so upset and it just seemed like a good idea at the time. She melted into him like she was meant to be there. She smelled delightful. He didn't want to go too fast or say anything wrong in case it messed up this great mood. Maybe it was safe to just continue the conversation as if nothing was different.

He pulled back a bit. "Now that we have a better idea of where he was headed, we can take a look."

"What, go to the lake?" she said.

"It's the best lead we have now," said Dave. "The only one."

"I suppose so," she said. "But when would we go?"

"I think we should go tomorrow," he said. "I'll just need to shuffle some things and get some stuff together first."

"Wait," she said. "Tomorrow's Thursday. Don't you need to get organized for the big Federal announcement on Friday?"

"I'd like to see where this all goes," he said, "before the mill visit happens. I have a feeling. As for the announcement, most is set up already. Besides, you said it's just a quick day trip, right?"

CHAPTER 35

Dave was in the detachment already when Sheila and Reese arrived. "You're here early," said Sheila. "Actually, you're not even scheduled on for today."

"I wanted to check over the details for tomorrow, that's all," he said.

He called Reese into his office, and closed the door. "I need you to keep this under your hat, especially from Sheila, but JB and I are going to Loon Lake today."

"Today? Where's Loon Lake?" said Reese.

"It's about 50 miles somewhere north of here. I'll show you on the map. It's supposedly an easy day trip. I'm following up a new lead." He explained his new theory about the disappearance, as Reese's eyes widened.

"I know it's a rush to squeeze this in today," said Dave, "but I think this disappearance and the pollution issues at the mill, plus those select few in town with unexplained riches, all these things may be linked together. And I'm concerned, both as a friend of many here in my town and as a police officer, that once the government dumps millions more into this project, they will do all they can to squash any investigation. I'll keep in touch on the radio to the Telecom Centre, so if there are any issues today while I'm gone give them a call."

"Does sound like a good lead," said Reese. "but what about the District NCO and that Minister's aide? Didn't we tell them we weren't going to do any investigating until the presentation is over? What if they call? What do I say?"

Dave looked thoughtful. "If the staff sergeant calls and asks, tell him I'm following new information that can't be put off. And if you have to, tell him the whole story. I think he'll understand that it has to be done now. We'll be back tonight and hopefully have evidence of something. And if the Minister's aide calls tell her I had to go to Winnipeg for a court appearance, but will be right back."

There was a buzz on Dave's intercom. "Mayor Palin here to see you Dave. Do you have a minute?"

Dave rolled his eyes, at this rate they'd never get going. "Thanks Sheila, send him in."

He smiled at Reese. "I like that she's not saying 'my husband is here' anymore."

Mayor Palin stepped in as Reese held the door for him. "Just need a minute Dave, want to make sure all is arranged for the big visit at 11:00 a.m. tomorrow."

"All under control, Mayor."

"I trust you've seen to it that there will be no protest?"

"Well, I can't legally forbid a protest," said Dave.

"Can't you make up some excuse, like no permit or security issues?"

"No," said Dave, "I can't just make up an excuse. I'm charged with upholding the law for everyone in town, including protesters. I have talked with the band representatives already. They do have a right to protest but must do it in a lawful manner. I have been assured they will do that."

"Well, some of the press will be here this afternoon," said the mayor. "And they'll be attending a presentation and reception at the plant. Might get a tour too—a limited one of course, as most of the equipment will probably too complicated for them to understand anyway. But I just want to make sure they can get in past any disturbance."

"We'll do our best," said Dave.

The mayor was not happy with that, but after a few more assurances he left.

A minute later there was another buzz. "Miss Bourbeau and her grandfather here to see you," said Sheila.

"Send them in please," said Dave.

He rose as they came in and extended his hand to the band elder, with a nod. "Welcome sir, always honoured to have you visit. And you too JB."

"Busy day," said JB. "We just saw Chief Storm Cloud stomping out —he wasn't happy. Oops, sorry Grandpa, go ahead."

Her grandfather touched her arm. "It pleases me to see the younger generation wanting to learn about the old ways and get involved in issues, but we also try to teach patience. Thank you for seeing me and my granddaughter. She told me about what you have discovered so far, and that you are hoping to find out more today. I appreciate you working quickly on this, helping us out."

"I'm just interested in justice," said Dave. "I try to be as impartial as I can."

"We appreciate that," said the elder. "You also have shown in your job that you have compassion—you have a good balance."

"Thanks," said Dave. "I reassured the mayor that all was in control —he was concerned about any protests that might go on. I told him that protesting is within the law, as long as it is done in a lawful manner. I assured him that would be the case, right?"

"Yes, it will be peaceful," said the elder. "Some of the younger band members wanted an aggressive presence, but the other elders and I negotiated successfully for something calmer. I have read Gandhi, you know."

Dave raised his eyebrows. "That's interesting, and reassuring. Thank you sir."

"But," added the elder, "I also have read *On Civil Disobedience* by Thoreau, *The Art of War* by Sun Tsu, and *The Prince* by Machiavelli. So I am aware of various possibilities. But I prefer Gandhi." He smiled at Dave.

Dave smiled back, "I think I'm still reassured. The mayor did mention there was a presentation this evening and reception at the plant for some of the press."

"Who else is coming," said JB.

"Besides Minister Gottman and her aide, there will be a business reporter from Toronto—Globe and Mail I think—the local MP, you and some other elders, the mayor and all his council, and, of course, more reporters. Not sure if anyone will be covering it live, though. The

Minister may bring someone to film, so they can do their own version for a press release. Mayor Palin mentioned a mini-tour too, but thought most of the press wouldn't know what they were looking at anyway. Would be a shame for the press to come all this far and miss seeing inside the plant."

"Yes, it would be too bad," said the elder. "I'm sure they'll have access."

"Would be a help if they gained an appreciation of all the fancy equipment in there too," said JB. "Perhaps some of the workers that are more familiar with the new equipment could explain to the press what sort of things to look for, and how to tell what is in service and what is not. Just to ensure they get full value from their tour."

Her grandfather smiled, "Such a clever granddaughter I have, my little Wisakedjak. Did I mention what a great catch she was?" He smiled mischievously at her.

"Grandpa!" She poked him in the arm.

CHAPTER 36

I t was after 10 when Dave and JB headed out past the mill. Dave hoped her estimate of a day trip for this was accurate.

"The trail is further down, by the reserve," said JB. "Your truck will be fine there for the day."

They wrestled the snowmobile off the trailer, and grabbed their two small packs. Dave had included an evidence kit in his bag, just in case.

"Just let me check in with Julie before we start off," said Dave. "She'll be waiting for my call."

"Julie? A friend of yours?"

"She's in our Operation Control Centre—OCC. We all talk to them a lot and there are regular shifts so we get to know each other well without ever meeting. She sets a timer depending on what I'm up to, so if I don't call in she'll escalate and eventually send someone to look for me. Nice to know she has my back, even if it's from Winnipeg."

After his call he locked up the truck and they followed the trail into the bush. At first they made good time in the shade of the trees, but as the day wore on the spring sun made the snow wet and sticky, forcing them to stop often to clear the track of slush.

'This is turning into quite a battle," said Dave. "We're either blinded by the sun or stuck under some dark trees—not the friendly forest Junior and I hiked through."

"Spring is a time of change," said JB. "Of new beginnings. Winter doesn't like to see an ending, doesn't want to let go of its grip."

"Do you think we'll make it, " asked Dave.

"Oh yes, eventually," said JB. "It's just going to be slow slogging all the way I think. I should have known better, wasn't thinking clearly. I have driven through this sort of stuff before, we'll just have to keep working at it."

At least they hadn't tipped over or become stuck in the mud. In spite of the hard work, Dave was enjoying the sunny day, as were the flocks of tiny birds that followed their progress. JB pointed out the animal tracks crisscrossing the snow – not only rabbit but also squirrel and fox.

"Bears will be stirring soon too," she said. "look, there are some green shoots coming up, in the bare spots. Spring is definitely here."

"We've been battling this snow for a couple of hours," said Dave. "Why don't we stop for a rest. I could use a bathroom break too. This bumpy ride isn't helping things. I'll call into the OCC again."

"Say hi from me," said JB. "And while you're doing that, I'll brew some tea."

They stopped in a sunny clearing, and shut off the machine.

"Wow," said Dave, "you don't realize the racket until this is shut off."

"I know," said JB. "Even the new ones are still pretty noisy. I definitely prefer being on foot or in a canoe in the bush, but these are good workhorses, especially in winter."

She cleared a spot on some rocks, while Dave went off to the side and checked in on the radio. He called over to JB. "How long to the lake?"

"I would say we're halfway," she said. "It's almost noon now, should be there by three. Then I guess we play things by ear."

Dave finished his call then gathered some dry twigs.

"Here's your firewood," he said.

"Very good," said JB. "Junior trained you well." She quickly lit a small fire and set a pot to boil on it.

"Did you also bring the traditional native lunch of pate and baguette?" asked Dave.

JB smiled, "But of course, *Monsieur*. No wineskin though, another time."

They sat and sipped their tea, jackets open and hats off. JB pulled out a small pouch and some papers. "Smoke?"

"Still trying to quit," he said," maybe I'll just steal a quick puff."

He watched as she expertly rolled a cigarette. "A skill you developed in Ottawa?"

"Actually my dad taught me, but it did impress the kids there."

"Likely some were rolling more than tobacco," he said.

"That they did," she said. "I'll admit I tried it too a few times. But I found that for me it just made my head fuzzy, made me less perceptive of things, less connected with the spirit world. So I declined—they were fine with that. But how about you? Must be *verboten* if you're going to be a Mountie."

"I can't say," he said. Then he glanced at her and remembered he was trying to be more open. It really was hard to break old habits. "Actually, I did the standard try-it-in-high-school thing. Just a couple of times, and ended being sick as a dog both times. That was it for me. Then when I decided to apply to the RCMP that was on the questionnaire of course—but they are realists about it. They think being honest under pressure is more important than concealing a teenage experiment. I didn't even have to pull a Bill Clinton and say I never inhaled."

JB passed him her cigarette. "Here, take that puff and then we'll get moving."

Dave helped clean up their little campsite, throwing the bread crumbs toward a flock of birds chattering near them. They quickly swooped in and grabbed for every scrap they could find. They certainly liked baguette.

* * *

JB had tried to push things, but as she feared they didn't reach the lake until mid-afternoon. The last few miles had been a fight through scrub bushes, under the heavy branches of dark pines. They'd had to backtrack a few times, sweating in spite of the deep snow in places, so it was a relief to break through into the bright light and relative warmth of the lake shore.

She pointed up at a cliff. "Is that the pine in your dream?"

"Wow, yes," said Dave. "And the hole was maybe 50 yards off-shore from it. But the lake is almost clear of ice. What do we do now?"

JB left her rain pants and coat draped over the ski-doo and led the way down the shore a bit. She pointed into a clump of birch. "There it is, a canoe. We often leave some near lakes, for whoever comes along."

It was a slightly battered aluminum canoe, sitting above the snow, upside down on some poles.

"What—not a traditional wood one?" asked Dave.

"No, they are too attractive to porcupines over winter, they like to nibble on the gunwales—especially where sweat has made them salty. These Grummans are a little noisy, and cold on the knees, but do just fine."

Dave helped her get the canoe down. As she'd expected, there were two paddles—plastic and aluminum—strapped inside, plus a couple of battered life jackets tucked into the ends. Dave helped her move the bow into the water, then she pointed. "You can be in the front, that's that end. Keep low and hold the sides as you get there. Then kneel in front of the seat, with your butt leaning against it. I'll pass you your pack."

Dave settled in, carefully, afraid to move.

"Ever been in a canoe?" she said.

"As a kid," he said. "Maybe twice. I'm thinking this lake water is barely above freezing temperature. The metal feels like ice under my knees."

"Don't worry, we won't tip," she said. "Anyway, what's a little risk seeing that we've come all the way out here based on a dream, right?" She then slid the canoe further out and hopped in. "I'll paddle," she said.

The day was hot, away from the snow in the woods. JB was excited to get out on the water again but she was also worried about what they might find. She quickly paddled over to the cliff, below the lone pine, then stopped the canoe. "Do you remember what direction the hole was in your dream?"

"I think it was straight out from here," he said. "It was lined up with that bunch of white trees on the other side."

She pointed the canoe toward the clump of birch.

"How far?" she said.

"Maybe halfway?" He looked over the side carefully. "Wow, can't see a thing, could be a bottomless pit."

"It drops right down at the cliff," said JB, "but there are several shallower spots further out, where the rock comes closer to the surface. Maybe only ten or fifteen feet deep and great visibility at this time of year, before pollutants and spring warmth get all the algae growing again.

Sure enough, as they paddled further out, gradually the bottom came into view, and she could start to pick out some shapes.

"Wait," he said. "There's something." He was pointing just a bit ahead.

JB let them drift slowly. She peered over the side, then pulled back suddenly in horror. "Oh no!" She dropped her paddle and started sobbing.

CHAPTER 37

Dave could see the ski-doo clearly in the water, with a body— bundled up in a snowmobile suit—just by the front end. He was trying to think about what to do when he realized JB was sobbing behind him. He tried to turn, but the canoe wobbled dangerously. "Let's get back to shore," he said, "before we tip over and freeze in this water. And decide what we do next."

JB slowly calmed enough to turn the canoe around. Somehow she managed to hold it together until they got back to shore, but then she just beached the canoe and collapsed in tears. Dave scrambled out and helped her out, hugging her, heedless of the cold water around his ankles.

"You're sure it was him?" he said.

"Oh yes, that was his Kawasaki, and the hat I made him. He loved that hat." And with that she started to cry again.

Dave hugged her. "I'm so sorry." He patted her back. "I'm trying to think of what to do now. Normally we call in a helicopter and the police dive team. They can put some wire lines under the snowmobile and haul it out. And a body basket for—" he trailed off. "But it's only a couple of hours until dark. There's no place for the helicopter to land. And it will take a few days to assemble the dive team." He paused and thought. "I'd really like to do some crime scene work like taking photos so I can show them the location. But it's getting dark pretty fast. We have to get going to still get back tonight."

JB was not sobbing any more but made no effort to break free of his arms. She looked up at the evening sky. "It's still clear so it will be cold tonight. This slushy mess is hardening up already, so would be a quicker trip back. It will be too rough a trail in the dark though. And we won't see much out on the lake, or under it." She paused. "I'm sorry, I'm beat."

"Didn't you say there was a cabin near here?" he said.

"There is," she said, "It's a small hunting camp—sort of a shared place for whoever happens to be out here. My dad has stayed there."

"That's settled then," he said. "We'll stay there overnight, let you rest up, then we can check out the lake again in the morning, and take off right after."

The cabin was close to the shore, and quite small. The late afternoon sun had warmed the front, but the air was starting to cool. Dave unhooked the shutters over the windows, removed the bar over the door and led the way in. There was a small wood stove against the back wall, to the right was a table and two chairs and some shelves. To the left was a wide built in bed. One bed. There was a mattress on it rolled up as well as a plastic bag of bedding.

JB lit a kerosene lantern, then opened the stove and lit it also.

"That was lucky," said Dave, "a fire laid already."

"Always like that," JB said, "we leave it ready for the next person. This place gets used off and on all year round. Never know when someone might get here too exhausted and cold to build a fire. There's likely more wood in the shed out back, too."

"I'll get it, and call in our status," he said. "I'll tell them we're staying over night, and to let your grandfather know we're okay. I'll wait until we get back to tell him about your dad. You just sit. I'll be back in a flash."

When Dave got back JB was poking around in the shelves by the stove.

"Did you get through?" she said.

"Yes, I managed to get things rolling. What are you up to?"

"I can't just sit," she said. "Water is boiling for tea, and I found some rice too, as well as an Oxo cube. Even found a can of Klik to fry up." She pointed at a trap door in the floor. "Down in the root cellar."

While she cooked supper Dave unrolled the mattress and spread out the bedding. He found a broom too and swept out the winter's dust. JB was quiet, so he just let her putter around at the stove.

She looked around. "It looks nice in here, thanks."

"Always is easier to clean somebody else's place rather than your own, " said Dave. "I found some drawings here too, mostly birds." He passed them over.

"Oh, those look like my dad's," she said. She leafed through them. "He had a great eye for this, was always doing rough sketches. Thanks, I'll keep them. Junior and grandfather will like to see them too."

They finished their meal off with a dessert of energy bars from Dave's pack. Night was falling already, so they just sat, tired after the day. Dave went over what he had found so far in all the interwoven issues, and what he thought the outcome would be. JB was pretty upset.

"We need to lock these bastards all up," she said.

"I agree it looks like they are responsible for a lot, but so far not things that will stick in court. But, I have a plan on how to maybe tease out a confession here and there. We'll see. Trust me."

She smiled, "That I do. Come on, I'm beat, we need to crash so we can get an early start." She looked significantly at the bed. "Come on, we can share. I don't want you all cranky tomorrow from sleeping on the cold floor. I'll add some logs to the stove to keep it warm in here."

Dave stripped down to t-shirt and long johns, as did JB. She doused the lamp, then they climbed under the blankets—not too close. JB lay facing the stove—back to Dave. They lay there for a while, then JB said, "Dave, could you just hold me please?"

Dave moved over to her, and cuddled up carefully. He put his arm around her waist, and his face behind her head. Her hair smelled nice.

"Thanks," she said, and squeezed his hand. He smiled, and relaxed.

Dave woke up in the middle of the night, the fire had died down and it was getting colder in the cabin. But it was still warm under the blankets, JB had rolled over and was snuggled right up to him, arm across his chest, and a leg over his. She felt very nice. He thought she was asleep, so kissed the top of her head. She tilted her head back and kissed him back.

"Hmm," he said, "I was thinking of getting up and putting some more wood on the fire, but —"

She hugged him harder. "Stay, we're just fine," she said, and then kissed him hard.

**

Dave woke to find JB still snuggled right up to him. He just lay there watching her until finally she opened her eyes and looked softly at him.

"Is it time to get up now?" he asked.

"Not yet," said JB. "We have time to cuddle for a bit. You're like a furnace, much better than my electric blanket."

"Thanks, I thi—." JB's kiss caught him off guard and once again took away his breath.

***

It was just getting light when they finally got out of bed. JB raced to the small outhouse, while Dave stood at the side of the trail. "Go ahead, it's all yours," he said. "I'm fine just here."

Breakfast was more tea, and something JB called bannock. It was like biscuits, but done in a fry pan, and delicious with some jam.

Before leaving the cabin JB raked the coals out of the stove and carefully laid a new fire in it, ready for the next visitor. She sealed up all the food tightly, while Dave cleaned the dishes and counter.

"We'll take our garbage with us too," she said, as she barred the door.

"Ready to face the lake again?" he said.

She nodded. "I knew he was gone already, but in a way it's good to have it settled. Let's do what we have to do now and get back."

As they drifted over the body again, Dave peered over the side. "It looks like the ski-doo came apart or something."

JB shaded her eyes and squinted at the machine. "No, I think he had taken the covers off to work on it, they are usually latched on pretty tight. There's a metal gas can down there too, from the mill I think, with the top off. After that long trip through the slush maybe he stopped to gas up."

Dave shielded his eyes and peered below the surface again. "It looks like his coat was caught up in some of the wiring. Maybe it broke through and he just got stuck."

There was a gasp behind him. "Sorry JB," he said. "I was thinking out loud. Not a good way to go."

"We always have a few people go through the ice in the spring," she said. "Problem is the water is ice cold, and all that clothing weighs you down. Plus the soft ice just crumbles at the edge when you try to get out. Friends can lie down and hold out a sapling or even flip a rope to you, but I don't know of anyone that has got out by themselves. So he probably went quicker this way."

"Well sweetie, I can't say how sorry I am about this," said Dave.

"Thanks, " she said. "Glad you're here with me. I just wish you could have met him, I think you two would have got along nicely." She paused, her eyes full of tears. "Dave, what are you going to do now?"

"I'll need to treat this as a crime scene for now," said Dave. "I know we have our suspicions, but now there's some things to do." He pulled out a small camera and a compass. He handed the compass back to JB. "Will this work in a metal canoe?"

"Yes," she said, "aluminum doesn't really affect it. Things like an axe head or rifle barrel will, though."

"Great." Dave turned toward the bow again. "If you could set us up over this spot, and point us as well you can to North, I'll take a photo of the shore from here. Then we can do it for East, just to triangulate."

Once they were done, he asked, "Could you pass me that baggie the baguette was in?" He then slipped the camera in, sealed it, and held it just under the surface. He pushed the shutter release. "Not sure how well this will work, but should be enough light for it."

He looked down again. "Looks like there is a small bag next to the snowmobile, but it is too cold and deep for me to dive for it."

"Maybe his logbook is in there," she said. "Would this fishing line help you grab it? I carry one as part of my 'just in case' supplies." She took a key from her key chain and tied it above the hook. "This will be a good sinker to keep it going straight down for you."

Dave slowly lowered the line over the side, and peered into the depths, jiggling the line up and down. "Got it!"

He slowly pulled the line in, then reached under the surface and pulled out the small knapsack. He opened the top, looked inside, and took out a sealed plastic bag, clear on one side, bright yellow on the other. There was a book inside. "Looks dry still—must be one of those map cases." The book was labelled 'Log Book.' Dave handed it to JB, "Does this look like your Dad's?"

"Yes," she said, leafing through it. "And it looks fairly new, it only has his notes since January of last year." She flipped to the last few pages. "Looks like he was on the track of something though, says he was coming here for a final set of readings to confirm what he had found several times before. Not sure what all the numbers and references are." She went to hand it back to Dave, but glanced again at the last page. "Wait, here's a note to me!"

My dear Jackie,

I'm up here to try to get yet more samples and measurements from the lake bottom, before this year's runoff disturbs it. I think I've collected enough evidence over the years to get this looked into officially. However, my place in Guelph has been broken into—just kids they said but no cash was taken. I have a feeling it was more than a simple burglary though. I didn't have any samples there, all my old stuff is in the lab. And this year's are in Rosie's freezer. I get the feeling I'm being watched, even here. If something happens, remember I love you, my little bird. Look after your little brother, help him learn from some of the things you had to deal with growing up here. I did try to be a father and a mother to both of you.

Love, Dad

Her voice broke, as she began to sob uncontrollably. Dave picked up the book and continued to read it aloud.

P.S. Tell Rosie to give you the turkey. I won it for you in the bonspiel, since you couldn't be here. It's in his freezer too, in the bottom. Make sure to clean it well before you cook it.

JB Managed a faint smile. "Not sure I'd want the turkey," she said. "It's a year old now. Rosie must have finally thrown it out."

"Actually, he didn't. Rosie mentioned it to me a few days ago," said Dave.

"Okay, but Dave, we need to get my father from down there. I need to bring him home!"

"Don't worry. Division in Winnipeg will send out a dive team. They will bring him home for you, and also figure out a way to get the snowmobile out. Might be able to winch it out, or finagle a helicopter out here. But it would help to mark it for them." He reopened the bag. "I'll leave this as a marker. If I blow some air inside it should float, and the bright yellow will keep it visible." He dropped the line over the side again, jigged for a bit, then gave a firm yank. "That's got it. I'll tie the line to the bag and we can head back to shore."

He climbed the cliff for another picture of the lake, with the yellow float faintly visible. He reported in and gave Division an update. "Julie, I'll open a file when I get back and send in copies of the photos I took. The body has been there a year. It's a fairly cold lake but the dive team will still need some specialized equipment, but they know all that. We're leaving now, will be back by noon."

He also got an update on the preparations for the visit. There was a bit of a protest underway, but nothing too serious yet. That might change when he got back with his news. JB's father had been very popular in Kirk's Landing.

CHAPTER 38

It was clouding over by the time they headed back, so the snow stayed firm and fast. Dave called the office as soon as they got to the SUV, to check in with Norris. She was not quite panicking, because dispatch had updated them on Dave's status, but it sounded like the office was a frenzy of activity with preparations for the event. He updated her on what they had found, but asked that she let him be the one to break the news to JB's grandfather.

"The mill tour went well," she said, "with no real protests organized outside. Not yesterday in any case. That business reporter came out looking like the cat that swallowed the canary. She'd apparently seen something newsworthy, perhaps with the help of her tour guides. She did talk to the mayor after that, but not for long. This morning there definitely is a protest, mostly First Nations but a few locals. Some students in the mix too, I think."

"Students?" Dave thought most of the local kids were behind this project.

"They're from Winnipeg," she said. "Only ten but they're pretty vocal. They're with some group that's been covering a lot of mill pollution issues over the years. All peaceful so far, but they've blocked the main gate and side ones and have ensured no one enters or leaves. Townspeople aren't that happy about it—a lot of anger at the thought this might cost them the grant money. And that Minister's aide has lost her air of sophistication. She's in panic mode. Babbling on about troops and putting people in their places. And of course throwing everyone in jail. She doesn't seem to do well under pressure."

Dave had suspected that Emily was more show than substance. "How about Minister Gottman?"

"She seems more competent than I'd given her credit for. Looks like she may have learned from some past mistakes and is less impetuous than before. All the same, she too wants to talk to you. Oh, and the local MP, the mayor's brother? He doesn't need to talk to you. He's disappeared, as in left town. Running from possibly bad publicity I think."

"One less worry," he said. "The Minister won't like that, though. Is Reese there?"

"I left him at the mill and came back to the detachment to make some calls. District is in the loop of course, I talked to Staff and he's sending four more constables, they should be here any minute now."

Dave had already discussed support with Staff, working from the chief's assurance that all would be low key. These extra protesters might ramp things up a bit, so the back-up might be needed. He'd asked that they be soft hat—no riot shields or anything. He wanted to keep things low key for now.

"I already mentioned the students to him, so he's putting the TAC team back at Division on alert, in case we need the extra crowd control."

"I assume he's still coming too?" Dave asked.

"Yes, he is concerned this might escalate, and even if not, he said the Minister sounds like she needs to see some rank here. I suspect most of the panic is coming from that aide though. He did say that it's all your show though, at least so far."

Dave was glad that Staff had his back. "I hope my show goes well, fingers crossed. You've done a good job Norris, thanks."

He turned to JB, "I think we can do a quick detour over to Rosie's first. I have a hunch we should check that freezer."

"Norris," he said, "I need to check something at Rosie's Cafe first then will go right to the mill. Make sure all the key players are there, but do try to keep them apart."

***

Dave slowed as they drove past the mill but all appeared to be under control—so far. Rosie's was almost empty, with most of the customers down at the mill. Rosie was full of questions about the trip, but Dave held up his hand.

"We found the body of JB's dad, and some other interesting things. We haven't told anyone else yet so keep it quiet. Details after, but right now, I need to see the turkey that JB's dad left in your freezer."

"Oh JB, that's too bad," said Rosie. He gave her a hug then turned to Dave. "You're not going strange on me again are you? You have all this excitement in town and you want an old turkey?" But as he was asking he led them out back. "This is strange. I've been thinking about it the past few days. I finally took it out yesterday."

"It's not a stew already, is it?" asked Dave.

"No, it's still thawing in the fridge, along with an old one of mine. I was going to clean out the rest of that old freezer too but suddenly things got real busy around here."

Rosie and Dave lifted the slippery bird onto a workbench. Dave looked at the back end. "Looks like there's something in here."

"Usually is," said Rosie. "There's a bag with the heart and liver and kidneys, some people add them to the gravy."

Dave reached inside and pulled out a clear plastic bag with a small black plastic object in it.

"Looks like this was a high tech bird," he said.

The three of them all stared at the memory stick in amazement.

"Neat," said Rosie. "I wonder what he left us on it. And I wonder if it still works? Let me grab Mike Donnelly. He's out front working on his laptop."

Dave explained what he had found, and held it out to Mike. "Can you read this?"

"Probably," said Mike. He plugged the memory stick in, and typed in a few commands. "It seems encrypted, but—just a sec." A few minutes later he smiled. "There we go, reads just fine now. Want me to do a copy too for a backup?"

"Please," said Dave. "What do you see on it?"

"There's a series of folders, looks like they're named after local lakes and rivers. Each one has some spreadsheet files and some document files. And there's a presentation. Let me just start that up. Here, take a look."

They gathered around the screen as Mike paged through a few pages of the presentation.

"Looks like he found clear evidence of pollution from the mill, starting right from the opening eight years ago. Before that, everything was clean. Big presentation, looks almost complete. There's a file called Read Me. Hang in there. Aha! Apparently his samples are in Rosie's freezer and back in a storage company locker in Guelph." He looked at JB, "Your dad did a damn fine job."

She smiled back, with a lone tear running down her cheek. "He was a damn fine guy."

Mike handed the memory stick back to Dave, "He certainly was. Looks like a slam dunk now, for proving pollution, plus a cover-up. Those murdering bastards."

"So far it's just a suspicious death, not murder," said Dave. "We'll have to see how it develops."

"Did you want to keep the turkey too?" asked Rosie. "Looks like there's nothing else in either end."

"No," said Dave, "that's OK. You're going to have lots of customers this week. Make it a special on the menu."

Rosie led him to an old chest freezer in the back, unlocked it and raised the lid. There was a layer of bags and bundles, all carefully arranged in the bottom. Dave looked at a few of them. "I think these are the samples from his work here last year, all nicely labelled and sealed, but I'll leave them here for now. I'll lock it up and hang on to the key. Oh, I'll need to buy a lot of coffees too, and a bag of muffins and donuts. I'm heading to the mill now to see if I can resolve this all and some free food might help."

"If you calm that crowd down I'll give you the coffee and donuts for free today," said Rosie. "Just help me load it into your SUV."

***

Dave was just getting ready to leave Rosie's when Sheila came bustling in with his uniform on a hanger and a bag under her arm.

"Tell me, how was Winnipeg?" she said. "No, don't worry, I guessed your real destination but kept quiet. But you're not going like that, are you?"

"Maybe not?" he said. He had his storm coat on, and a spare hat in the truck, but other than that was still in a wool shirt, jeans, and boots.

"Definitely not," she said. "I've already pressed a shirt and your pants. Boots are polished too. I've a cordless razor and a hot washcloth in a baggie. You can pop into Rosie's washroom and get changed. People will never remember you were three minutes late, but they will always remember that you looked competent on camera. The media are all over this already and we have an image to maintain."

Dave smiled at her use of 'we' and nodded as he headed for the washroom. "You're right, thanks Sheila."

***

Dave and JB arrived at the mill, snowmobile still on the trailer, and pulled up just short of the crowd. As they got out he called over Norris, then, catching Sheila Palin's eye, motioned her over too.

"Ladies, I don't mean to stereotype but I want to defuse this with a bit of psychology. Could you both make sure that the coffee and muffins and donuts in the SUV get shared around to all the groups? Mix in assurances that we've got it all in control with a bit of a motherly look too. Watch Sheila, she's good at that. And I mean that in a good way."

His staff sergeant came over and greeted Dave. "Just here so far for support, and to keep the Minister happy. Looking good so far, but we're ready just in case. Only a few journalists, reporters and still cameras—no film crews from the networks. Not yet."

The four constables he'd brought from Winnipeg were by the gate, just in caps and vests. They were less intimidating to look at that way, but Dave knew they were still tough and ready.

Dave then gave Staff a quick summary of what he'd discovered so far, and what he hoped to do to resolve this.

Staff looked at him with wide eyes. "For someone that was supposedly here just for a year to put in time, you've certainly been busy. If Bourbeau's death isn't accidental, we're talking murder. I'll make some quick calls for you to get some things rolling."

"Thanks," said Dave. "Now let's cut some of these protesters out of the herd." Dave headed along the fence, and as expected, the students followed him in a clump. He stopped and turned, and the students realized that three of the newly arrived police, as well as the staff sergeant, were now standing quietly between them and the rest of the crowd.

"Hi, I'm Corporal Dave Browne, I'm in charge of the Kirk's

Landing detachment. Thank you for joining our peaceful protest." One of them was about to speak, but Dave smiled and held up his hand. "Please, hear me out, we don't have much time. First, this is my town and I'm responsible for security here. I am aware of the pollution issues and concerns, and in addition have news, some just hours old, that will be of interest to everyone. And hopefully will resolve this to everyone's satisfaction. But people need to hear what I have to say and discuss some solutions, which means we need to stay peaceful about this. I appreciate your strong views and focus on these issues, but long after you have gone the people on both sides of that barricade will still have to live and work with each other. Division headquarters has a large crowd control team on standby, but I've told my staff sergeant here that we don't need them."

"We demand to be part of any negotiations," said one of the members of the group. Dave nodded at him, "Your request is noted." He held up his hand again, "I'll let you know if I feel you can be part of the solution." He looked the group over, and pointed to one of the women. She was holding back a little, quietly, yet several of the others had glanced back at her. "What's your name?"

"Susan Suzuki." She smiled. "No relation."

"Okay Susan, you'll be my contact, I'll call on you if need be. Now excuse me, I've more groups to talk to."

Staff spoke to him quietly as he walked by. "Looking good so far, keep it up." Dave held up a hand, fingers crossed, and smiled. "Thanks."

As he got back to the gate, he saw that the ladies had been able to spread both calm and refreshments. The two sides were mixing a bit now, trading donuts and good-natured jibes, but he knew it might not last. He saw some elders on the plant side of the gate, talking with several angry-looking First Nations youth. The crowd was thicker now, right up to the gate, so he'd have a hard time making his way through. He called JB over.

"I need to sneak around and help your grandfather with those youth. And I'll have to tell him about your dad too. He'll want to know as soon as I see him."

"Don't worry," said JB. "You're a good friend to him. But how will you get in?"

"I think my 'fade' is okay to use now," said Dave, "but I need to double-check I don't go black again. Tell me how it looks."

He concentrated for a moment, felt that shift, and looked at JB anxiously. She grinned, gave him a thumbs up, and slapped his butt, "Looks good. Go get him, Captain Fade-Away"

Dave quickly ran to the side gate. It was closed, with only a small group on either side, sipping coffees. Dave spotted Junior in the group, so gave him a little wave as he squeezed through the opening, then jogged back to the main gate. Charlie Bourbeau watched his approach from the corner of his eye, but kept a straight face, talking quietly and slowly to the group, trying to calm down two youths in particular.

Dave made his way into the middle of the small group, then unfaded. Both youths yelped and jumped back in surprise, but Chief Bourbeau just nodded to Dave, and said, "Corporal, what wisdom do you have for us all."

Dave gave the same little speech he'd given the students five minutes before, and asked for patience and an open ear. The two youth lost some of their bluster, and walked back to the main crowd, looking over their shoulder as they did so.

Charlie chuckled. "They will be jumpy for a few days I bet. Good for them to learn that they don't know everything. We'll enjoy adding this to our winter stories." His face saddened. "But I think you also have some news for me, from your search yesterday."

"I do," said Dave. "You know that your granddaughter and I went to Loon Lake to follow a lead?"

"Yes, she had asked me if the cabin was still there."

"She did, did she?" Dave put his hand on the elder's shoulder. "Well, we went out in the lake and found your son's body, maybe ten feet down, still with his snowmobile. Looks like he went through the ice and got trapped and drowned. I'm very sorry sir."

Charlie sagged for a moment, then said a few words in Ojibwa and put his own hand on Dave's other shoulder.

"Thank you for believing us and still looking. I could sense the change last year in his spirit. We will have a proper ceremony for him. But first, we need some justice. Do you have any more news?"

"I do," said Dave. "I think it's time to gather some people together. We'll do that right here, inside the gate but away from the crowd itself." He got on the radio and started giving orders.

"Reese, I'm setting up a little meeting and I need you to help me collect some key players. I'll want them all inside the fence, where I'm standing now. Ask Staff to get the student I pointed out before, Susan Suzuki, and bring her in here with him. Also, Klein, the mill manager and the security chief, Tony Barretto. Minister Gottman, but not her aide —she's more of a liability now I think. Tell her we need her skills outside for liaison or something. The Minister will agree, I'm guessing. Get the mayor, as well as his wife Sheila, she can take notes. If you have to, tell everyone it's a pre-press conference. That business reporter too, Amanda O'Leary. We promised an even better story if she waited for just a bit. Let's see, ask Donnelly to come along with his laptop. Norris too, I may need her for some backup—things could get complicated here. As for you, I'm counting on you to keep everyone calm out there, so that my little group can resolve some things."

CHAPTER 39

A few minutes later Dave stood in front of a small group. "This feels like an Agatha Christie novel," he said. They all just looked at him.

"Never mind," he said.

He cleared his throat. "I would like to thank you for attending this unscheduled meeting. I realize you are all busy in preparation for the presentation formalities but I feel that together we can work out a civilized solution to our current situation." He gestured to the crowd gathering in front of the fence. "Also, I've uncovered a number of new facts recently that will help our discussion."

Dave was a little nervous about this strategy. Most of the people here thought they were going to talk about how to deal with the protest group, but he had another agenda. He was going to gradually reveal some facts from the investigation, and see who would react. Staff had reluctantly agreed, but muttered something about sensationalist drug tactics. Although it worked in detective novels, Dave had never heard of it tried in real police investigations, but he figured it was worth a try. What the heck, this was supposedly what he was good at, thinking outside the box. He saw the mill manager start to raise his hand, so he continued quickly. "We don't have much time so I will go through the material I have on some issues, clarify how each of you is involved, and then take any questions at the end."

The group looked confused and peered suspiciously at each other..

"Do we need to get lawyers?" asked the mayor.

"It's up to you," said Dave. "Anyone that feels they need one can certainly get one, but no one is obligated to stay and listen, and you don't have to say anything that you don't want to. Anyone?"

The mayor looked around then shrugged, "Not for me, I've done nothing wrong."

Dave continued. "I want to emphasize that for those staying now I expect your focus will be on a solution and not just winning while someone else loses. We could just let the protest continue, until everyone gets dug into their positions. Then a few months from now we or a similar group will be here trying to do the same thing. We've all seen it and read about the towns and people and officials that were involved. Or we can be known as the town—and group—that worked together, solved this problem, and went back to living their lives together. Is that us?"

Dave looked at them all, "I'm seeing nods, so let's go."

" All right then," said Dave. He took a deep breath. This was it. A few key people knew what was about to happen: Norris, Staff Scully, JB, Mike Donnelly, and Gottman, who had refused to attend until Staff discretely murmured a few phrases in her ear. Now Dave had to roll it out smoothly so the rest would be interested enough to stay to the end.

"I'm not sure if you know each other," said Dave, "so I'll point out who's who. Myself, most of you know, Corporal Dave Browne, Detachment Commander. Staff Sergeant Scully. Constables Norris, here, and Reese, over helping with the crowd. Sheila is our detachment clerk, she will be here to take notes. Susan Suzuki, representing some of the protest group here, is concerned—as are many—about pollution issues. I am hoping after this meeting she will be assured of our intention to address those issues, and take her group home. Her role here is observer only. She's one of the few not involved in the web of conspiracy I found."

At the word 'conspiracy' several heads popped up attentively.

"Charlie Bourbeau is here because it's the reserve land that is downstream from the mill. And it was his son, Jacques Bourbeau, who was investigating local pollution and disappeared last year. Jacques Bourbeau's daughter, JB, was with me recently out in the bush when we made a significant discovery. Mike Donnelly, from the IT department of the mill, has been using his unappreciated database skills to help document some of the events last year at the mill. And helped me investigate a high-tech turkey."

Mike smiled smugly.

"Amanda O'Leary, a reporter with the Business Network, came here initially to just cover the funding announcement, but has discovered it's a much bigger story."

"I'm wishing I'd brought a crew," said Amanda. "But I'll manage." She held up her smartphone.

Dave smiled. "We've the mill manager Frederick Klein, as well as Tony Barretto, the mill security chief. And finally, Madame Gottman, Minister for Northern Economic Development. Thank you Madame Minister, for allowing me to capitalize on your event."

The Minister nodded. "Carry on," she said.

"Thanks," said Dave. "Oh, and not here is Frank Risso, one of the mill quality inspectors. Unfortunately he's still in jail for violation of a Protection Order, but he will figure into this too."

Dave noticed a quick glance between Barretto and the mill manager. Good. The bait was out. He had everybody's interest.

"I'll start with my arrival here a few months ago," said Dave. "There was an unexplained disappearance still on file, that of Jacques Bourbeau, a local resident and biologist at the University of Guelph. He was apparently up here investigating pollution from the mill. I also found a number of complaints on file about pollution, mostly downstream in the water, and discovered it was not a new concern."

"Wait a minute," said the mill manager, "we've had do-gooders whining for years, trying to blame all their problems on some imaginary pollution, and spreading their lies every time someone new comes to town."

Several others started to speak, Dave just held up his hand. "Calm down and listen everybody. You'll all get a chance. I'm not making accusations, not yet. I'm just sharing with you what I have found out so far.

"Keep in mind that for us to initially look into something, it doesn't have to be backed with hard evidence and be an obvious criminal charge. If we get a complaint from anyone we use our best judgement to see if we need to look into it further. We may find nothing, we may find enough to turn it over to another RCMP group, we may find enough for an immediate criminal charge. Is everyone fine with that?"

He looked around, and got back some nods and some sour looks.

"As I talked to people," he said, "I found out that this mill was designed to be cutting edge technology as far as pollution control was concerned, so it would seem there couldn't really be any pollution issues. The mayor and other business people were proud of the example this mill was setting in terms of pollution control, as well as being grateful for the boost to the economy and job creation this Federal funding had given, for both the town and the reserve. However, "most of the local jobs were menial labour, and the upper and mid-management jobs, whether supervisory or technical, these had almost all been outsourced, with no attempt to do any local training."

"This is sophisticated equipment that needs an expert touch," said Tony. "Can't expect someone to just walk in from welfare and start pushing random buttons."

JB pushed forward. "What's that supposed to mean?"

"Calm down everyone," said Dave, touching her arm. "Tony, that's out of line."

Dave continued. "There also were reports that much of this fancy equipment was down for maintenance. Often. Some had never even been turned on. I tried to get a closer look at the equipment on my tour but was told it was too dangerous on the floor."

He held up his hand at Tony, "Maybe it is, maybe it isn't. Let me continue to my next item. Part of my job is to keep our eye on any outstanding warrants in this town. We ran a check and found an outstanding warrant on a Frank Risso."

"That loser," said Tony Barretto. "He's always in trouble, I'm sure you'll find a lot if you dig further with him, I was always suspicious of what he was up to."

The mill manager and mayor both nodded vigorously.

"He's been a pain in the butt for years," said the mayor, "terrible worker. Don't rely on anything he might have told you."

"That's interesting feedback," said Dave, "given that he had been given a senior position in quality control in the mill. A lot of responsibility for someone that people feel is not that reliable."

He waited a moment, but there were no comments.

"So, we have lots of money into this project," said Dave, "but not a lot to show for it. Part of an investigation like this is to look for signs of excess money, such as you would get from gangs and drugs, or money laundering." He held up a hand again as the mayor looked ready to start off protesting. "I'm not saying there are necessarily gangs or drugs up here, but as I drove around town I saw a lot of big houses, flashy vehicles, powerful boats. Many acquired back when the funding started to flow in. I'm sure mill work can be rewarding if you add in a lot of overtime, but this was mostly management, who would likely be on salary."

"You need to realize that housing costs are much cheaper here," said the mill manager, "and that we are a very performance-oriented company. We expect hard work from our employees, but do reward managers with performance bonuses."

"I realize that," said Dave, "and I'm sure any further investigation will take that into account."

He waited, again no comments. Just a few worried faces. And the mayor, mill manager, and security chief all made a point of not looking at the parking lot and the nice trucks in their reserved spots.

Dave pointed at the lot, "Looks like some of you have worked very hard then and been rewarded well."

The business reporter, Amanda, snapped a quick picture of the trucks with her camera and smiled at the manager. "Congratulations on a successful year."

"Hey, you can't do that," said Tony, "this is a restricted area. And put away that tape recorder too."

"Actually, I can," she said, "and no, I won't."

Dave just looked at Tony and smiled. He noticed Sheila was still taking her notes, and Staff was nodding at the crowd, seemingly fascinated by the story unfolding.

"So, getting back to your friend Mr. Risso," Dave said. "We saw some possible links between him and some of the current issues. I asked Constable Norris to keep her eyes open on the mill floor when she went in to make the arrest. I assumed you would continue to treat her as just an uninformed woman, baffled by machinery."

Tony started to look a little concerned.

"Fortunately, Constable Norris worked at a mill before joining the RCMP, and was very familiar with what she saw—or what she didn't see—in terms of equipment. And when she went back for her cell phone she dropped, she took the liberty of taking some photos, just for my own curiosity of course."

"You can't use those, you didn't have a warrant," said the mill manager.

"We do now," said Staff Sergeant Scully. "For all records and documents, including the database."

The manager didn't seem that concerned, but Tony did step aside and key his radio.

"Tony, put that down," said Dave. "Too late to try to cover up. Mike here can explain why."

Tony put his radio down. "Mike can?"

The whole group turned with interest to see Mike setting up his laptop on a portable table.

"Thank you Dave," he said. "I'm glad to assist your investigations. At the request of the RCMP I put together an assessment of data activity from the mill systems." The Minister leaned in closer as he pointed to some charts. "You will see here that over the past few years the actual data has been significantly different from that used in the official reports. The reports used a sanitized version of the data, designed to make it look like the new systems—government funded systems—were running properly. But they weren't."

"What!" Tony exploded. "Those numbers are lies. You can't just show up here, make up some figures and charts, and expect us all to believe them!"

Mike smiled. "These are not made up numbers, they are part of the database records. When I first noticed these discrepancies I created a process to not only collect both sets of data—raw and adjusted—but to have it backed up. As per that audit policy, signed off on by you, as manager of security, all the backup data is stored off site." He turned to Dave. "Data that is available for police review when you are ready."

"You're lying! Give me that computer!" Tony started toward Mike and the laptop but Norris grabbed his arm. He shook her off and glared at Dave. "He's making it up. Our systems engineer can get you the correct data from that backup, wherever it is."

Mike shook his head. "Actually Tony, you can't. Only the head of IT —that's me—or somebody with a warrant—he looked at Norris—can access the data. It's in policy and provincial law."

Klein gave Tony a shove. "I thought you said he was stupid?"

Mike smiled again. "I was, but I trained up."

"Oh, and that engineer?" said Dave. "That would be John Hammel I believe. He's been working with us as part of our investigation."

Amanda stepped forward. "Excuse me, but does that mean all the pollution sensors are still operating?"

"Yes, they are," said Mike. "It looks like they were disconnected from the mill displays, but the data was still being collected. It's all here." He pointed to the screen. "And I'm not an expert on water or air pollution, but it seems pretty evident that the results are bad."

Amanda looked puzzled. "But I thought this mill was state of the art for pollution control."

Dave pointed out that while the mill was state of the art that was only if run correctly. In this case, many of the critical systems were either not installed or not turned on. Constable Norris had noticed this when she was in the mill, and the records Mike had accessed confirmed this.

"Furthermore," said Mike. "If the investigators want it, this database also collected the year-end reports to stockholders and government oversight departments, including earlier versions showing how the data was changed to give better results. Also shows the ID of the person doing the reports." He looked significantly at the Klein, the mill's manager.

Staff Scully was now standing at Klein's right arm.

Dave looked over and noticed Amanda dialling her cell-phone. "Amanda, could you hold off for a sec? Everybody?" He smiled then looked around at the grass and gravel. "This is obviously not a court of law. However it may be that there will be a trial in court and we don't want anything deemed inadmissible because it was reported incorrectly. Amanda, we certainly appreciate that you need to get a story to your editor, but could you talk with Staff Sergeant Scully first to make sure what you report will not affect our evidence? Also, you might want to wait five more minutes. There is more to this story."

Amanda put her phone down. "No problem Dave."

"This is part two of my story," he said. "After I asked Mike to focus on a few days in particular last year he found a peculiar spike in water flow levels over a period of a few hours. Specifically, there was an unusually large surge of water released out of the spillways. A surge that would have required a manual over-ride to the regular program."

"What would that do?" Amanda said.

"Sometimes it does nothing," said Mike. "It's just used to manage the levels. But this was spring, and a warm week, with the ice on the lakes starting to soften. Most local residents who travel by vehicle or snowmobile use the ice on the lakes or rivers, and it's usually fine, but this spike in water flow would damage all the ice, both on the river and lakes. They usually send out a warning bulletin—which didn't happen this time it seems. But still the locals know enough to see it's weaker, so usually avoid it."

"Sorry to interrupt," said Susan Suzuki. "I can see how this could be bad for the fish downstream. We've been pushing for tighter regulations on these control dams for years. But I'm curious, why those particular days?"

"Good question," said Dave. "When JB's father went missing, Tony said that Jacques had dropped by the mill that day and said he was on his way to Dexter Lake. So that's where the search focused, with major support by the mill."

"We sent all we had," said Klein.

""Yes, you did," said JB. "But not until the next day. In the meantime, there was a bit of a snowfall, covering any tracks up."

"And based on Tony's information," said Dave, "the police and search teams all went to Dexter Lake and dutifully searched the trails along the way, around the lake, even out on the ice. They found nothing."

"He could have got lost and wandered past the lake for miles," said Tony.

"My son did not ever get lost," said the elder chief. "I taught him well." JB gave her grandfather a hug.

"I was troubled by that data report of water level change," said Dave, "so I asked JB what was downstream, and what ice might have been affected. She told me it was the Hawk River, which flows into Loon Lake. If that was the path her father had taken, he may have run into weak ice, so would have to stay off the river, slowing him down a lot. He probably would have had to stay the night and would have missed a big conference in Toronto he was presenting his pollution findings at. We decided to check it out, just in case."

Dave didn't mention his vision. Maybe another time, in another setting. "We went to Loon Lake yesterday, and found her father's body in the lake, ten feet down and still with his snowmobile. Looks to me like he drowned, but we'll know for sure at the autopsy."

There was shocked silence at this news, and then mutterings of sympathy from almost everyone, except for Tony and the mill manager.

"We managed to retrieve his log book, and found in it notes on his recent work, as well as information on where he'd hidden his samples. He suspected he was in danger over his work. Looks like a very complete study, and seems pretty damning about pollution from the mill. I will be passing that information on for further action."

"What about the body?" asked the Minister.

"A dive team is on the way to the crime scene "said Dave.

"Crime scene?" asked the mill manager. "For accidentally falling through the ice?"

"Yes," said Dave. "I'm considering a charge of 'Criminal Negligence Causing Death'. That's a murder charge. It will depend on if the person who caused the water surge intended to cause harm to Mr. Bourbeau.

Tony's face had a look of horror, quickly replaced by fury. "That rotten bastard Risso," he sputtered, "he was always meddling in things. Who knows what crazy idea he had. He was always going on about people poking around the mill operations."

"Well, we asked him, and he denied any knowledge of this," said Dave.

"He would," said Tony, "but I think you'll find that the spillway console was part of his area that day."

"Interesting that you'd know that specifically. Is that where he usually worked," asked the staff sergeant.

"No," said Tony, "but we like to shuffle people around, especially quality managers, gives them better background."

"Knowing Risso," said Mike, "he was pretty clueless about any of the equipment, I doubt if he could do more than sit there and fake it."

"So who assigned Risso there on that day?" asked Staff.

"I don't remember, probably the shift supervisor," said Tony.

"Dumb backup guy here," said Mike. "I think if someone were to check the data records they would find it was in fact you, Tony."

Norris chuckled, then gave Mike an admiring look. "Good one Mike."

"Doesn't matter who assigned him," said Tony. "It was his station so he's the one that played with the levels."

Mike smiled and explained how someone had changed the water levels, but tried to make it look like was Risso. "Someone else with a higher security level, as an over-ride. Tony, in fact."

Tony looked ready to explode again when Klein put a hand on his shoulder.

"Calm down here. All this speculation doesn't prove anything. How could anyone think that would be a murder plot?"

"There is another fact that would support the charge," said Dave. "It looks like, from the position of the body, that Mr. Bourbeau stopped and was repairing his snowmobile motor when it went through the ice. He had a gas can marked with the mill logo with him too. That doesn't mean anything on its own, there are lots of them around. But Mr. Risso was, ah, concerned that he was being unfairly implicated in a murder, so told us that on the morning that Mr. Bourbeau disappeared Tony gave him a can of gas. Risso was instructed to mention that the river might be soft, meaning a longer trip, and give him the gas. I suspect contaminated gas. We'll know after we run some tests on it and the ski-doo. "

"You, you murderer!" The accusation came from the mill manager, catching everybody off guard, including Tony. All eyes went to Klein, whose face had finally lost its complacent smile and was now an incredible purple mask of rage. "You said you would just slow him down for the day!"

"What do you mean, me?" Tony glared back at his boss. "It was all your idea, you told me to get rid of Bourbeau, frame Risso, everything!"

Tony threw himself at Klein. Staff Scully pulled Klein back and held him away from Tony, getting an elbow in the stomach from Klein in the process. Norris grabbed Tony from the other side but before she could get a good grip on him, he twirled and punched her square in the face. He yanked away from her grasp and suddenly was standing behind JB with a knife to her throat.

The crowd froze in disbelief.

Tony snarled at Norris. Her nose was bleeding but she had her pistol trained at him. "Drop it sweetheart," he said, "or your friend here is dead. And that goes for the rest of you do-gooders, back off. One move and I'll slit her throat. And you!" He glared at Klein. "You can rot in hell. I'm not going down alone for this. You tell me to look after things and now you turn on me like a mad dog."

If anything it was Tony who now looked like a mad dog, eyes wide, spitting froth out of his mouth. But his hand on the knife was steady and there was no doubt in anyone's mind that he was capable of carrying through his threats.

Norris lowered her gun.

Dave was in shock but fortunately years of adrenaline-soaked police take downs, plus the fact that it was JB under the knife, converted his shock into an ice-cold focus of intensity. He had only one idea but it might mean revealing to the crowd his fade power. That didn't matter now, only JB's safety mattered and the glint of the hunting knife on her soft neck. But maybe there was a way—

He glanced at Chief Bourbeau and made a hand gesture he hoped the chief would interpret as 'make a diversion.' Sure enough, the Chief nodded imperceptibly, then let out a loud wail of anguish. All eyes shifted to him in surprise and Dave took the opportunity to fade and quickly run around behind Tony. He pulled Tony's knife hand away, yanked Tony backward, then unfaded.

As the crowd looked around, confused, they saw Dave and Tony rolling around on the ground. Norris bent down and, seeing an opportunity, pulled back on Tony's fingers and took the knife. Suddenly it was all over.

Dave got Tony to his feet and handcuffed him. Staff was already handcuffing Klein, and JB had run to the arms of her grandfather sobbing. Mike was busy using a handkerchief to dab at Norris's face.

Dave took a long breath of relief when he saw JB was all right, and then looked around the crowd to assess what to do next. "Norris, would you do the honour of reading these men the police warnings. We have the initial murder charge, then Aggravated Assault for Tony." He glanced at

Scully. "Thanks, Staff. We'll be adding Assault Peace Officer. The rest of you, we will be taking statements from you shortly about what you saw and heard today. Please don't discuss it among yourselves until we get your statements."

He turned to the business reporter, "Amanda, please check with Staff to see what information you can release to your paper. And we will need a copy of that recording you were making on your phone."

He looked over to the gate, where Reese looked ready to break through the crowd. He keyed his radio, "Reese, all okay here. Send over a couple of those constables to help us with statements and transporting the prisoners."

"Staff, we can handle the prisoners. Could I ask you to talk with the Minister about the press release?"

Finally Dave could go over to JB. Although he wanted to wrap his arms around her and hold her tight with relief, he restrained himself and merely held her shoulder as he inspected her beautiful warm neck, that thankfully had only a pink mark to indicate where the knife blade had rested.

"It's been quite a day, hasn't it?" he said.

She grabbed his hand and held it tight. "I'm fine. Thanks for saving my life." She smiled at how inadequate that sounded, but her eyes held his and said so much more.

"I have to go deal with the prisoners," he said, "but I'll see you later, to take your statement." He smiled at her.

"You'd better get going," she said, "before people start to talk."

Dave put the prisoners in separate vehicles and on their way to the detachment, and then joined Staff and the Minister as they talked.

"Staff, Mike Donnelly is able to secure the computer evidence we need to support the charges, but I think we will want to do a search of the mill equipment and their personal computers to collect other evidence. I'd like to do it tomorrow before these guys can contact their buddies to hide things. Can we keep a couple of these constables for an extra day?"

"I think that can be arranged Dave. And good job by the way. A bit sensational but very effective! While I make a few calls, I think the Minister here has a few questions for you before we talk to the press."

Dave turned back to the Minister. "Now, how can I be of help?" he said.

The Minister looked at him with a smile, "This has turned into bit of a mess, but maybe it's salvageable. I have some ideas for damage control, but after seeing what you just did I'd like to hear any suggestions you might have."

"Well," said Dave. "There are a few things that we can't—and shouldn't—sweep under the carpet. We've a murder charge, misuse of government funds, bribes, years of cover-ups, all sorts of environmental infractions I'm sure."

He paused. "Not my expertise, but this award was to recognize advances in technology. And I think this mill is still an example of an excellent design, except that it wasn't being used correctly. It looks like most of the employees were not involved in the cover-up, either. They are a good team. Is it possible to still give the town the money, but maybe with better controls? I'm sure there will be new management running this mill, after today's events."

She nodded thoughtfully but made no comment

Dave glanced across the field at Chief Bourbeau for a few seconds. "Madame Gottman, again, it's not my expertise but if you do decide to give the grant to the town there are a couple of areas where it would really be put to good use. When the mill was first opened, the company promised employment to local people, but little of that materialized." He pointed to the young people still standing by the fence. "Many of them are smart people, they just never had enough opportunity to show it. So part of that new money could go toward an aggressive training program in the mill, with a focus on those from the reserve."

Dave took a deep breath. He was in it now, he might as well go for the whole pie. "The mill will have to clean up the pollution of course. But it's obvious from this case that it's very difficult to monitor how much they're doing. There aren't enough inspectors to watch everybody and so you need to get more people involved. What if you established a Centre of Excellence here, to do pollution research, as well as add a focus on the environment at the local schools? That way you can keep a closer eye on everybody to make sure the money is being spent appropriately. And you might even be able to get funding from multiple ministries. How does that sound?"

"Sounds like you might be in the wrong job," said the Minister, "All good ideas. I don't want to rescind the grant because we went to quite a bit of trouble to get it approved in the first place. But I can't make a detailed commitment today about where it will go. I like your suggestions. Let's see, I can make an announcement saying the grant will be awarded and my department would be pleased to work with all those here on developing these ideas. I'll need to get the mill's owners in the loop right away too. My phone has been buzzing like mad, and I see my aide bouncing up and down over there like a pogo stick to get my attention."

She turned toward the gate, then paused. "Oh, and Corporal? This has been one of the most interesting functions I've been to in years. Thank you. And thank you for making the effort to resolve the case before I made the presentation. Oh, and by the way, I do like Agatha Christie!"

Dave contacted the staff sergeant and updated him on his talk with the Minister. "Just one more thing Staff, honest, then I promise I'm done. " To his surprise Staff laughed—that was a first.

Dave walked over to update JB, the Chief and Suzie.

"What do you guys think?" he said. "Is this something you can live with?"

Chief Bourbeau nodded. "I like the ideas, but we have been hurt in the past by promises that never materialized. But having a presence on the committee is certainly a way to stay in everybody's face. Certainly more effective than this protest. If you'll excuse me, I'm going now to go talk some sense into those young guys and tell them they've protested sufficiently for today."

Susan smiled. "I need to get back to my friends and give them an update. I expect they too will feel like their work here is done for the day. This was a great example of problem-solving here. Not what I'd assumed a cop would do. And what they say is right, you guys always get your man."

"Actually, our motto is 'maintiens le droit,' or 'defending the law'," said Dave. "You were quoting the Hollywood version. But thank you for the compliment and your patience. Here's my card, if you've any other peaceful protests planned, let me know and maybe I can hook you up with a local cop that has an approach similar to mine. We're not all bad guys."

"Neither are all protesters." She smiled and walked back to the main gate.

***

Once again Dave was alone with JB. "When I saw that knife against your neck, I almost ... I can't tell you how much ..."

JB put a finger to his lips. "I know. We can talk about that later. Now I have to help Sheila with your housewarming party."

CHAPTER 40

Dave drove slowly back to the detachment, still dragging the snowmobile behind the truck. He was exhausted. Thankfully Reese and the extra constables were there to clear the crowd and get the mill access open again. After hearing the announcements from the Minister and Scully the protesters had all waved at the cameras and happily trotted off to Rosie's to plan their next protest and eat the special—turkey curry.

The press conference was almost anti-climactic. The Minister made a brief statement, focusing on the economic benefits of the new program. The reporters tried to drag some criminal details out of her too, but she was experienced at being tight-lipped. Staff handled the police portion of the press conference—an edited version though. Financial irregularities were alluded to, but as it was an ongoing investigation most of the details were left out. Before the press conference Staff made some phone calls to HQ to arrange to keep two of the constables overnight and bring in a couple of specialists to assist in the search of the mill the following day. He told all this to Dave just before the press conference and looked particularly smug after a quiet conversation with the Minister. After the press conference he headed back to the office to see if Norris needed any help with the prisoners. "It's not every day we can take down a conspiracy ring, solve a murder, and make a Minister happy," he said.

When Dave finally left the site Mike was talking intently with the assistant manager, but both were smiling at whatever they were planning.

Dave had agreed a few days earlier, reluctantly, to let Sheila coordinate a party at his place both as a house warming party and to celebrate the visit from the Minister. Really, where did Sheila come up

256

with these ideas? At the time he'd had no idea there would also be protesters, a murder investigation and people arrested. He'd meant to call her to cancel but then he'd forgotten. His mind wandered briefly to why he forgot and to this morning when he woke up with his arms around JB and his nose buried in her hair. It felt like an eternity ago. He didn't know where this was going, but he definitely wanted to do that again.

He arrived at the detachment and could see a party already going on in his house next door. Not quite yet! Instead he backed the trailer into the garage and then went into the detachment, expecting to see Norris under an explosion of paper.

Four smiling faces greeted him: Norris at her desk, beside her a new unknown police officer typing at the computer, an older man Dave knew to be the Justice of the Peace happily grinding coffee beans, and Reese at the radio giving orders to somebody. Dave smiled and raised his eyebrows at Norris with a quick glance at the JP.

"Corporal!" she said. "The JP has remanded Barretto and Klein in custody until tomorrow night after the search of the mill is completed. He's hanging around to sign the search warrant for tomorrow. This is Corporal Bob Standish from Commercial Crime Section. Staff sent him out to help write up the search warrant tonight and stay for tomorrow. Reese has some constables at the mill so nothing goes missing tonight, and they also agreed to handle any local calls so Reese and I can go to the house warming party.

Dave glanced at Reese, who looked very smug about having bossed around senior constables for a couple of hours already. He looked back at Norris with another glance toward the back room where the cells were located.

"Oh yeah. They're in separate cells. We already interviewed them separately, and took statements but Klein lawyered up pretty fast. The two constables going back are going to take Tony with them to Remand Centre so they don't yell at each other through the walls. I'm just getting their appearance papers together right now."

Dave smiled, what a difference from a few months ago. "Great work both of you, and thanks Corporal Standish for your assistance. You and the JP are welcome to come next door for a little house warming party when you're finished here. Norris, is there anything you need from me now?"

Norris replied, "I'll need your notes for the past day, but that can wait until tomorrow. Why don't you head over and make sure they aren't going through your old love letters?"

Dave laughed. "No worries there, no love letters."

He really wished his house was not full of people. He just wanted to be with JB for some quiet time. Almost losing her today made him realize how much she meant to him, and how empty his life would be if she wasn't in it. This morning in the cabin they hadn't got past all those layers of long johns, and now he realized what he felt for her was far more than physical. He didn't want to mess it up by moving too fast. Or too slow. He definitely didn't want it on the front page until they figured out where they were, but who was he kidding? In a small town everybody would already know.

***

He walked next door to find 'his' party in full swing, with a warm fire in the fireplace and a crowd that was already spilling over onto the deck.

"Hi Dave," said JB. She gave him a quick hug and kiss. "We took the liberty of getting your party rolling for you. Brought some beer and wine from the Roost, and frozen munchies from the grocery store. Rosie talked Junior and his friends into being servers—it's going quite well. Here, have a cold one."

"Great, thanks," said Dave. He took the beer from JB and looked around his crowded place as she continued her update. He saw people both from town and the reserve, although some of the high-rollers he'd seen about lately were conspicuous in their absence. Sheila was helping with the party but the mayor couldn't make it because of some previous engagement he'd forgotten about until just now. Dave suspected their mayor was in the dark about much that had been going on, but he'd probably be laying low for a while. The Minister and her aide had dropped by earlier, just for a few minutes. Dave guessed that JB had been glad to see the aide leave.

There was beer in a tub of ice, several open bottles of wine, and someone had ordered pizzas from the restaurant up at the highway. Dave realized he'd missed the social life from down south, and since he really couldn't hang out all the time at the one and only pub in town, maybe he'd do this again. His place did look comfy with a bit of a crowd in it.

After a few quick hellos Dave grabbed another beer and walked out to join the few on the deck. The day had ended with a beautiful sunset, bathing the back of his place in an orange glow.

Mike nodded to him. "Nice open house Dave, a little late, but nice."

"How's it look at the mill?" said Dave.

"Going along fine I think. That proposed training program will be fine with head office, as they assumed all along something was in place. More doctored status reports. As for personnel, the assistant manager was already doing a lot of Klein's work for him. He's a good man, and was always pushing for the junior managers to take more responsibility."

"He'll have a lot of new faces to work with as well," said Dave. "Barretto already named enough names for many of the current ones to be either sacked or put on leave."

"How about drugs?" said Mike.

"Off the record, we'll be getting warrants over the next few days," said Dave. "I suspect we'll uncover some links outside of the mill too. This all will be pretty disruptive for the town, so your unofficial council and the real one are going to have to work together to manage this. How about all that pollution control stuff?"

"We turned all the sensors back on line," said Mike, "and the boards lit up like Christmas trees. It won't be easy getting everything running properly, but the concept and design are good. I'll have a busy few weeks. In the meantime, I promised your Constable I'd bring her a glass of wine."

"Go for it," said Dave. He then wandered over to where JB was talking to one of the native youth from the mill yard encounter. JB introduced them.

"This is Robin," she said. "We were just talking about ideas for some programs. I'd grabbed the Minister for a bit to talk about the youth programs I'd seen in Toronto and Ottawa, the ones using some hip-hop culture to engage them in a program. She liked the idea, and said someone in her office would help me follow up on it. Not Emily, I think she may be on her way out. Anyway, Robin's a pretty good artist. He used to hang out with Junior. There's some good kids and potential here, just waiting for something like this, right, Robin?"

The youth smiled shyly and nodded. "Gets pretty boring in the winter here."

"Be glad to help," said Dave. "We'll talk more. Right now I see another waving hand."

Amanda O'Leary was talking to JB's grandfather and beckoning at Dave. "What a fascinating man," she said. "Apparently he follows my show, and reads the Globe and Mail business section every day. I hadn't realized how much money some bands control—his isn't huge but he is a shrewd business manager, it seems."

"This quiet gentleman is indeed shrewd," smiled Dave. "I'm sure any deals will be to his advantage."

Charlie smiled back. "You have been busy today, like one of our finger string games. As you tug on a few ends, we see a new pattern—a good one too."

Dave continued to walk around and work the crowd. It was a big change from his old ways, he used to avoid crowds whenever he could. Now he had to admit he enjoyed it, and people seemed to enjoy being with him and listening to his ideas. Ideas that lately had been not that bad, he admitted. He wondered if this sort of positive feeling was related to the new way he had of using his powers as Captain Fade-Away. He smiled at the name JB had given him. And smiled even more as he remembered their night in the cabin.

"Hey Dave," said Norris. "What or who is that little smile for?"

"For JB," he said. "And for everything that's happened so far. I'm getting to like the north more and more. I do miss some of the big city lights, and the winter is a little long, but the small town life is getting more attractive to me. Need to do some long-term thinking, after I deal with some short-term issues."

"Well, you're glowing," said Norris. "I know that look."

"Nonsense, " said Dave, "I just was standing a little close to the fireplace earlier." Norris didn't look that convinced as she walked off. But he did have a nice warm feeling whenever he thought of JB.

CHAPTER 41

Dave bade the last visitor goodbye, then turned to JB. "Stay for a bit?"

"I need to go to," she said. "Much as I'd like to stay and show my appreciation for all you did today, I am barely keeping awake. One of the constables from Winnipeg is just starting her shift, she said she'd drive me back to the Grande."

"I'm pretty beat too," said Dave, "but couldn't have done it without your support, we made a good team." He gave her a big hug and a long lingering kiss. "Are you sure you're tired?" he asked.

"Sorry, yes, it's been quite a day," she said. "Don't worry, I'll see you tomorrow. Why don't we meet at Rosie's, say at ten?"

It was after 2:00 a.m. By the time Dave locked the door and turned out the last lights. His last few guests had cleaned up most of the mess before leaving, and he'd take care of the rest in the morning.

He poured himself a scotch, sat down in front of the fireplace, and sipped his drink in the dim glow of the embers. He thought about the day, the past few months here, his life, his future.

Not long ago he could hardly wait to get out of here, to get back down south to the bright lights and noise, and the excitement of major gang busts. Yet here he was actually starting to enjoy the place and the people.

He'd made a number of friends here; a new experience for him. He wasn't naive enough to think today's excitement would be at all typical either. He was willing to bet nothing ever would happen here again even remotely close in excitement. He'd always had a vague sort of plan to go back down south and slip back into the gangs program, but hadn't been thinking much past that. Nothing that big up here, but he could see some smaller challenges for the coming year, and perhaps beyond.

Running a detachment was more interesting than he'd thought before. It was nice to see the changes in his staff and think that some of it was because of his influence. Staff Scully was really warming up, although he was not ready to count on that all the time. Now that he'd been away from drug squad for a couple of months, he could see what a lonely life it had been. Somebody had to do it, but he was starting to realize it was no longer for him. He might consider starting that snowmobile patrol program that Reese was all excited about. And then there was his fade power. He was pretty confident the black spirit was no longer there, but he still had no idea what he did have or how to use it. Perhaps he could get some answers on that from the Chief and the elders. And then there was JB. He'd been a loner for a long time, but he was starting to realize this too was no longer for him. He realized he really liked her, and would miss her if he left. He was looking forward to spending more time with her up here.

These thoughts were still swirling around in his head as he walked next door to the office to check on the prisoner Klein and the guard. One was asleep and the other was happily playing with the coffee machine. While he was there he logged on and sent a quick message to Chuck, updating him on his activities and advising him that he would not be adverse to extending his stay here in Manitoba. That should raise some eyebrows.

Tomorrow he would tell JB he was staying. He was already looking forward to the look on her face when he surprised her.

***

JB barely stayed awake during the short drive back to her place. She peeled off her clothes on the way to the bathroom and cranked on the shower. Some of the other rooms might have the latest in flow-reducing shower heads but she liked her showers hot and hard. She let the needles beat into her shoulders, and slowly relaxed. When she was done, she put her hair up in a towel and slipped into a warm robe and fuzzy slippers. Slippers lined with rabbit fur, a present from her dad.

She poured herself a scotch and sat in her favourite chair, feet up on a footstool. She thought about the events of the day, and of the past year since university. And her life.

She realized she had been coasting. She'd gone to university without any clear goal, then hung out with her new friends in Ottawa just to enjoy the laid back easy life, then came back here to—to what? Working in the bar, hanging out with some old school friends, watching her younger brother and his friends go through the same issues and problems she had. Most of them the standard problems of youth, plus the issues of small town life, plus those of life on a reserve. She liked the idea of the Centre of Excellence, plus the focus of a new program targeting the local youth. She was sure she could get her brother to help too, to show the kids that there was a better path. First things first though. She'd return to University, this time with a specific focus on both art and social work, and then come back here to teach. She liked Dave too, and would miss him if he headed down south without her. This way they could be together—especially if he got sent to Ottawa.

Tomorrow she would tell him she was leaving, she was already looking forward to the look on his face when she surprised him.

***

Dave stepped out on his back porch, sipping a coffee. It was a beautiful spring day. He filled the feeders—disturbing the flocks gathered around—and gave a special greeting to his old friend the Whisky Jack. He'd done the dishes from the night before, emptied the ashtrays on the deck, and made an ambitious-looking grocery list. Now that he'd decided to stay, to begin to put down some roots for a change, he felt different. He might get on one of the committees for the mill grant projects, or maybe snowmobile patrols—once he learned to drive one. He considered a second cup, but was heading for Rosie's shortly to meet up with JB so decided to wait. He pulled on his parka and boots, then popped his head into the detachment office.

"Hi Sheila. Just going out for a few minutes to meet JB for a coffee, I'll be at Rosie's if you need me."

"No problem," she said. "Staff wants to talk to you later, he said to give him a call. Warrants are being coordinated still for the searches today—should be by noon I was told."

***

JB had woken up to the sound of the delivery truck down below at the hotel. She'd slept in, to just past nine. She felt rested, and relaxed, now that she'd picked a direction for her life. She was already excited about the new things she'd be doing, new people she'd be meeting. She remembered she was meeting Dave at Rosie's, so took a bit of extra care in getting ready. In fact, she worked her way through most of her closet before finding something acceptable. She really must do some shopping once she was back down south, and at more than Value Village. She managed to find the University forms, filled them out, and wrote a check for the semester. On her way out she checked in at the bar, to find Sid busy setting up for the day.

"Looking good Sid, I'm impressed."

"Thanks," he said. "After a few years in the trade you learn to be efficient, and pick up a lot of tricks. And this place is relatively easy to run, your dad and you have worked out most of the kinks already. Plus, I do prefer this small town life. Glad I moved here. I do wish I had more hours though, but with summer traffic I'm sure that will change."

"Be careful what you wish for, Sid." JB smiled and raised an eyebrow. "We'll talk later. Right now I'm heading up to Rosie's to meet Dave for a coffee, be back soon to give you a hand."

She glanced at her watch. "Yikes, I gotta run. I have to mail some stuff on my way there."

***

Dave and JB both arrived at Rosie's door at the same time. JB held it open, and did a curtsy. "My turn to be gallant," she said.

Rosie greeted them as they came in, "You're lucky, the last reporter just left to catch the morning flight. I made sure they all knew what a great job both of you did—they seem to be looking for a crime-buster team sort of spin. Who knows, could be a book in there."

"No thanks," said Dave. He turned to JB. "Let's sit over there at the end booth."

After Rosie had brought them both a coffee, and retired discreetly back to the cash, they looked at each other for a moment.

"I've been thinking, and have some good news," said JB.

"Me too," said Dave. He leaned forward and took her hand in his. "You first."

264

MIKE YOUNG

Mike was born and raised in Kirkland Lake, a small northern mining town with a nearby First Nations reserve.

He grew up with a love of the north, even in the midst of winter, exploring the surrounding woods with his friends, and his grandfather. He moved down south in his 20's to follow a career in quality management, but his real pleasure was still heading outside the city, with canoe and tent. While in Toronto he also developed an interest in back-alley murals, in artistic graffiti, and worked with some police there that saw its potential as a community building exercise.

He'd always been a voracious reader, so several years into retirement he decided to try writing, and hasn't stopped since. This is his first book, but he has several more drafts waiting in the wings.

ACKNOWLEDGEMENTS

I owe my thanks to the many people—and places—that helped me develop Kirk's Landing from just an idea to a published work of fiction.

The National Novel Writing Month—the concept, the website, and the local support group—gave me the encouragement in 2010 to meet their November writing challenge of 50,000 words in 30 days.

Ian Shaw of Deux Voiliers Publishing liked both my initial pitch and first draft enough to commit to working with me for the past nine months, reviewing each version to offer constructive criticism on all levels, including structural changes, character development and filling in of some 'plot holes.' Two other talented members of the Deux Voiliers team, Betty MacEachern and Nicole Chardenet, kindly dedicated long hours to copy-edit and proofread the final draft. My Beta Readers, Millie Norry and Lynne McGuigan, added valuable encouragement, perspective and suggestions. As far as content for the North, police work, and First Nations, I relied on my early years in Kirkland Lake, plus various police and First Nations friends, and of course the Internet. For the aboriginal content in particular, my intent is to present it with both accuracy and respect. I hope I have achieved that.

Finally, a very special thanks is owed to Millie Norry, as my friend, consultant, and muse, for her continued encouragement and occasional 'nudges' when I lost focus.

As for writerly places, there were many in addition to the office in my home in Ottawa. My local Bridgehead café and O'Connell's pub offered a relaxing atmosphere in which to create and craft, whether inside in a corner or out on the sunny patio. My 'local', the Carleton Tavern, provided free Wi-fi, affordable beverages, and more than enough character studies.

I hope that you enjoy Kirk's Landing, and won't be shy about offering me your comments at ravensview@gmail.com.

Mike Young

ABOUT DEUX VOILIERS PUBLISHING

Organized as a writers-plus collective, Deux Voiliers Publishing is a new generation publisher. We focus on emerging Canadian writers. The art of creating new works of fiction is our driving force.

We are proud to have published *Kirk's Landing* by Mike Young.

Other Works of Fiction published by Deux Voiliers Publishing

Soldier, Lily, Peace and Pearls by Con Cú (Literary Fiction 2012)

Sumer Lovin' by Nicole Chardenet (Humour/Fantasy 2013)

Last of the Ninth by Stephen Lorne Bennett (Historical Fiction 2012)

Marching to Byzantium by Brendan Ray (Historical Fiction 2012)

Tales of Other Worlds by Chris Turner (Fantasy/Sci-Fiction 2012)

Romulus by Fernand Hibbert and translated by Matthew Robertshaw (Historical Fiction/English Translation 2014)

Bidong by Paul Duong (Literary Fiction 2012)

Zaidie and Ferdele by Carol Katz (Illustrated Children's Fiction 2012)

Palawan Story by Caroline Vu (Literary Fiction 2014)

Cycling to Asylum by Su J. Sokol (Speculative Fiction 2014)

Stage Business by Gerry Fostaty (Crime 2014)

Stark Nakid by Sean McGinnis (Crime/Humour 2014)

Twisted Reasons by Geza Tatrallyay (International Crime Thriller 2014)

Four Stones by Norman Hall (Canadian Spy Thriller 2015)

Nothing to Hide by Nick Simon (Dystopian Fiction 2015)

Frack Off by Jason Lawson (Humour/Political Satire 2015)

Wall of Dust by Timothy Niedermann (Literary Fiction 2015)

Please visit our website for ordering information

www.deuxvoilierspublishing.com

879002

CPSIA information can be obtained
at www.ICGtesting.com
Printed in the USA
LVOW08s1454080817
544259LV00013B/760/P